WHEN APRIL FINALLY OPENS THE DOOR TO THE PAST, SHE COMES FACE TO FACE WITH HER GUILT.

Inspired by true events, **Supreme Sacrifice** takes you on a journey spanning three decades, which begins in a steel mill town in the Midwest during the height of unionism in the 1960s. April is the pride and joy of her father, Josef Straka, a first generation American, once a successful businessman at the top of his game, whose alcoholism soon brought the family to the depths of despair.

April's spiritual journey begins when her father dies in a mysterious car crash. Every night she is plagued with a dark cloud of haunting, recurring nightmares. Her days aren't much better living in this blue-collar, steel city shrouded in post-industrial gloom and overcast skies. Married young, she struggles to complete her academic studies, which launch her into the business world. She and her husband move to the South.

Just when she thought she had left her past behind forever, nightmares return coincidentally on the heels of a stormy, complicated relationship with a new friend. April is introduced to new spiritual tools and friends who help pull her back from the edge and into an obsessive search for the answers to her father's accident. Storm clouds slowly begin to part when she learns how to tap the power and strength from within by changing how she sees her past, forgiving herself and others.

Malie spins a compelling story of a young woman's journey to self-discovery, and the transformation of April's awakening and ultimate redemption to accomplish her dreams.

SUPREME SACRIFICE

*A woman's journey from the bondage of
guilt to the freedom of forgiveness.*

RITA MALIE

BALBOA
PRESS
A DIVISION OF HAY HOUSE

ISBN: 978-1-4525-3990-4 (sc)
ISBN: 978-1-4525-3989-8 (e)
Library of Congress Control Number: 2011917315

Balboa Press books may be ordered through booksellers or by contacting:

Balboa Press
A Division of Hay House
1663 Liberty Drive
Bloomington, IN 47403
www.balboapress.com
1-(877) 407-4847

Printed in the United States of America

Balboa Press rev. date: 10/10/2011

"This book is dedicated to my husband and children.
They are my reason for being."

"To those whose lives have been affected by alcoholism and addiction. My hope is that this book offers encouragement to others who have traveled a similar path that the spirit to heal and the continued struggle of family never quits."

PART ONE

PERDITION

Inside yourself or outside,
You never have to
Change what you see,
only the way you see it.
—*Thaddeus Golas*

PROLOGUE
March 1953

Ohio's ominous, cold, northeasterly March winds howled through the large maple and buckeye trees that lined the front of the Straka's ranch-style house. Lightning lit up the sky, and thunder rumbled in the background. April heard the trees' bare branches pound against the wooden siding and windows and clutched her teddy bear more tightly. Just last week, her sixth grade teacher had said people shouldn't sit near windows when it stormed, but April wouldn't move. *Daddy's going to get really mean tonight,* she thought. *It might start sooner if I move.* April sat across the room, frightened and frozen in her chair, as a shiver passed from her shoulders to her tailbone. The living room was dim and distorted by a flickering sixteen-inch Philco TV and streetlights peeking through the curtains. Neighbors were all tucked in for the night, secure and protected within their quiet homes. This looked to be another typical night at the Straka house: father ready to pass out after a long day of drinking at one of the family-owned bars; baby brother sound asleep, oblivious to what *might* occur; and mother preparing to work the late shift at the bar.

"Give 'em hell," said President Harry Truman, who was being interviewed on the evening news. April glanced across the room to her father, Josef. He was slouched on his worn, green chair with his arms perched high on his protruding belly. His sweat-stained undershirt clung to his body. He wiped his brow with a dirty hanky.

April was disgusted by his appearance, and she needed to do her homework, but she dared not move, because her father had a gun tucked against the cushion next to his thigh. This night was different. Her eyes traced the barrel of the gun, wondering if it was loaded. She watched his hands, which were massive, considering his short frame. Pure terror set in. A current ran through her insides, causing involuntary shivering. Fear welled up in her stomach as she sat on her hands to steady her arms and legs, which were shaking like riveting jack hammers.

In a drunken stupor, with bloodshot eyes and reeking from alcohol, he wiped a film of sweat off his brow with his dirty hanky. "Shut-s-shut that goddamn TV off," he stammered. "Listen to me, ya hear? I don't want ya to be like me! Ya got too many big ideas! I'm tired of hearing 'bout your big college ideas. You're too smart for your own good. Look at me. Where did it get me?" The more he lectured, the louder and further enraged he became.

She hugged her stuffed bear and tucked it under her thigh. A strong odor of rancid sweat permeated the living room. April listened to her father's heavy breathing, waiting with fixed anticipation until the liquor would get the best of him. Then she could slip away. It was getting late. She wanted to finish her homework and go to bed. A car pulled into the driveway. *Maybe someone's coming to rescue me. Be strong.* Seconds later, she heard the clicking of her mother's heels on the hardwood floor. Her mother hurried past, but never looked her way. Her mother's ride had come. The walls vibrated when the door slammed shut.

To survive in the Straka family, it was "sink or swim" and "survival of the fittest." April knew things had a way of preying on her father's mind when he was sober and would surface as soon as the booze took over. She vowed she would break free someday and escape this nightmare in Milltown.

Suddenly, Josef slowly leaned his body against the arm of the chair to steady himself. He stood up, coughed into his fist, and drew his gun. His large, stubby fingers unbuckled the belt around his barreled waist. Inch by inch, he slowly removed the belt like a two-edged sword ascending from its scabbard.

April began biting her nails to relieve her nerves. Her breathing was rapid but shallow. Sweat trickled down her ribs. She tugged at her wet pink cotton blouse to peel it away from her skin. The intense pressure of panic continued to build as she awaited her father's next move.

"Stand in the middle of the room!" he commanded. Wrapping the belt tightly around her tiny waist with one hand, he menacingly waved and pointed the gun in her direction. Slowly, he circled her, his head bent below his shoulders, repeating over and over and over, "If ya don't change your ways, I'm never gonna pay for your college. You're toooo much like me, toooo many big ideas. Get down off that damn ivory tower and high horse. Ya think you're so smart. Well, you're not! Where did it get me? Do you want to end up like me?"

Why is Daddy so mad at me? What did I say to set him off this time? What did I do wrong? I made the honor roll again. That's what he said I'd have to do for him to pay for college. That's all I want, but I never know what he wants. It's so confusing. First he wants me to be like him, and when I am, he doesn't like it. What's happening to me? Her big brown eyes darted away to hide her tears as she turned from him to avoid looking at his face. Ashamed and terrified at his outburst, she glanced at her reflection in the picture window, sucking on a strand of her long brown hair and then tucking it behind her ear.

"Let's go!" he barked.

"Where?" she answered quietly, trying to stay composed.

"Just go!"

"Daddy, we can't leave Junior alone."

"Go!"

For a moment, she felt lightheaded and lost her breath. She had to reach for the wall to balance herself, causing the belt to fall. Stepping over it, she grabbed the bear, stuffed it in her pocket, and marched like a victim ready to face a firing squad. Her heart was pounding so fast and loud she was sure he could hear it. *Is that gun loaded? Where is it?*

When they walked outside, the storm was over, but the rain hadn't washed out the smell of sulfur from the town's air. Milltown, a nickname given to a growing city that prospered because of its raw material production of World War II armaments, provided a generous pride to its community while helping to quarantine many of its citizenry from active duty. Once proud that her father was a Milltown businessman instead of working in the steel mills, she wasn't happy when he bought the taverns.

5

Her father opened the car door and made her get into the driver's seat before he got in on the passenger's side.

"Get in that car and drive!" he demanded.

"Me? Daddy, I don't know how to drive." Another jolt of fear shot through her.

"You'd better learn fast! Get in that car and drive!" She tried to remember everything her mom did when she drove. First, April turned the key in the ignition, and the car started. Her eyes traced the floorboards. Her feet barely reached the pedals. Then she put the car in reverse and lifted her foot off the brake. Slowly, she put a little pressure on the gas pedal. "Look over your shoulder while you back out of the goddamn driveway," her father yelled.

She struggled to obey, but couldn't really get much of a good look behind her. She prayed no cars were coming. The steering wheel was so cold, she had trouble keeping her hands fixed in any one position. She fumbled with the buttons on the instrument panel, hoping to look for the heat, but gave up. She saw no headlights coming down the road, so everything was okay to go. The station wagon slowly crept down the steep driveway. The tires smashed the crunching buckeyes along the way. Breathing a sigh of relief, she shifted into drive and asked, "Where do you want me to go?"

She received no answer. There was no moon. The darkness was heavy. The roads were deserted. Her eyes were fixed on the white lines separating the lanes on the street. She held the wheel with white knuckles, her face a mask of concentration as she focused on keeping the car moving slowly and straight. Still, she was given no directions—just silence. Headlights from cars passing from behind lit up the St. Michael statue perched on the dashboard. It was a gift she gave him on Father's Day. She bought the statue with her allowance when she was at church with her grandmother, who she lovingly called BaBa and who told her St. Michael helps to keep people safe. Now she prayed St. Michael would do his work for *her* tonight.

The night was surreal. She motored past her school—a place she would be arriving on foot in a few hours. She inched the car along at twenty in a forty-five-mile-per-hour zone. She felt she was driving on instinct alone. Still, no directions were given.

Her heart pounded painfully; her breathing was slow and labored. Not knowing how to adjust the car heater, she shivered from the cold and her wet blouse.

Joseph slumped low in his seat, elbow against the armrest, slobbering chin resting on his chest. The silence was deafening. She was afraid to take her eyes off the road to see if he was awake. Her body shook so badly, it was difficult to keep the steering wheel steady. She swerved to avoid hitting a pothole big enough to swallow one of the tires. Glancing back to look for any signs of police, she drove slowly across the Butler Bridge. Fog was beginning to lift. The mill's smokestacks, spewing out thick, colorful coke and sulfur pollution, obstructed her view from the windshield.

Within minutes of starting this terrifying night ride, she heard snoring. Struggling to hold the gearshift with sweaty hands and stretching to work the pedals, she finally maneuvered the car safely home.

Tiptoeing into her bedroom, April knelt down on a little, padded stool below the window for a momentary respite from the craziness she had just experienced. She covered her eyes, pressing hard to block out her thoughts. It took a while to quiet her shivering. *I could've wrecked the car and even killed us,* she thought. Only the streetlight was visible in the dark night when she finally opened her eyes. The croquet court across the street was masked by the fog. She stared at the streetlight with a predatory gaze and vowed that someday, she would leave Milltown, never to return.

CHAPTER 1
March 1961

April organized her desk to prepare for the one Monday of the month she had to work late at her Sears office job. She held an icy can of Nehi lime soda against her forehead, daydreaming that things would finally work out for her and Karl. It had been well over a year since they were married, and the life growing in her the past three months brought hope and contentment that she had never felt before. She was so deep in thought, listening to the clattering of typewriters, adding machines, and murmurs of her colleagues, that she was startled when the phone rang. She sprang like a Mexican jumping bean, jamming her knee against the desk as she attempted to get the swivel chair under control.

"April Dunlap, Sears-Roebuck correspondent. May I help you?"

A weak voice answered, "It's me."

"Hey, Mom. What's the matter?" she whispered. She held the phone in one hand while soothing her bruised knee with the other. "Are you okay? I can barely hear you." Waves of nausea passed through her. She put the soda can down and took a long, slow breath, attempting to regain her equilibrium and calm her stomach.

"You need to do something."

"What's something? What's the matter, Mom? I can barely hear you. Can you speak up?"

"April, you need to help me." Her quivering voice cracked, fading in and out.

"Tell me what's happening." April noticed people in the office leaning forward to listen to her conversation.

"Dad wants to move back tonight. Do you understand? I can't handle it. I can't handle 'im comin' back."

April could hear her mother crying. "Mom, I'm working late tonight. I don't know ..."

"That's okay," she interrupted. "Just get here when you can. I need you today. Junior needs you."

April heard a click and then a dial tone. The phone went dead. She stared at the floor. "Damn it," she whispered as she sank lower into her desk chair, listening to the air collapse into its vinyl covering. Her abdomen contracted violently with the anxiety that she always felt with every discordant encounter with her father. She drank more Nehi and nibbled on a saltine cracker.

******

April fastened her navy blue Misty Harbor raincoat, punched out her timecard, and slipped out the back door. The wind kept whipping her hair into her face. For a moment, she wished she hadn't traded her long ponytail for a shag haircut. It was another overcast night in Milltown, a city full of train whistles, clanking railroad sounds, and roaring blast furnaces—a dreary city blackened by its prosperous steel production. The sky was cloud-covered. The streets glistened with rain. The wind whipped against the car, which made a whirring sound that foretold impending, ill-omened events. Punxsutawney Phil's forecast was right on the mark. He spotted his shadow during the early morning hours. Winter had not yet given up.

Karl, the dutiful husband, was waiting for her in their black and yellow Ford convertible that she called her bumble bee—the car they bought in Virginia the day he was discharged from the Navy. She jumped into the car.

"Honey, you look terrible. Did you have a bad evening at work?"

"Dad plans to move back home tonight. When I talked to Junior last week, he said Mom was sleeping a lot and that he was taking care of himself. I mean, for God's sake, he's only ten. I think she's on the verge of another nervous breakdown, honey. She begged me to not let Dad move back yet. We need to drive over there right away. Now maybe you know why I never wanted to leave Virginia and come back here. I would've loved making it our home. I would've loved living anywhere else. Then at least I would've been oblivious to all their problems."

"Honey, maybe it'll be different this time. Is there anything I can do to help?"

"There isn't anything anyone can do. Can you understand why I wasn't happy when your father promised you that job with the steel mill offices if we would come back to Milltown? As soon as we found out that the job fell through, we should've turned around and moved back to Norfolk. Then I could've brought Junior to live with us."

"Let's not bring that up again."

"Well, we are where we are. No use arguing. I can't turn my back on my poor brother now. And there's no one else my mother can turn to. I'm all they have."

"So what's the deal? What are you gonna do?" he asked calmly. "He might already have moved back by the time we get there. And even if he hasn't, it's still gonna be pretty hard to tell him he can't move back into his own house."

"Yeah, but what choice do I have? I'd gladly have Junior come live with us if only my parents would go away and leave us alone. But that's never gonna happen. Dad's getting worse, and so is she, but I've got to protect her until she gets back on her feet so she can take care of herself and Junior. When we get there, just stay in the living room. I'll talk with him in the kitchen. Don't be surprised at anything you hear—but as long as it doesn't seem he's getting violent, just remain calm. I'll handle it. Just pray he's sober when he gets there."

While Karl drove, she closed her eyes and conjured blissful memories from her childhood when she was Junior's age. Sundays were a ritual. The family would visit relatives, eat at a fashionable restaurant, take in a movie, and finish with a drive through the beautiful Mill Lake Park in their shiny Buick Roadmaster. Josef bought a new one every year. She imagined the cool summer evening drives they took, winding along the tree-laden park roads, smelling the intoxicating fragrance of lilacs and lilies of the valley while listening to the Jack Benny, Walter Winchell, and Amos and Andy radio shows. Then, her father was at the top of his game. His businesses were flourishing.

"Baby, which one of those mansions would you like to live in someday?" he'd ask almost every time they drove around the beautiful estates that glittered along the park lakes and ponds.

She visualized the luxurious furnishings inside those mansions—the people and their lifestyles that must have matched their opulence. She wondered who lived in those houses and what they did to get there. She was determined that someday, somehow, she would live that life. Her father bolstered her self-confidence by stoking internal fires to excel in whatever she set out to accomplish and rise above Milltown's labor strata. After all, she was her father's daughter—she was smart, ambitious, and liked the finer things in life. She had big plans for her future. He told her the sky was the limit and that she could achieve anything she wanted as long as she was willing to work for it. When she was little, he'd tuck her into bed and leave with the same words: "Time for bed. Don't read too long." One time, with pad and pencil in hand, he drew the structure of a one-story, sprawling t-shaped home with a flat roof that doubled as a sunbathing area overlooking an in-ground swimming pool. He had lofty plans for their future and big plans for his dream house.

"Josef, stop filling that child's head full of dreams," her mother would counter.

"Julianna, that's what you need—a few dreams! April has the brains to go far in life, just like me. She's not afraid of anything—are you, baby? You mark my word, baby; someday, we're gonna live in one of those houses in the park." But it seemed later that the more she began to emulate him, the more his demeanor changed. He began berating her for wanting to follow in his footsteps. She remembered him yelling, "I don't want you to be like me!" It was very confusing.

The car was quiet. April was lost in thoughts about her father. When she was young, she had believed in his ability to accomplish anything he put his mind to—he was a force of nature. He was smart and self-taught, and he broke away from the steel mill legacy that shaped the town's social divisions. He had become a successful, self-made businessman with the fearlessness and stamina of a Paul Bunyan, regardless of his stocky, five foot nine frame. No one challenged him when he drank;

yet when he was sober, no one could match his quick mind, his wit, or tell a joke in any dialect as well as he could. Whenever he walked into a room, he became the life of the party—until his persona was altered after a few drinks. People both loved and feared him.

He bought a small house at the unfashionable tip of Milltown Lake Park, just a stone's throw from the colossal towers where the affluent professionals lived among well-manicured gardens. It offered a consoling proximity to those he hoped to emulate one day and enough distance from the dark valley of narrow-mindedness so prevalent in Milltown. He was determined to someday move up and out of that dark valley, breaking out of the caste system between worker and elite.

But life took a turn for the Straka family. A downward spiral of pressures occurred with the addition of another child, a long steel strike, and more businesses, which brought more responsibilities. April's parents became more distant with the distractions and increased demands. It wasn't long before the alcoholic binges increased. April's plans didn't work out as she intended. One year at the prestigious Western Reserve University, where she chose to pursue pre-med, was quickly extinguished when a bomb was dropped, causing a tectonic shift one summer morning after she returned home from school. Half-asleep, she overheard her parents arguing in the kitchen about money.

"But I promised her I'd pay her college ..." her father yelled.

"Well, there's no money left, and we're in debt," her mother interrupted. "You haven't been able to sell the other tavern, and the overhead is killing us. It doesn't look like the strike is gonna end soon. The men have been out of work for weeks. You need to tell her now. Don't let her keep thinking she's gonna go back."

When a marriage proposal from Karl, who was in the Navy and stationed in Virginia, occurred shortly afterwards, the opportunity to escape Milltown with the man she loved was irresistible. Her plans would have to wait.

She peered out the windshield. Although the windows were tightly closed, the sound of roaring blast furnaces from the steel mill could still be heard. The sight of dirty smokestacks and the polluted river reinforced her nausea. It reminded her of the depression she always felt living in this community, entrenched in its blue collar culture, incapable of transcendence, and resistant to change. The putrid smells of mill smoke choked out the beauty of the city's lush, green hills and the park's gardens. Shrouded under clouds of yellow, blue, and black smoke, the area's claim to fame was having been selected as the city to store the arsenal during World War II, because it offered over three hundred days of cloud cover protection. At the turn of the twentieth century, immigrants were encouraged to migrate there, because it was a thriving community with high-paying jobs. The American dream of homeownership was almost guaranteed.

April and Karl approached the white, shingled house on the hill. The porch light was on. The covered entrance had a sloping roof and was partially hidden from the street by two buckeye trees in front. Their barren branches were hardly visible in the darkness. Josef planted the trees the year the house was built, naming them April and Josef Junior. Karl eased the convertible in front of the dark house that was buttoned up for the night. He shut off the motor. Her eyes traced the floorboards. They sat in a strained silence, listening to the crackling of the engine cooling down.

There was no car in the driveway. She felt a temporary reprieve. "Thank God he's not here yet. That'll give me an opportunity to take an inventory of what's going on inside before he arrives. Everyone must be asleep."

Shivering in her raincoat, April felt happy she didn't live there anymore, yet sad she had to return under the present circumstances. She began biting her nails. The slow pressure of panic began to build inside. Creeping stealthily through the back door into the dark landing, her stomach tightened into a knot. Karl followed closely behind. She covered her abdomen with warm hands. The kitchen was dark except for a sinister glow from the oven light. She shut off a dripping faucet. "I know Dad's never on time, but I hope he isn't too late tonight."

The flowered wallpaper in the archway leading into the hall from the kitchen revealed an indelible dried bloodstain that was left untouched for years. That bloodstain served to be a milestone in the Straka household. It symbolized the end of the family secret about

Josef's drinking that was sacrosanct before his violent tirade. April's mother had a habit of challenging him at his worst moments—when he was drinking and impatient. Then the two would argue, and he would attack. The family worked hard at keeping his drinking a secret from the neighbors. When her dad hit her mother on the head with a salt shaker, she ran to the neighbor's for help, blood running down her face. April heard her mother's screams and the door slamming shut. The neighbors drove April's mother to the hospital. April was upstairs, bathing Junior. The police arrived when she was putting him to bed. They arrested her father. He slept his buzz off in jail and was released the next day.

"I'm going to check on Junior and Mom. Wait for me in the kitchen," April said. She peeked into Junior's dimly lit bedroom—an innocent angel, sound asleep. She tiptoed toward her mother's room, following the sound of loud snores. April adjusted her vision to her mother's dark bedroom and squinted at the surroundings that were illuminated by the hall light. Clothes hung from drawers, a desk chair, and a lamp. Throw pillows were strewn on the floor. Piles of school papers were stacked at the foot of the bed on top of blankets that were rolled into a wad. She snored like a drunken sailor. A thin sheet barely covered her silhouette.

April pulled the blankets and sheet over her mother's fetal-positioned body. She finger-combed her mother's dark brown hair from her face and nudged her shoulder. "Mom, it's me. I'm here to talk to Dad tonight. I'll make sure he stays away until you get on your feet. Do you understand what I'm saying?"

The snoring stopped. Julianna barely opened one eye and turned over in bed. She flailed her arms and moaned, "Don't let 'im come back home, don't … don't let 'im … lock the doors. Don't let 'im in." Her shoulders heaved. She laughed hysterically, like a patient in a mental institution.

April grabbed her shoulders and gently shook her. "Stop it, Mom! Be quiet. You're gonna wake Junior! Get a hold of yourself. I'm here to help you." Gently, tenderly, she stroked her hair.

It was déjà vu. The past was returning. The hysterical laughing caused a flashback. April was eight and heard similar sounds coming from this very bedroom. She remembered asking BaBa how her mother could laugh when she was so sick in bed. She never did get an answer. Later, she overheard the doctor say her mother was having a nervous breakdown. Some things never change—only this time, BaBa wouldn't be there to help. It would be up to her. She wondered how her mother's life had gotten so twisted and confused. Would Julianna come out of it this time? She sat gingerly on the edge of the bed and didn't realize a coffee cup had turned over until she felt something wet on her skirt.

"Don't worry, Mom," she said. Even as she said those words, they were not words she believed. She rubbed her mother's head to soothe and quiet her. Her hair smelled like soiled, oily rags. Saliva moistened her chin and pillow. Julianna rolled over and began snoring again. April was determined that she, herself, would never be dependent on any man.

She straightened the bed and returned to the kitchen—a place frozen in time—yet everything about the beautiful new home had become worn and damaged. She and Karl sat across from each other at the old, red, chrome-trimmed Formica table. The kitchen chairs were ripped and their stuffing exposed. Paint on the walls, once bright yellow, had faded to a dirty white and had begun to reveal cracks throughout the plaster. Mustard and brown print linoleum had lifted up along the baseboards; faded yellow daisy wallpaper on the drop ceiling had begun peeling at the edges. The stove looked as if it hadn't been wiped for days. April opened the refrigerator. There was a dry, sour smell. A saucepan with leftover chicken noodle soup, a jar of grape jelly, some eggs, two cans of orange soda, and a carton of milk stood on a rusted metal shelf. A wastebasket at the back door was overflowing.

"This place is pathetic. At least someone did the dishes and tried to clean up. I'll make some coffee. God, what am I gonna do, Karl? They've hit rock bottom. When's this ever gonna end? He's addicted to booze, and she's addicted to him. She's always telling us that he's just tired; he's sick. We're the ones becoming sick and tired. You wonder if she ever had a lucid moment and thought about getting out of this situation. She had to know things were never gonna change. Instead, she greeted his abuse with compassion."

"Don't you think you're being pretty hard on her? Maybe she felt stuck. Maybe she thought things would get better."

"I know I am, but I'm frustrated. I'm sick of it. Things won't get better. Daddy's never gonna quit drinking as long as she condones it. And when she finally faces reality, her fantasies begin to collapse, and she detaches from reality by trying to sleep it away. She's falling apart, inch by inch. And before you know it, I'm scared she'll have left us forever, once she feels there's nothing left to save. She has such a big heart. She's tried all these years to save Daddy, and it's ruined her health. Now she can't seem to face that there's nothing more she can do—that he's beyond saving. If I don't do something to change things, we'll lose her too. Poor Junior—he came along just about the time things started getting worse. Now all Daddy's businesses are gone—the taverns, the beer and wine chain stores—and he's back in that old shop that was once his first thriving business—his electric shop." April got up and put on a pot of coffee, thinking it might be a good idea to have some when her dad arrived. Karl just remained quiet and listened.

She continued. "I swear, they remind me of Mr. and Mrs. Willy Loman. It's all they can do to get through each day; they're completely self-absorbed with their problems. Mom used to be the local Ann Landers, giving people advice about their problems. What a joke. She can't even handle her own problems. When I was a kid, I used to tell myself, 'Someday, I'll be old enough to get outta here.' Now I'm old enough, but I still can't get outta here. You know that old saying, 'you can't go home again.' Unfortunately, I *am* home again."

They went into the living room and drank coffee, waiting for headlights to appear on the driveway. This moment had been repeated over and over in the remnants of April's childhood memories. She had spent many nights kneeling quietly on a little maple, padded, three-legged stool beneath the side window in her bedroom, looking across the street at the Croquet Court, dreaming about studying hard and becoming a doctor someday. She loved to learn and was even voted the most academic in her graduating class. Staring at the corner streetlight, she would lose herself, fantasizing how much better life would be far away from home and wondering how it would feel to live without fear.

She wanted to be where the skies were clear and the sun always shining. She thought that once she walked away from her old life, she would never come back.

April paced and checked the wall clock, remembering when she wanted to be anywhere else in the world but on that little padded stool, seeing those headlights creeping slowly down the street again, hiding under the covers, wishing her father would never arrive. She had fantasized about what life would be like if he never took another drink. If there was a God, why wasn't he doing something to help her? She always felt alone and hopeless—like she was the only one in the world this was happening to.

While Karl dozed off in the rocker, she paced back and forth in the kitchen, checking the wall clock. Biting the side of her mouth, she thought about her father's stern looks that could stop her dead in her tracks. He never had to speak a word. His looks spoke volumes. When she was a child and he entered the house after a long day's work, she'd dive at his feet to remove his shoes and scurry into the kitchen to make one of his favorite highballs—Seagram Seven, ginger ale, two ice cubes, and a maraschino cherry. The kids in the neighborhood loved him, because he always brought home bags of candy for them.

It was getting late, and she wondered if she should try to call the shop, but at that moment, approaching headlights came into view as the car slowly crept up the driveway. *He's here*, she thought to herself with a deep sigh. *Buckle your seatbelts and prepare for a crash landing.*

CHAPTER 2

April started biting her nails again—a habit she had extinguished after she married and moved out of the house. The palms of her hands were sweaty from nervousness and dread. Except for the crackling sound of the furnace turning on to warm the house, a deafening silence filled the room while chilled air rose up around her as Josef entered the back door. He dragged himself up the creaking stairs, then stopped and looked her squarely in the eye. His trousers were so baggy, the crotch hung midway to his knees.

"What the hell are *you* doin' here?" he growled. The look on his red face was furious. Dark stubble shrouded his unshaven, strong jaw and dimpled chin. He looked terrible, with protruding, puffy, bloodshot eyes. He still wore the old pair of reading glasses he had bought years ago at Woolworth's five and dime store, but now they were patched with tape over his right ear. He wore a dirty plaid shirt with buttons missing at his waist, exposing the soiled undershirt that covered his bloated stomach. He looked like a derelict from the wrong side of the railroad tracks. April realized both her mother and father had hit rock bottom.

Suddenly he stopped, leaned his elbow against the kitchen counter for balance, dropped a Kroger shopping bag filled with dirty clothes on the floor, and lowered his head to peer over the glasses perched low on his nose.

April couldn't tell from his expression what he was thinking or who would appear this time—Jekyll or Hyde?

"Daddy, I need to talk to you."

He made a guttural sound. He had a habit of snorting loudly to clear his sinuses and expelling their contents into a soiled hanky. He wiped away lines of perspiration that collected on his upper lip and cracked the knuckles of each finger. When he finished, he laced the fingers of his large, stocky hands together, ran them across his hair, and stretched his arms above his head, almost touching the ceiling. "Ahhhhh," he yelled. He glanced at the clock on the wall. "It's late. I'm tired. I don't feel like talkin'. It'll have to wait till tomorrow. I'm goin' to sleep."

"It can't wait, Daddy. I need to talk to you tonight. Please sit down. I can make you something to eat if you're hungry." April struggled to keep her voice steady and low so as not to raise his anger, but a tremble began creeping in. His body reeked from a disgusting, strong barroom odor. His black hair, twined with strands of gray at his temples, was slicked down with Brilliantine.

"No, I don't want to sit down! I'm not hungry! I'm just tired. Leave me alone. I want to go to bed. I don't know what ya—why you're here, anyway? Just leave me alone!"

"I can't leave you alone. It's important we talk tonight," she continued.

"Then make me a cup of coffee," he growled. "I heard you're pregnant."

"Yes. I'm due in September. Who told you?" She tried to sound calm, answering in a quiet voice, making small talk, as a sudden surge of uneasiness and a rising trepidation continued to erupt. Quietly, she set two cups of coffee on the table. April's throat instantly became so dry, she could hardly swallow. She smiled and eagerly grabbed her cup, sloshing the steamy liquid with her spoon. She took a full-size gulp of coffee to wet her tongue. His face looked pained, and his slurred words meant that Hyde was hovering close by, but on his way in.

"Karl told me. Doesn't he tell you anythin'?" he snarled. "He stops at the shop once in a while. I'm teachin' him some handyman tricks. It's no wonder he doesn't know anythin'—his father never even owned a hammer." His eyes were half-closed as he rambled on.

It seemed he couldn't hold a normal gaze. April noticed his inability to make eye contact with her; he always looked above her head. "Daddy, this isn't a good time for you to come back home. You can't stay here tonight. Mom's in a bad way. She's on the verge of another nervous breakdown." Her voice began fading into a murmur. "She needs to get on her feet before you come back, and Junior ..."

"Junior what?" he yelled.

For a moment, April leaned forward to answer; her lips parted, but nothing came out. Finally, she spoke up. "He needs her." She glanced at Josef, who looked pained, and saw the muscles in his jaw tighten.

"So what does that hafta do with me comin' back home, for Chrissake?"

"Junior said Mom's been closed up in her room for two days. She needs to get back on her feet before you come back home to stay."

"So, what the hell does my comin' back home have to do with your mother not gettin' back on her feet? Besides, she never threw me out. I left on my own."

"I know, but I'm afraid she'll have another nervous breakdown if you come back now. Junior needs her. He says he's been pretty much on his own—that she sleeps most of the time. We need to give her time to get back on her feet. She can only deal with one thing at a time right now, and that one thing needs to be taking care of Junior and herself." She leaned against the sink to consider her next plea and said, "If you come back ..."

He cut her off. "Wait a damn minute! What about me? This is my home too, ya know. I've been livin' at the shop now for a month. I'm comin' back, whether you like it or not. I pay for this house!" He wiped the drool dripping from the side of his mouth with his thumb. His eyes opened wide, and he stuck out his chin, waving his hands wildly in the air. He pounded on the table with a heavy fist, yelling, "This is my house too, you know!" He began grinding his teeth and breathing heavily, sounding like the bellows of an accordion losing air.

He seemed to be overwhelmed with impotent anger. April wondered who he was angry at, but guessed it was probably himself.

"Daddy, please sit down, and lower your voice. You'll wake Junior. Listen. We know this is your house, but Mom's sick. If you come back now, it'll be too much for her to handle. I'm not able to be here to take care of them."

There was a long pause that made her uncomfortable. Two conflicting emotions flooded her thoughts for the man who used to be her role model—fear and pity. She wondered if he ever understood the pain his behavior caused the family. Would he throw them out of the house, like he did to so many of their friends and family? She knew she had to remain steadfast, regardless of the consequences, yet remain calm and placate him as much as possible. This would be her balancing act—delicately walking on eggs while keeping the shells intact.

"Daddy, I love you and Mom. I want the best for both of you. It hurts me to have to ask you to stay away, but it'll only be for a little while. I promise."

His head hung down below his shoulders, like he wasn't in any hurry to respond or argue further. Finally, he staggered to the table and dropped onto the torn kitchen chair. April followed and sat across from him. They had spent many happy hours together at this table on Sunday afternoons, laughing, listening to polka music on the radio, and counting and stacking neat piles of money earned during the week from all his businesses.

Settling into a moody tone, he asked, "Don't you think I know the kid's important?"

"Yes, I do. Don't you think it's even harder for me to have to ask you to leave?" Her nausea returned, but she had to put it out of her mind to focus on the task at hand. She was glad Karl was nearby, but knew it would be unfair to involve him, since he had only been in the family a short time.

"Daddy, say something. You're just staring into space." Josef's eyes glazed over. It seemed he worked hard to avoid making direct eye contact. Obviously, he wasn't in any mood to talk. She couldn't leave until her task was complete. It was now or never. Her heart began to beat faster. *Damn! Why can't I find the right words when I need them? I'll wait until he says something—something about his feelings. Something! Anything! Please, God … help me live through this. Help me be strong. Tell me what to say, what to do, and how to do it.* She wondered if her bladder would hold out long enough to finish this undertaking. She nervously crossed and uncrossed her legs, finally pressing her knees together to keep them firmly planted in her chair.

He slowly lifted his head to look at her. "Ya just don't unnerstan, baby. Ya don't unnerstan …" April's father kept repeating the same phrase while he ran his heavy, calloused hands up and down his chipped coffee mug.

"No, Daddy, I don't. Help me understand, so I can help you."

"There's nuthin' to talk about. I'm sorry for anythin' I've ever done in the past to hurt you or anyone else. Ya want me to leave my house and my family. What do ya want me to say?"

"Don't you agree that we need to think of Junior—that Mom can't deal with you coming home just yet? It's enough for her to even care for herself."

Tears welled up under his drooping eyelids. He pulled out a soiled hanky again and blew his nose. She reached across the table and wrapped her hands around his grease-stained fingers. "Daddy, we love you, but just give Mom some more time—just a little while longer. Give her a chance to get on her feet."

He dropped his head again. The muscles in his shoulders and neck seemed to tighten. "I'm sorry, baby, but ya just don't unnerstan." By now, tears were streaming down his face. He removed his glasses and wiped his eyes with a napkin.

"You keep saying I don't understand. Help me understand," she pleaded. "Tell me what's troubling you. Maybe if you tell me, I can help." She knew his resolve was slowly crumbling. Thankfully, Hyde had completely retreated. They both sat in silence.

"How long do ya think it'll take for your mother to get well?" he asked as he slowly rose to his feet.

"I don't know. We'll just have to wait and see."

"Then there's nothin' more to say."

"But I want to help you, Daddy. What can I do?"

"April Baby, there's nothin' more to say tonight. I'm tired. I gotta go." He shook his head, mumbling under his breath, "Gotta go, gotta go, gotta go."

He swallowed his coffee, jerked his head back sharply, grabbed his bag of dirty clothes, and struggled to get to his feet. He walked slowly toward the living room, where Karl was fast asleep in the rocker. He bent over Karl and touched his hand. "Karl, if I've ever hurt you in any way, I'm sorry."

Karl opened his eyes, wondering what was going on. He sat up and answered, "No, I'm fine."

April ran after Josef, wrapped her arms around his neck, and kissed his rough cheek. His tears wet her face. She kissed him again. Silently letting her tears flow, she drew him into her and held him tightly, like when she was a little girl. She felt his heart beat against her chest. She closed her eyes, wishing things were different, wanting to tell him how much she loved him—but the words wouldn't come. He let her hold him, but only for a moment. He pushed away.

She hated seeing him penitent and emotionally fragile—a hollow man. She felt guilty she had to turn him away from his own home, but it had to be done. She sobbed as she watched a beaten man slowly stumble out the front door and into the dark shadows of the night. She thought of a hundred things she should have said—but would it have made any difference? Thankfully, he was sober.

He never looked back, nor said goodbye.

This was the man who just a few years ago was all-powerful and in control. Or was he ever in control? What happened to the man I adored—the man who used to be my role model? Where and when did it all go wrong, Daddy? What's gonna happen now?

He dragged his feet along the front porch and into his rusty 1954 Pontiac station wagon. Feeling spent with exhaustion, she watched the departing car creep up the street until the two tiny specks of blinking red taillights disappeared into the night.

I love you, Daddy.

CHAPTER 3

April collapsed into her swivel rocker, grateful she didn't have to work late this Monday night. Resting her legs on the matching ottoman, she examined her living room and enjoyed the brand-new smell of everything. BaBa's handmade multicolored rag rugs covered the shiny hardwood floors. Although the furnishings were sparse, she and Karl were able to accumulate some furniture with her Sears discount: a brown, early American, winged-back sofa with a golden eagle pattern; Cushman cherry step tables; brown ruffled lamps; and country accessories. They lived in a newly constructed development with other young married couples. All the ranch-style houses were similar and built by the same contractors. Karl's parents, younger sister, and brother had moved into the neighborhood shortly afterwards. In-laws living that close never work out very well, and April's in-laws would promise to be no different.

She sat in the rocker and stared out their big picture window framed with white Priscilla crisscross curtains hanging limply on each side of the panes, letting in the night. The room was dark except for the hazy beam of light from the gas outdoor lamp post. She pushed against her feet into a steady rock, causing the hardwood floor to squeak. Rocking back and forth, she stared at the Big Ben clock on the mantle.

"Did you have any luck finding a job today?" she asked when Karl entered the room.

"I'm going for an interview tomorrow. Sealtest is hiring some milkmen. Wouldn't that be a hoot—from a sailor to a promised steel mill office worker to, finally, a milkman? Will wonders never cease?"

"Anything at this point would be an improvement. So much for President Kennedy telling us we're entering a time of good possibilities, because it sure hasn't played out that way for us, has it? You know, if I wasn't pregnant, and we hadn't bought this house, we could've left and started ..."

"I know," he interrupted. "You keep reminding me. It didn't happen, so let's just drop it."

"Well, you know we'll need to get a lot before the baby comes, and Sears won't let me work past my six months, and that's just around the corner."

"You worry too much. Everything'll be okay, honey. You'll see."

"Somebody has to. I don't know how we'll be able to continue to make $116 monthly house payments much longer, plus pay college tuition with unemployment checks. At this rate, we'll never be able to repay my godparents for the down payment they loaned us for the house."

"Trust me. It'll all work out. We'll be fine. We'll pay them back."

She knew Karl would do anything to prevent her from worrying how they were going to make ends meet. When he got laid off, he acted as if nothing ever happened. For weeks, he made his lunch every morning and left the house as if he was going to work, but there was no work. Instead, he scoured the city, looking for another job, before having to finally confess what had happened. Whenever April thought about the lengths to which he would go to prevent her from worrying, she realized how much he cared and loved her. She had confidence in his ambition. For all that was happening to her parents, the one great constant in her life was Karl's unconditional love, devotion, and ambition.

His father moonlighted at used car lots to regroove and cut new treads in old tires. Karl would beg his father to take him along to assist and make some money to supplement his unemployment, to no avail. Instead, his father would make Karl's younger brother play hooky from high school and take him. When Karl and April bought their home, they needed an adult to co-sign the mortgage papers, since neither was yet twenty-one. Karl's father refused. When Josef heard Karl's father didn't trust his own son enough to co-sign, Josef also refused. April's godfather came to the rescue and co-signed the mortgage.

Karl reached over to pat her shoulder, giving her one of his soulful looks with the big brown eyes that always melted her insides. They had much passion for each other. She always felt hungry for his touch, his kiss—a longing that began their wedding night when they stopped at a motel off the Pennsylvania Turnpike on their way to Virginia. He had an irresistible smile and an innocence that enchanted her. She swore he was the most handsome guy she had ever seen. Tall, with dark brown eyes, curly hair, long eyelashes, and a confident stride like a champion Kentucky Derby stud, he was a dead ringer for the actor, James Garner—a likeness that never failed to arouse women's emotions. His greatest attraction was his incessant drive, control, and ambition that matched hers and her father's. He had the energy required to build a successful future. She was the hard-nosed money manager and never shied away from challenging Karl or anyone else.

"Let's go for a walk, honey. The cold spring air and exercise will do us good. Maybe it'll help you get rid of that nausea."

The walk in the brisk March air was far from anything spring-like. Cold temperatures and damp air prevented the trees and flowers from early budding. A refreshing, light mist sprayed their faces. Overhead, a thickening of dark clouds masked everything in a somber gray and black background. There was no moon, and another early spring snowfall was hovering just above the dark, starless sky.

They heard the phone ringing as they returned. Karl quickly unlocked the door and picked up the receiver. He listened intently to the person on the other end of the line, mumbling, "Yeah, uh-huh, okay, okay, I will."

April removed her coat, hat, and gloves and collapsed once again on the rocker. This would be her favorite nesting place with the baby. Karl was right. The walk did help. The nausea was gone. "What was that all about?" she asked as he hung up the phone.

"It was your aunt that lives near the park. There was a bad accident near the entrance to the park a few hundred feet from her house. She could see the rescue trucks, police cruisers, ambulance, and a wrecked car that looked like your father's. I'll drive to the hospital. You stay home. Have some dinner. You've had a long day."

"I'll go with you."

"No, I'm sure it's a false alarm. I'll be right back. You relax. You worked all day. Put your feet up. Have some dinner. I'll be home before you know it."

"I'm going," she insisted, hoping to mask her anxiety.

"Then get your coat on. Let's go."

His eyes looked serious. April wondered if he was telling her everything and felt lightheaded from anticipation. She slumped over her purse, her head between her legs in the front seat of their Bumblebee. The car smelled of Karl's pipe tobacco. She forced herself to swallow and take deep breaths with every bump in the road, but felt clammy and weak, waiting for the cascade in her belly to end.

The trip to the hospital seemed to take forever. Snowflakes were beginning to fall, and the night air was ominously still, as if at any second, the wind was positioned to whip up into a storm. Their breath was beginning to fog the windows. Karl turned on the defroster to clear the windshield of heavy condensation. Few cars were on the road at this late hour. They drove along the steel mill's railroad tracks, then shot across a bridge. Blasts of rising multicolored smoke were spewing out.

On the radio, the Inkspots were singing, "You always hurt the one you love, the one you shouldn't hurt at all ..." Immediately, she receded into a dark place after listening to a few bars of that song. She sat up. Her face locked into a frozen stare to conceal her sadness. The haunting melody burned a sorrowful spot in her heart. The first time she heard it was on a Sunday morning while she and her father counted and stacked money on the kitchen table. She had laughed lightheartedly and asked innocently, "Isn't that your theme song for Mom?" He found no humor in her question, giving her a frightening, contemptible look. She knew she would pay for that comment later. Spontaneity is off-limits when living with an alcoholic. There was no such thing as being carefree. Families of alcoholics lived in a world all their own, walking a tight wire, always waiting for the next shoe to drop.

She tried to hold on to pleasant memories of him when she was little—the fun they had roller skating together when her mom was at club with the ladies or his delight listening to her practicing the accordion, and later, the piano. But the good times quickly vanished once he succumbed to a life mired in alcohol, losing all his hopes and dreams. Now he was at war with himself and the world. Poor Junior—he never had a chance to see the loving side of the dad she knew. She wondered how her dad was getting along since they parted last week. She remembered him stumbling out the door and leaving in his car. *Was it really him in the accident? What if he is in a coma? What if he ends up a paraplegic? How could Mom handle any more stress?* By the time they reached the hospital, she had bitten the side of her cheek raw and started on her nails.

Karl was quiet and didn't say a word throughout the ride, finally bringing the car to a shuddering stop several feet from the emergency entrance. The hospital portico had a huge concave roof that was laden with soggy English ivy. A policeman stood at the imposing doorway, smoking, a newspaper under his arm, talking to another cop. Karl and April rushed past the men through the automatic double doors. April led the way into the emergency room, with Karl following behind. Once inside, he grabbed her elbow and whisked her through a crowded corridor lined with gurneys. The smell of Isopropyl alcohol permeated the halls. The nurse pointed them to a room marked *Grieving Room.*

The room was filled with a deafening silence. Julianna was the only one there. She looked ruffled and bent over with her elbows on her knees, sitting in the corner like a lost soul, fixed in time. Her salt-and-pepper hair was unkempt. She had a weary look of shock and terror on her face that April swore she'd never forget. Her mother's skin was pale, and she stared into space as if she was lost in a twilight zone, all the life drained from her body. Her eyes were swollen and red. She held on tightly to the arms of the dark mahogany chair as if it was going to move out from under her, and her knuckles were white. She burst into tears, sobbing into her handkerchief the instant she saw them enter the room.

April felt her mouth suddenly go dry and her throat tighten as she blurted in staccato, "Well, was it Daddy? How is he?"

"He's gone."

"What do you mean, he's gone? He can't be!" She grabbed her mother's cold hands, then dropped them. With her heart thumping and unable to breathe, her body went numb as she immediately collapsed like a deflated balloon. Karl grabbed her as she collapsed into the chair. A sudden sadness gripped and enveloped her body. She felt like she was overcome by a crushing undertow. Her knees were mush—all wet and spongy. She doubled up as if she had been kicked in the gut.

"Dad's dead. He hit a tree."

The nurse brought a medicine cup with some pills and a glass of water. "Mrs. Dunlap, your mother said you're pregnant. These pills will help calm you."

April swallowed the pills. Karl sat down next to her, cradling her in his arms. She tried to remain stoic, but instead laid her head on his shoulder and wept. Her body would not stop shaking. She was numb.

The nurse returned. She gave her some pills to take home, then handed Julianna a plain brown bag. "Mrs. Straka, these are your husband's belongings."

As Julianna reached to grip the handles of the bag, a small, bronze statue dropped to the floor.

"The policeman said your husband had a firm grasp of the statue when they found him," reported the nurse. "It must've been very important to him."

April quickly retrieved St. Michael. She froze, then slowly traced its outline with her fingers, remembering her father's surprised look as he unwrapped his Father's Day gift. "So, where should I put this beautiful statue?" he asked, holding her on his lap.

"BaBa said St. Michael is an archangel and protects people. I think you should put it in your car." The statue would remain in a place of honor on top of the instrument panel of every car he owned. She held it tightly in her sweaty palms, as if she could connect with some mystical vibrations left by her father. Returning it to the paper bag, she placed it on top of a blood-stained shirt—the same plaid shirt he wore the last time she saw him. *Oh, Daddy. What happened? Why are you leaving us like this? I'll never be able to hold you again.*

April watched her mother open the bag with an unstable hand

and search through its contents until she removed his worn leather wallet, which was covered with blood. She brought the wallet within an inch of her face and then turned it so the light from the floor lamp illuminated it. She stared at it for a long time, passing her trembling fingers slowly over every spot of blood. She was emotionless while she unhurriedly examined each compartment. She clutched it to her chest with both hands for what seemed like minutes, then she finally removed its contents: only four one-dollar bills. Her chin quivered when she asked Karl if he had a pen. "Karl, please write today's date on each dollar bill. I want each of us to have something of Dad's that he had his last moments of life."

Karl wrote *March 21, 1961* across George Washington's forehead on each bill. He kept one, gave one to April, and returned the other two to the wallet for Julianna and Junior.

"Mrs. Straka, the hospital needs your signature to perform an autopsy. It's necessary for all accidental deaths," stated the nurse.

Julianna signed the form without examining the document. "Can I see my husband now?"

"I'm afraid that won't be possible."

"Then please tell the policeman to come in. I want to talk to him."

Within seconds, the officer who had been standing outside with the newspaper under his arm arrived. His grave face looked like he was about to jump out of his skin. "Yes, Mrs. Straka, how can I help?" he spoke in a low voice, nervously tugging up and down on his chin with his thumb and forefinger.

"How did my husband's accident happen?"

"We don't know the details yet. There will be an investigation. We'll get in touch with you as soon as we receive the results of the report. We're hoping the autopsy will help us determine if the cause of the accident was medically related."

As the policeman exited the room, he motioned for Karl to follow him.

Karl returned in a few minutes.

"Mom, I think we should go to your house to notify the family.

There's nothing more we can do here." April dried her eyes. "I'll ask the nurse if there's anything more they need from us." The medication was working. The tears were gone. April felt calm and knew it was time to take charge. Although her mother always criticized her for being unemotional, just like her father, it was times like these she relied upon and admired her strength. April gave the nurse the name of the funeral home, and they began to leave.

"What did the policeman want?" asked April as she and Karl walked through the parking lot to their car.

"He wanted to know if Dad's car was in poor mechanical condition and if he had any health problems. I told him no to both questions. He said he was curious about the accident, since neither drugs nor alcohol were found, and yet there was no evidence of any skid marks."

CHAPTER 4

The sun began to peek over the dark horizon. April felt a gnawing ambivalence as she returned to the house a week to the day after her confrontation with Josef. She felt a guilty relief he was gone, yet was sad and heartbroken his life was filled with such tragedy and despair. She gasped, feeling a chill shimmy from the base of her neck to the bottom of her feet the second her foot stepped onto the kitchen floor.

She remembered how he had looked sitting across from her last week. Closing her eyes, she could still see his hands, watery eyes, patched glasses, and the worn grocery bag filled with dirty clothes. She wondered what his last thoughts were moments before crashing into the tree. Imagining his lifeless body mangled in the front seat of his car was more than she could bear. Sitting again at that table, she was afraid to look toward the back door. She had an eerie feeling that at any moment, he might appear. She almost felt as if he could be walking up those steps again, but she knew it was impossible. His presence was everywhere. She could feel his energy, but then suddenly, it was over. He was gone.

Julianna patted her arm. April jumped a foot, drawing her breath in sharply. Startled, she opened her eyes to see her mother standing beside her.

"Sorry. I didn't mean to scare you. Are you all right? You look like you've seen a ghost."

"Thankfully, no. I'm fine."

"Where did Karl go?"

"He went home to get ready for his job interview with Sealtest. For a moment, I thought you were Dad. I could've sworn he was gonna walk through the back door."

"That's something we never have to worry about again. We wondered how this was going to end. It's over. Thank God, it's over, and your dad didn't have to suffer. They said he died instantly."

"God has nothing to do with it. If *he* did, our lives would've been a whole lot better, Mom, but God has never been there for us all these years. It's sad to say, but maybe this'll be a new day of hope for us—a new beginning. You know what? Isn't today the first day of spring? Don't they say it's the season to celebrate the earth coming back to life—the season of renewal? Maybe it's time for us to come back to life. Let's sit down and have some coffee."

April noticed the dark circles under her mother's expressionless eyes. She had lost so much weight that the skin on her face was pale and haggard. Her cheekbones were protruding and jagged. She looked years older than she was—a young widow at forty-five. April sensed it would take some time for her mother to recover from years of nervous exhaustion. It was unlike her not to always be perfectly coiffed, with fresh lipstick, and dressed in a neat outfit. Her fragile self-esteem and vanity always required she maintain an acceptable appearance. April remembered her mother's daily rituals: exercising on the floor each morning as she watched Jack LaLanne on TV, applying lotions and creams to her skin every evening to preserve her youth, and staying on a perpetual diet to maintain her svelte good looks. This nervous breakdown had surely taken its toll on her.

"When did you last see Dad?"

"He came over around 2:30 yesterday. He was in a hurry to get to the bank before it closed and wanted me to sign some papers."

"Was he drunk?"

"No."

"What papers did he want you to sign?"

"I'm not sure, but I think he said he was applying for a second mortgage or some loan. I'm not sure. He said he had to get to the bank on time, or we could lose the house. I guess he hadn't been keeping up the payments. He looked terrible. He hadn't even changed his clothes or shaved for a couple days. He asked how I was doing, kissed me, and left."

"What else did he say? How were his spirits?"

Julianna had a blank expression, and her eyes were unfocused, as if she had wandered off again into another dimension. "They were the usual. He seemed to be okay, but in a hurry." She rose from her chair to leave the kitchen. "I'm gonna lie down for a few minutes. I need to get some rest."

"Junior's still sleeping. Do you want me to tell him about Dad when he wakes up, or should I send him into your room?" April felt her mother's anxiety the minute she asked the question.

"You do it, honey. I don't have the strength to face anything else this morning."

April always wanted to be there for her younger sibling, given the hopelessness he had growing up with two absent parents. Her responsibilities to care for Junior were thrust upon her throughout her teens, since her parents were totally consumed with their problems and preventing the family businesses from financial collapse.

Drifting away in thought, April watched her mother, reduced to such a state of disheveled emotion, leave the room. Both parents were first-generation Americans, yet different in every other way. Josef was driven by fear—fear of not enough money, liquor or food—while Julianna was driven by love. Julianna believed love conquers all. She believed in God's will and prayed to God for everything—as if *he* was going to help her. Josef hadn't believed in any higher power except money. His God was green. He often repeated, "My dollar is my God"—to which Julianna would respond, "Money is the root of all evil."

While the Straka family believed in God, not much credence was ever given to religion, the Bible, or its teachings. They only attended church sporadically. Religion didn't play a central role in the family. Josef mocked the "so-called religious people" who faithfully attended church every Sunday, sat in the front pew to show off their finery, then lied and cheated during business the rest of the week. While he was ambitious and had a strong desire to overcome his Slovak peasant ancestry through educating himself, Julianna seemed content with her station in life. She accepted whatever hand she was dealt, always wanting to seek approval, always trying to please others. She was a sweetheart to everyone, regardless of the situation. One of her many favorite sayings was "Kill them with kindness"—and kill them she did, bending over backwards to please and cater to everyone to a fault, while suffering later with stomach ulcers. Her passion was escaping into the fantasy world of movie stars. Hollywood magazines were always scattered throughout the house. She was like Laura Wingfield, the sensitive, young woman in *The Glass Menagerie* who played with glass animals to escape reality.

Julianna expressed her love, pride, and talent through cooking. Everyone acknowledged her culinary skills. She was the "hostess with the mostess." Julia Child had nothing on her.

April recalled many loving memories of her mother. They had fun walking to April's dance lessons on Saturday mornings and stopping at the bakery to pick out her favorite date-filled cookie if her lesson went well. Later, there were the private accordion and piano lessons. They would ride the bus to a downtown studio. April never had stage fright and would perform on cue for anyone in any place. Best of all were the times she spent alone with her mother after arriving home from school in the afternoons. Together, they would watch their favorite TV soap opera, *Secret Storm,* while Junior was napping. April had her mother all to herself. They would taste-test dinner and talk about the day. Julianna loved her children unconditionally. It was heart-wrenching to watch her fall apart piece by piece, succumbing to nervous breakdowns.

In the beginning, everything had started out well for her parents. April heard stories of how her father completed an International Correspondence Course on electric motor repair. Before World War II, he used nickels and dimes to buy scrap motors, which soon became priceless and scarce commodities following Pearl Harbor. Profits from the repair and sale of those motors started him on a lucrative path that accumulated the wealth needed to develop other businesses.

Initially, all he wanted was to quit his job at the steel mill and run his own business, with the freedom to be his own boss. He quickly became known in the local community for his ingenious creativity and business savvy. Within ten years, he was able to build his empire, moving from one business to another, beginning with an electric motor repair shop. Before long, he was pulled like a moth to a flame to move into businesses involving alcohol: first, a chain of beer and wine carry-out stores, then onto two taverns located adjacent to the mills. Josef was totally consumed with the building of his empire by the time Junior was born. His alcoholism had become so severe, he ended up at a psychiatric hospital, which unfortunately didn't help remedy his addiction.

A talented, self-made man, he soon was on top of the local community's business world, turning everything to gold. He would brag about all the partnership offers he received from beer distributors, promising April that when the time came, her wedding would be an event of the season, with all the town VIPs attending. But everything began to unravel like a ball of yarn when he entered the bar business.

An alcoholic owning a tavern is nothing less than daring certain disaster. It was his undoing. He sank deeper and deeper into a sea of alcohol, drowning with no hope of survival, ending up a failed businessman—a has-been running a second-hand swap shop. His descent occurred as quickly as his meteoric rise.

He was the oldest son and only alcoholic of seven children. He developed an addiction for the almighty dollar. He got lost trying to live the American Dream. A man of extremes, he was consumed by food, drink, and money.

April kicked off her shoes and began making phone calls to the family. The sun ushered in a beautiful morning. An alarm clock went off, and within seconds, Junior came out of his bedroom like an obedient soldier, ready to start the day.

"What are you doin' here?" He walked toward her, looking half-awake, rubbing his eyes to adjust to the bright sunlight pouring through the kitchen window.

"I have something to tell you." April opened her arms wide, and her little brother walked into them. They clung to each other, their warm bodies embracing and foreheads touching. They were sheltered in the hug. As they came out of their huddle, April began to rub the skin along the back of Junior's hands and gently kissed his cheeks. She looked down at his face. He looked puzzled at this early visit from his older sister.

"Let's sit down," she said.

"You need to hurry, 'cause I have to get ready for school."

"You won't be going to school today, honey."

He sat across the table from her. Junior, troubled by his allergies, sniffled and wiped his watery eyes with his blue-and-white-striped flannel pajama sleeves. April lovingly grasped both his hands.

"Daddy died last night. He had an accident. His car hit a tree in the park."

She watched his reaction closely and waited for his response. He didn't look any more surprised than if he had been told a neighbor's dog died. There was no emotion—not even a wince. April never remembered Junior ever smiling much. It wasn't surprising, since he never had much time with—nor love from—his dad. "Are you all right?"

"Where's he now? Was it a big tree?"

"He's still at the hospital. They'll be taking him to the funeral home. I guess it was a big tree. I don't know."

"Where's Mommy?"

"She's lying down. She needs to rest. We've been at the hospital until early this morning. The next several days are going to be very stressful for all of us, but especially for Mom."

Junior bolted out of his chair, heading toward the hall.

"Stop! Where are you going?"

He turned to look at her and shrugged his shoulders. "I'm gonna go be with Mommy."

"Not now, honey. Let Mommy sleep. She's been up all night."

April jumped up to give him a warm embrace and patted his head. He had big brown eyes that always looked sad and deeply dimpled cheeks. He wore a flattop that he kept straight and firm with crew cut wax. He loved watching Davy Crocket on TV while wearing the coon skin cap throughout the program. He was so cute, you wanted to kiss him on the spot.

Julianna revealed to April her worry that he didn't care much for school and hollered at Josef when he'd let him play hooky. Josef would take him to the tavern to help clean up, letting him play shuffleboard with the customers. She said Junior was always in trouble and becoming known as the neighborhood bully, getting into fights and raiding the neighbors' gardens.

"You know something? I've never been to a funeral home. Is Daddy gonna be at the one down the hill on Poland Avenue? That place always gives me the creeps when I ride past it on my bike. It's scary."

April reached down and put her arms around him, then touched his hand and intertwined her fingers in his. "There's nothing for you to be scared about. I'll be with you for whatever you need. Daddy asked me a long time ago that if anything ever happened to him, he wanted me to take his place. I will always be here for you. Yes, he'll be at Novotny's Funeral Home. You're the man of the house now, and I'm not going to call you Junior anymore. From now on, you're Joe. Is that okay with you?"

"It's okay," he said, and he smiled. "That's what they call me at school."

"You have an important role. Mom needs you to be strong the next few days. Together, we'll all get through this."

April slipped her hand into her pocket, came up with something, and held it toward him—palming it, like a secret. As she opened her hand, there was *the* one-dollar bill.

"This is for you," she said.

"For me? What's it for?"

April placed a finger under his chin, turning his face up. "Mommy wants each of us to have something of Daddy's that he had during his last moments of life. This dollar was in his wallet."

"I know what I'm gonna buy with my dollar."

"You need to give it to Mom for safekeeping. This is something you want to keep and cherish, not spend. Dad had this with him when he died."

"Will God send me to hell for being glad that Daddy's gone?"

"No, of course not. God would not do that."

"Then I want to go see Mommy now."

"Okay, but promise you'll not wake her." April watched him tiptoeing out the kitchen, thinking how ironic it was her dad was left with only four dollars. Josef was known to have a wad of bills fastened with an engraved sterling silver money clip. The four dollars gave another testimony to how far he had fallen. He never realized that his riches were his family, not the money in his pocket.

CHAPTER 5

"Mom, hurry, the local news is about to start!" April wrapped her arms around her bulging abdomen. She felt like she might have to throw up any minute, but her eyes remained fixed on the television. She dragged the beige leather ottoman closer to the screen to get a front-row seat. From the corner of her eye, she spotted her mother entering the room. Her heart beat fast as the lead story showed pictures of the twisted front end of the rusted station wagon and the damaged driver's seat. Waves of anxiety passed through her body as she turned away from the television for a split second to make sure her mother was okay.

Julianna was expressionless as she wiped her eyes and bobbed her head back and forth like one of those bobble-headed dog statues seen in car windows. April turned her attention back to the TV to see the mangled wreckage that filled the screen. She listened to the journalist's report. "Mill Lake Park recorded its first traffic fatality in many years when a well-known former Milltown businessman crashed into a tree near the Park Avenue entrance about 8:30 p.m. last evening. Joseph Straka, forty-seven, was pronounced dead at Milltown General Hospital. Park police said Straka was traveling alone in his 1954 station wagon west on Park Avenue when he failed to make a turn. Apparently traveling at high speed, Straka splintered three guard posts before crashing violently against a huge oak tree twenty yards inside the park limits. Park superintendent Henry Masters said this is one of the few auto fatalities to occur in the park since the early 1900s. The county coroner ruled the death a traffic fatality and said death resulted from a compound fracture of the skull. The coroner's investigator said the accident occurred in a comparatively straight stretch, requiring just a slight turn to the left. Instead of turning, Straka went straight, shooting off the right side of the road for fifty-seven feet before striking the tree. There were no skid marks, indicating Straka didn't apply the brakes. An investigation is underway to discover if his brakes were defective. Straka was last in the news in March, 1958, when he was stabbed in the abdomen with a butcher knife during an argument in an apartment over one of his taverns."

Julianna cleared her throat and whimpered, "Oh, God. Oh, God. Now why did they have to bring up that stabbing? They're making your dad out as if he was some kind of criminal when it was just one of those crazy mill workers refusing to pay their rent. By the way, where's Junior? I don't want him to hear all this."

"He's playing in the basement with his train set." April only half-listened to the rest of the television, because she was stunned as the news report brought all those embarrassing memories back. The stabbing incident occurred during her senior year in high school. She was summoned from class to rush to the hospital. A rusty butcher knife penetrated her dad's abdomen, which was protected by five inches of fat. Three days later, he was discharged, and within a month, only a tiny scar remained as a remembrance of the unfortunate episode.

"Mom, wait 'til Daddy's family hears there were no skid marks. They'll have a field day with this news. You know their infamous reputation as the town gossipers in Hamilton Township. Now the Hamilton people can gossip about them."

"You're so cynical. Remember, we're Strakas too. What they do and say also hurts us."

"I'm not a Straka anymore. I'm a Dunlap now." April ran to the kitchen to answer the phone. "Hello."

"April, this is Mack. Don't bother your mother now. I just wanted to know how you're all doing. I was shocked to hear the news this morning. Just tell her that I'm glad we got together to take care of the insurance papers when we did, and I'll get everything ready for her to sign and have the money as soon as possible after the funeral, which will relieve a great burden from her shoulders. Just tell her I'll see her at the funeral home, and she can call if she has any questions about anything. By the way, let her know that the Strakas have been calling and asking questions about the accident and if it might be a suicide. Tell her not to worry. I'll get a copy of the accident and coroner's report and take care of everything."

April returned to the living room. "That was Mack. He said he was shocked when he heard the news and wanted to know how you were doing. He'll see you at the funeral home and will take care of everything for you.

"Thank God for Mack. He's been such a trusted friend to your dad and me for years."

"He also said some of Daddy's family have been calling asking about the accident and wanting to know if it might have been a suicide."

"What? You can't be serious!" shrieked Julianna, bolting upright in her chair. "Why do they care about that?"

"Knowing Daddy's family, they probably don't want you and Junior to get any money. It sure didn't take them long to stir things up, did it?" The phone rang again. "I'll get it," April said, jumping from her chair. Returning to the living room, she said, "That was Uncle Ted. He and Aunt Joy just heard some of the family gossip and offered their condolences and apologies for their family's insensitivities. Uncle Ted said that Dad had been making visits to their homes the past week, crying that I threw him out of his house. He never mentioned anything about Grandma and Grandpa, just that Uncle Andy's leading the accusations and is the one who called the insurance man to report his suspicions."

Julianna sat on the edge of the sofa in disbelief, quietly squeezing, twisting, and rolling her white handkerchief taut as a cigarette. She stared into space at a place above April's head, mumbling something under her breath, asking herself questions that had no answers. "Nothin' that family ever does surprises me anymore. Haven't I suffered enough? Maybe they're right; maybe Dad did commit suicide. Who knows?"

"Stop that, Mom. Don't buy into their nonsense. You know that family well enough. When money's involved, they're like vultures, waiting to feed off dead animals. How could you even think it was suicide?" rebuked April. "Put it out of your mind. It was an accident! Dad wouldn't do a thing like that."

"Maybe he did. Maybe you shouldn't have sent him away last week. I'm sorry. I don't know what to think anymore." Her frown faded into a puzzled, blank look, her head waving back and forth. She mumbled in an almost incoherent ramble, "I'm gonna lie down. I'm tired." She left the room.

April thought how she and her mother sometimes had the uncanny ability to hit a nerve with each other. She grabbed the papers from the front porch. Right next to the lead story about President Kennedy and his plans for the Peace Corps, a new U.S. government organization that would train volunteers to work in developing countries on educational and agricultural projects, was the headline:

MILLTOWN BUSINESSMAN KILLED
AS CAR HITS PARK TREE

Police first believed that Straka suffered a heart attack, causing him to leave the road, but a postmortem conducted at Milltown Hospital's morgue revealed no evidence of a heart attack. The coroner's investigator checked with Rosa Brothers Auto Service to see if the steering, brakes, etc., had been defective, but the front end of the car was so badly smashed, it was impossible to determine if there had been any defect there. The front end was split and telescoped, and the steering wheel broken. Rosa employees and police worked twenty minutes to extricate Straka's lifeless body. Using a crowbar, workers extracted the front seat and then pried up the brake pedal and broken steering column in order to free the body. A son-in-law, Karl Dunlap, said the car was in good mechanical condition, that Straka had no heart trouble that he knew of, and that Straka was always a careful driver.

Karl was right about one of his facts. The family knew that Josef did not have any heart problems, but they all knew his car was in disrepair, and his driving skills depended upon his sobriety. Sober or not, he never was a fast driver. April read the article over and over, hoping to find a clue: no skid marks, no heart attack, traveling at high speed. She wondered if the truth about the accident would ever be fully understood. *What a coincidence that he died one week to the day and hour of my last meeting with him.*

The funeral director called to tell April her dad's cosmetic work would be complete soon and ready for viewing in two days. He cautioned that no one should touch his face. The funeral would be held on Good Friday.

When Karl arrived back from his interview, he and April sat down with Julianna and Junior to discuss Josef's last day. "Joe, you need to join us. The man of the family should be in on this too."

From the calls they received during the day, they began to piece together everyone who saw or spent time with Josef his last day. After Josef left Julianna, he arrived at the bank to drop off the papers shortly after they closed the doors at 3:00 p.m. The bank teller remembered the exact time, because they had just closed the doors and heard someone knocking.

An acquaintance by the name of Earl was the last one to see him alive. He said they were together from 4:00 until 7:00 that evening. They met at an auction they both attended routinely. Josef bought some odds and ends for the shop. From there, they went to the Hilltop Bar, a quarter mile from the park, and had a couple drinks. Josef said he was going to visit his daughter and left. The accident must have happened a few minutes later.

******

Dressing for the wake in her mother's house, April stepped into her skirt and examined the dust balls clumped along the bedroom floor and closet doors. She wondered how long it had been since the house had been vacuumed. She and Joe would have to clean before the funeral. She walked around the room, brushing dust from the lamp, making the bed, and straightening the painting on the wall. It was a picturesque water color of Mill Lake Park painted by her godfather, a talented artist.

With misty eyes, she watched her reflection in the mirror, remembering happy times as a child with her dad whenever they visited BaBa on Sundays. While the women were in the kitchen, April had his undivided attention. Together, they read the papers and talked about politics in the living room. It was one of the few times she could remember feeling grown-up. She loved to discuss current events, because he made her feel that she had worthwhile ideas and opinions.

On the closet floor were his clothes. Seeing them brought back some precious moments. April smiled, remembering the expression on his face when she begged him to buy a new suit to take her to college. It turned out later to be a family joke. He'd always laugh heartily and recount the story about how he spent "$120 to buy a new gray suit to carry my daughter's suitcases into her dorm room—that took only about fifteen minutes." Then there were the times he would sit her on his lap and call her his baby. She'd stroke his black hair, smelling the sweet Brilliantine lotion on her fingers. She loved that smell when she was a child.

April emulated her father, and she resembled the Straka family in every way: proud forehead, sharp jaw, determined chin, dimpled face, and no lack of self-confidence. He focused his adulation on her. There was no denying she was his pride and joy. Her role in the alcoholic family was that of the strong one. The family depended on her when things got rough. There's a lot of responsibility on the favored child, who goes through life trying to measure up to all the expectations. April believed she was super-competent, yet kept well-covered any fears, self-doubts, and vulnerabilities. Born in the month of April, she was the typical tenacious Taurus the bull. She persevered at all costs to achieve success and abundance and studied voraciously to maintain the top rung of the ladder in her class standing.

With a perpetual undercurrent of tension and anxiety, it was impossible to be carefree, as she never knew what to expect when she walked through the front door. The family was unable to share joy and happiness together during holidays and important events, because those were the times when the alcohol took over.

April tasted her salty tears as they streamed down her cheeks. She scanned the room while combing her hair, and she had the feeling of being watched—almost sensing his presence. She felt that if she turned around, she might see his vision in the mirror—his ghost, head down, ready to say, "You don't unnerstan, you'll never unnerstan, baby." Many thoughts raced through her mind.

The autopsy report gave a detailed account of Josef's injuries, but no evidence of any prior medical history that would have accounted for the accident. A mental picture of him lying on a table in the morgue flashed before April's eyes—and disappeared just as quickly. She wondered how he would look, given the description of his accident in the newspapers. She remembered a saying—"In the dark night of the soul, it's always 3:00 in the morning." It was sad her father lived so much of his life at 3:00 a.m. in a world all his own—one that no one could reach, one that varied from ecstatic highs to morbid lows.

The bedroom filled with the afternoon sunlight. April stared at her wedding picture on the bedside stand, a picture of a youthful bride and groom. Karl looked quietly handsome with dark, thoughtful eyes while April revealed a spontaneous smile, laughter in her eyes and warmth in her gaze. She and Karl did not have enough money to buy the picture. It was a surprise when Julianna gave it to them on their first anniversary. April stared at her beautiful satin wedding gown she bought on sale for $75. Karl proudly stood beside her in his rented tux, wearing the only pair of shoes he owned—his Navy regulation shoes. Together, they looked at each other with hope and love.

Having been in the Naval Reserves during high school, Karl went active following graduation, and April went off to college. One Sunday afternoon, when he was home on leave, they drove to the Milltown Cemetery, where he proposed and gave her a beautiful diamond ring. After they married, they always laughed whenever they passed that cemetery.

What could two nineteen-year-olds possibly know about life, except escaping into each other's loving arms? April nervously twisted her wedding ring as horrible thoughts of the eve of her wedding day came back.

Julianna had met Karl and April at the door when they returned from the church rehearsal to tell April her dad had left the house on foot. There was a horrible drizzling rain on that foggy and cold October night. April and Karl had to find her father. She was a minor, and her parents needed to sign the permission form in the morning. She and Karl jumped in the car and drove about a mile up the street before finally spotting a dark figure walking along the side of the road. April jumped out of the car and begged Josef to come home. He wouldn't talk, but kept walking. There was no convincing him to return. Julianna called the priest to explain the situation. Josef returned days later. No one ever knew where he went. The first time April saw him after the wedding, he sat her on his knee, and with tears in his eyes, told her she would always be his baby, no matter what happened in the past. Her wedding day had taken a different turn of events, given what Josef's dreams had always been for his daughter. April realized later that he left because he knew he would have spoiled her wedding day with his drinking. His absence was his gift to her.

******

Getting ready for the wake, April couldn't understand what took Karl so long to shower. She watched him as he returned to the bedroom to inspect the limited choice of clothes he brought from home. She dabbed some Prince Matchibelli Wind Song behind each ear, took his hands, raised them to her lips, kissed them twice, and put them on her belly. "Our lives will be different now, you'll see," she said. "Just think, maybe we'll be normal, like everyone else. And soon, you'll have started a new job. What do you think it's gonna be like? I've been so consumed with what's going on here, we haven't even talked about it."

"Well, it's certainly not rocket science, honey." He smoothed her hair from her forehead and kissed her nose. "I'm gonna spend the first week in orientation with the guy whose route I'll be taking over. They're gonna show me how to do the month-end bills for my customers. Then it's up to me to collect the money, keep track of the accounts, make my deliveries on time, and smile a lot. It's pretty simple. As soon as I get familiar with it, I'm going back to college. Didn't I tell you everything would work out?"

April admired the common sense and balance Karl offered whenever she was troubled. He had a way of convincing her that together, they could move mountains—even when the mountains seemed as tall as Mount Everest. She thought how it seemed as if they had known each other for eons, yet it had only been three years. She thought about the first time they met their senior year. They attended different schools. He was dating her best girlfriend. He told her on their first date he was going to marry her. She laughed and said he probably wouldn't want to wait long enough for her to finish college, but they were madly in love. He would always tell her she was too good for him, but the passions they had for each other bolstered his confidence and overcame his fleeting moments of unworthiness.

Joe knocked and stepped into the doorway. "Are you guys ready yet? Mom said we need to get there before calling hours."

The doorbell rang. A black wreath with a black velvet bow from Grandma and Grandpa Straka had arrived.

CHAPTER 6

As they approached the funeral home, Karl held Julianna under the arm. She fished a hand-knit embroidered handkerchief from the pocket of her black wool coat and held it to her face. April struggled to her feet getting out of the car. Her heart pounded as she held on to Joe, thankful the antidepressants would help her mother get through the next few days.

A bald man with thick gray eyebrows that looked like the edge of a whisk broom met the family at the funeral home's double doors. Mr. Novotny, the funeral director, greeted them with a nod as he introduced himself, then led them down a foreboding corridor. The sign-in book was perched on a lighted ledge attached to the wall with stacks of Mass cards and envelopes. Catholics consider it a very beautiful thing to receive a Mass card letting them know that a Mass is being said for someone they miss. Aside from the gift aspect, the soul of the departed receives the benefits of the greatest prayers of the Church and the infinite value of the offering of the Son to the Father for the remission of sins.

Above the ledge was a brass plaque with gold letters that read *Josef Straka*. To the right was an archway leading into the room where Josef's body lay in state.

The viewing room felt cold—crypt-like. It was adorned with dimly lit candles and low incandescent lights. Espresso-colored heavy drapes encircled part of the room from floor to ceiling. The matching thick carpeting exuded a solemn atmosphere. Soft organ music filled the room. Baskets and vases of flowers from family and friends bordered the area and clogged the room with heavy smells of roses, gardenias, vanilla candles, and furniture wax. Chairs were placed at right angles to the coffin to allow the immediate family to view visitors as they entered the room and completed their prayers at the kneeler.

Mr. Novotny nervously rubbed his balding head and explained, almost apologetically, that he did his best preparing Josef. He cautioned that no one should touch his head or face. He said that the entrance was locked to give them privacy, and he would need to know before opening the doors if they desired to close the casket. Then he disappeared into his office.

Everyone inched closer to the coffin. Eggplant-colored drapes behind the body gave a drab, depressing energy to the room. Inside the ivory, satin-lined open lid was a beautiful spray of red roses and a gold foil ribbon streaming from end to end with the words *Loving Husband and Father* printed on it. To April, it seemed as if the shiny bronze casket symbolized the tough veneer Josef exposed to the world while concealing the hole of unworthiness in his heart he never revealed to anyone—not even himself.

Karl and Julianna knelt first. April held on to Joe and remained close behind for support.

"Josef, Josef, why did it have to end like this for you and me? Why?" cried Julianna.

Karl held Julianna's shoulders as she leaned over Josef's body to caress his face. He grabbed her hand in time. "Mom, we're not supposed to touch Dad." He grasped her tightly around the waist for support.

April thought for a moment she was going to throw up, but stood riveted as she held tightly to Joe for support. She took a deep breath and collected herself. With his sister at his side, Joe stood like a soldier with a stone-cold expression. She held him firmly as they approached the kneeler. A sick feeling left her stomach and floated to her head.

"Why does Daddy look so funny?" he asked as he fidgeted with his tie.

She closed her eyes and counted to ten, but his question forced her to finally take the first look at her father's face. The subdued lighting outlined the face of someone who vaguely resembled the man she loved. He was partially shrouded beneath a white satin cover in his infamous gray suit. She examined some unfamiliar features. There was a noticeable contour of makeup, smoothing the area around his nose that was shorter than usual. His hairline was higher than she remembered, and the dimple in his chin was gone. Seeing the man who somewhat resembled her father was like a scene from a horror movie. *Stay strong,* she said to herself.

"Joe, the accident disfigured Daddy's face, and Mr. Novotny had to repair it as best he could. You'll understand more when I show you the newspaper picture of Daddy's wrecked car."

She tried to remain stoic for her brother but was unable to hold back the tears. As she cried, she thought that in life, her dad was a man of extremes who tried to fill the hole in his soul with money, food, and alcohol. It was sad that he was on a collision course with life, and those around him had to go along for the ride, but he took his last one alone. It was a ride to the park—not the place he dreamed he would live one day, but the place where his life would end.

Karl told Mr. Novotny the family wanted the casket to remain open.

CHAPTER 7
REMEMBRANCES
Julianna

Joe, Joe. I'm staring at you—at this face that's even hard for me to recognize. How could the man I loved for so many years be lying in a casket? Why can't I even cry? How did we get here—a funeral home—after all these years? It ended too soon. Now we'll never have a chance to make it better. How did everything get so bad for us? Was it the long steel strike that ruined our businesses? Was it when Junior was born? Was it when you bought the first tavern?

I have so many regrets. I regret we made such a mess of our lives. Our children had to suffer for it. I regret I was so afraid of you all these years. I was scared for my life when the psychiatrist warned me you would destroy me if I ever left you—scared when he said you would never be able to overcome your mother's rejection and that my love was the only thread you could hold on to. I was scared when Al-Anon told me Junior might become an alcoholic because your drinking was the worst when I was pregnant with him.

But we had good memories too, didn't we Josef? You could be so gentle. You nursed me back to health when I suffered from that breast infection after Junior was born. You were so generous, buying my mother's house, because she would've lost it because of my stepfather's drinking and unemployment.

I'll never forget our wedding day almost twenty-five years ago—a typical Slovak wedding—our beautiful bridesmaids with white ribbons in their hair, wearing gorgeous silk dresses, and the men in their black suits. Musicians played the czardas while the gypsy dancers entertained us. Oh, how I loved dancing with you to the *Anniversary Waltz*. Do you remember? We were drunk with happiness, singing along with the band, "Oh, how we danced on the night we were wed. We vowed our true love, not a word was said."

After everyone left, we were alone in bed. We talked about all the dreams we had. Where did all that go, Joe? Your family ruined things from the beginning. I knew our marriage was in trouble when your family wouldn't accept me. I was afraid I could never please your mother—I wasn't Greek Catholic. The criticisms started when I didn't have them in the wedding party. You could be such a good provider—so ambitious—working two jobs in the steel mill and the A&P while studying motor repair at night. In only three short years, we bought our first little house.

Our best times came after the children were in bed. I loved when we worked together in the basement, repairing motors into the wee hours of the night. You taught me how to do minor repairs, and I felt a part of what you were doing. You'd tell me how much you loved to watch my long fingers carefully rewinding the copper wires. I was happy to be your partner—contented, secure, and committed to our goals. I never wanted anything else. But it wasn't enough for you. You always wanted more.

You were like King Midas. You made money beyond our wildest dreams—buying me a fur coat, new cars, vacations—but you couldn't understand why *things* didn't bring me happiness. You quit your jobs, bought a building, and when you started your own motor repair business, we stopped working together side-by-side. You hired an assistant to do some of the jobs I once did. Things were still good then.

I was so happy I was able to give you a son. You cried when he was born, and I insisted we call him Josef Junior. I was happy with our success, but missed the closeness we shared working at home. We thought our success would bring us happiness, but it only pulled us apart. Couldn't you see our love began to change when you were busy building your empire? You didn't seem to need me anymore.

When you were too drunk to work, it was up to me to fill in at the taverns to keep our businesses afloat. In time, there was nothing left to save. Our money was gone. Now I've lost you. It's all over, Josef.

Julianna closed her eyes and laid her head on Karl's shoulder. Her mind faded to black.

April Remembers

Deep in thought, April stood behind her mother at the kneeler, thinking about her.

As I look at you, Mom, I wonder how you were able to fool yourself that Daddy was sick. You just couldn't face that he was an alcoholic. Your life has been one big fantasy. Daddy never acknowledged his problems. Instead, he imposed them on everyone else. Why should he own up when he had all of us pretending life in our house was just peachy?

April turned her attention to her father in the casket.

Daddy, you had such high expectations of me that I always wanted to fulfill. The happiest moment I'll never forget was when I had the lead in that fifth grade President's Day Celebration. I played Abraham Lincoln. I was so disappointed Mom couldn't attend because she had just delivered Junior. I did everything I could to prepare myself as I stepped onto the stage. I could recite that Emancipation Proclamation backwards and forwards. The auditorium was packed. Every seat in the house was filled. The lights dimmed when the curtains lifted. The principal sat in the front row and smiled at me, but she wasn't holding any flowers. As I panned the audience, it was a sea of strange women's faces with one man sitting in their midst, holding a bouquet of gardenias. It was all I could do to remain in character. When our eyes met, you winked at me. You never gave a hint that you were coming. I was thrilled that you took the time out of your busy day to be there for me. I'll never forget that. I will treasure it forever. That will always be my best memory of you.

The worst one was the vacation we took to Baltimore and Washington while Mom stayed home with Junior. I remember when we left, it was a scorching summer day. Mountain breezes in the Shenandoah National Park and Blue Ridge Parkway cooled us off. It was a beautiful drive. We viewed the rhododendrons, the Rose River waterfalls, and natural wonders of the Luray and Skyline Caverns, but you had to ruin it all by stopping along the way to drink.

In Baltimore, I remember touring the Premium Brewery and your business appointment with the general manager. After dinner at a posh restaurant with him, you dropped me off at our hotel room. I begged you not to leave me alone, but you wouldn't listen. You never listen to anyone. I knew you went out drinking. I stayed awake all night, listening to the strange noises in the big city while pacing the room. I was so worried. I wondered how I was going to get home if something happened to you. You didn't return until dawn.

Later, in Washington, you embarrassed me when you made a scene on the ferryboat trip down the Potomac River following our tour of Mt. Vernon, George Washington's beautiful estate. You wouldn't leave the bar. You bullied the bartender, because he refused to serve you any more whiskey. Everyone stared at us.

While all my friends had fun at the beach and park during summer vacations from school, I couldn't be with them because I had to work long hours at the beer and wine stores. I hated sorting bottles, stacking cases, dusting shelves, and waiting on customers. By the end of the day, my hands were so chapped, my fingers cracked and bled. I had to coat them with Vaseline and cover them with socks, hoping they'd heal overnight. Mom was busy at home. and when I wasn't working at the stores, I took care of Junior.

On Sunday mornings, we did have fun, though, counting the money together. I never had an allowance, and yet you'd complain you were broke when I said I needed school clothes.

People say whomever you lose in death can be replaced—a spouse, a child, a friend—but you can never replace a parent. I'll never have another daddy. Only last week, we were sitting at the kitchen table. I never thought that our hug would be the last one we would have forever. This is all like a bad dream I can't wake up from.

Joe Remembers

With an edge of sadness in his eyes, Joe squeezed April's arm. "Will you stay with me? Can I touch his hands?"

She smiled and stroked the dimpled peaks on his knuckles. Some trick of light shining over the casket made his big brown eyes appear almost black. The moment he touched Josef's folded hands, he grabbed April's arm and sprang back like he had been shocked with a live wire. April watch him closely. His eyes were shut, as if he was afraid to look at his father. Then he opened his eyes wide and stared directly at Josef's face. Slipping his hand slowly into his pocket, he pulled out his dollar bill. His eyes moved from the money to his dad's face and back to the money. He lowered his head and stared at it a long time as if it he was looking for some answer about his accident.

Daddy, I only remember two times I was happy with you: the time you took us to the drive-in movie to see *Please Don't Eat the Daisies* and the time you got me that three-fingered baseball glove for my tenth birthday. All the other times, I was ashamed—really ashamed—when you showed up drunk at my Little League games. Your belly always hung over your baggy pants. I'd hide in the dugout, afraid my friends would make fun of this fat man and find out later that fat man was my dad.

I hated bedtimes. You always slept with me. I could see you stumble around, taking off your clothes in the dark. You'd hang those smelly pants on the door and drop like a big whale next to me in bed. I had to struggle to move away from your fat, sweaty body to get comfortable again. I'd wrap one arm under the mattress and hold tight so I wouldn't sink into the middle of the bed. I'd sleep holding on to the mattress all night. I was stuck sleeping in only two ways—either on one side or on my stomach. If I wanted to switch from one side to the other, I had to wake up, turn, and hope to fall back asleep as soon as possible. I stuffed cotton in my ears and pulled the blankets over my head to drown out your snoring. You sounded like a roaring airplane engine. The bedroom smelled like BO.

I remember playing in the backyard with my friends the day before Thanksgiving. There was snow on the ground. Mom bought a rocker with her tips from the tavern. It was delivered that day. You came home from the bar. You were mad. You carried the chair into the backyard, dumped gasoline on it, and set it on fire. You went in the house to holler at mom.

Everyone in the neighborhood heard and saw what you did. Then you pulled the phone out of the wall. You broke the glass on the TV. You threatened to kill us. You got in the car and left. I keep thinking what April said when she told me you were dead. She said I'm the man of the house now, and I need to help Mom be strong. I guess I need to do better at school. Maybe it's up to me to bring pride and honor to our family.

CHAPTER 8

Uncle Ted, Aunt Ellen, and their two children were the first to appear. They stopped to sign the book and completed a Mass card. April always admired her uncle. He and her aunt lived the life she imagined as perfect: lavish home, clothes, vacations, and most of all, they seemed to be happy and loving. They were the beautiful people. Aunt Ellen's raven hair was cut stylishly short. She looked as if she had stepped out of the pages of *Cosmopolitan;* she was flawlessly groomed—an Elizabeth Taylor lookalike. Uncle Ted's angular features, dimpled chin, and dark curly hair were identical to his older brother. He had a striking, military-like stature and posture very fitting for a police captain. He and his wife approached the kneeler together to pray, then took turns embracing Julianna.

April accepted her uncle's wide-armed hug, sobbed, and held on to him, rocking, not wanting to let go. Hugging him was like having another chance to hold her dad. Tears flooded her eyes; a lump in her throat made it impossible to swallow. She turned away to compose herself. "We haven't seen you for such a long time. We've missed you," said April.

"Maybe we can change that now," he said. "We want to help in any way we can." He slipped an envelope into her hand. "Give this to your Mom. I'm sorry my brother's life had to end like this and that you've all had such a tough time. Aunt Ellen and I are here for you if you need anything."

For a minute, Ted held Joe at arm's length, apparently amazed at how grown-up Joe looked, and then gave him a big hug. They took their seats directly behind Julianna to show their support for the family.

Mourners queued up to sign in and complete their Mass cards. The room filled slowly with many people April didn't know. After viewing the body, they dutifully offered their condolences—some with limp hands, their fingers soggy like dishrags. They handed their envelopes to Julianna. April heard voices across the room. She saw her mother's friends—two men and women—hand their envelopes to Julianna. April's three bosses from Sears followed behind. Catching their eyes, April raised her hand to them—a gracious gesture of thanks to them for coming. Next, an old man kissed her cheek and pressed something into her hand. It was a twenty-dollar bill folded tightly into a small wad.

Next, April saw one of Dad's twin sisters and her husband arrive. She was also pregnant. She kissed April, handed her a fifty-dollar bill, and sat next to her in the front receiving line. April knew that sitting next to her aunt, she would be a victim to her verbal incontinence—a one-sided conversation.

She dreaded the arrival of the rest of the Straka clan. There were always "us and them" in the family—like the Hatfields and the McCoys. The players always changed, depending on what latest alterations Grandma Straka made to her will. Unlike his siblings, Daddy never talked ill of his mother, nor anyone else in the family—but his siblings gossiped and cursed her cruel and conniving ways, her gambling at the Jungle Inn, and obsession with faith healer Kathryn Kuhlman. It was obvious that April and her family, along with Uncle Ted and Aunt Joy, were the "them."

She caught Karl's gaze across the room. He stood at the archway, pointing to the funeral home's double doors to give her a heads-up sign. Men and women stood in groups, smoking and talking. The Straka entourage had just made their grand entrance—Grandma and Grandpa Straka, with twelve members trailing behind. She waited for the spectacle to begin. April's grandparents were from the old country— immigrant farmers who emigrated from the Austro-Hungarian Empire in the early 1900s. As usual, Grandma led the Charge of the Light

Brigade, with Grandpa trailing far behind, as if he wasn't related to anyone in the group. People turned from their whispered conversations toward the sound they heard from Grandma as she stepped foot into the main room. She lingered at the entrance until she was sure everyone had noticed her, and then made her grand entrance like Queen Elizabeth, sans the crown.

Grandma had the reputation of being a very shrewd woman who blackmailed her children and doled out feigned affection summarily whenever they demonstrated prosperity and accomplishments to her liking. She was a cold and unfeeling actress who could put on a good show when necessary. She obsessed over and hoarded her wealth. Money was at the core of her children's allegiance. She amassed her fortune from the labors of her children, who were expected to relinquish their earnings while living at home. With the exception of Josef, each child not only worried who was the top recipient in her latest will, but also cursed and disparaged her. There never was any way to satisfy her, nor win her affection; that was how she retained her power. She openly encouraged her children to compete against each other, which caused bitter rivalries for her love and money. April heard stories about her brutal discipline. Her routine punishment was making her children kneel, bare knees on rice, while tethered to a tree.

She was a tall, stately woman with an unbelievably youthful face. She wore a bulky-shouldered, three-quarter length coat, a nubby, black affair circa 1940; thick, dark-colored hose; black oxfords; and a heavy cotton flowered babushka. She knelt at the coffin and kept opening and closing the palms of her arthritic hands in front of her face, crying in Slovak, "I lost my boy, my oldest boy. What happened to my boy? Why did you join God so young?"

Grandma put on a good show, erupting into cries of, "Oh yoy yoy, oh yoy yoy. Josef, Josef, what have they done to you?"

April watched as her grandpa stood behind and gazed at everything and everyone except his son's lifeless body. She remembered her grandfather as a speechless man who usually escaped to the basement whenever they visited on Sunday afternoons. He was a reformed bootlegging alcoholic who never demonstrated much love for his children and looked the other way when they were abused by their mother. It was Josef who helped the midwife deliver his twin sisters. April's grandparents' beautiful, L-shaped, three-story brick house was structured as solid and obdurate as the discipline they demanded of their children.

As April watched her grandmother perform for the audience, she wondered what it must have been like for her father as a young boy, growing up in this family. He was intent on changing his name from Straka to Stanton, but it was never formalized. He wanted less and less to do with his family—except for Aunt Joy. He was jealous of his brother, Ted, who usurped his mother's love.

April heard Uncle Andy say, "Okay, Mommo, let's sit down." He lifted her from the kneeler and walked her to the back of the room. Grandma stared at Julianna with her steely blue eyes as she turned away from the coffin, murmuring, "Yoy, yoy, yoy." One by one, the members of her entourage slowly positioned themselves in the back of the room, whispering to each other throughout calling hours.

With expressionless eyes, Julianna sat with her body curled into a C-shape, her elbow resting on her chair. She held her chin with one hand, seemingly oblivious to Grandma's stares and performance.

A red-haired woman who once worked at the tavern came next in line and said a prayer. There was a run in her hose down the back of her leg, and her slip hung beneath her coat when she knelt. She quickly approached April's mom to tell her what a good boss Josef had been.

April took a break and joined Karl, who was smoking his pipe. She attempted to silence the murmured conversations of people sitting in the back of the room by placing her index finger to her mouth as she passed them on her way to the parlor. She walked past the Strakas and made sure she made eye contact with each of them.

April and her family arrived home that evening, exhausted. A neighbor stayed at the house to receive the food that was delivered in preparation for the arrival of family and friends. The table was set with Easter food prepared by Slovak women from the church. Platters were filled with oplatki (wafers), Easter bread, Easter cheese, Easter rice pudding, kielbasa sausage, sauerkraut and dumplings, crepes, kolachi, and ham. It was 11:00 by the time the last of the visitors ate, did the dishes, and left.

******

The second night of calling hours, the Straka clan arrived first. They sat stone-faced and once again isolated themselves in the back of the room. April and her family arrived minutes before the priest and the two altar boys, who arrived swinging pots of incense on golden chains. They knelt and began to pray aloud, "Our Father, who art in heaven, hallowed be thy name." The mourners followed their lead. It took forever to recite the entire rosary while the altar boys stood behind, praying. Everyone repeated the prayers on cue. April just listened, but never joined in.

Her thoughts drifted to a pivotal moment when she was a little girl in church one Sunday morning with her BaBa. Listening intently to the priest's strange words that she thought were Slovak, she whispered to her saintly grandmother, "What is he saying, BaBa? I don't understand him."

"Shush. I no know." BaBa chuckled and shrugged her shoulders. "It's Latin. I no understand either."

When April left church that morning, real doubt had set in about religion, and she had more questions about its value. If everyone seemed so devoutly intense during those masses, yet didn't even have a clue what was being said, this religion stuff seemed like a lot of mumbo-jumbo.

Karl waited in the foyer for the rosary to end. April was nauseous from the sickly sweet incense pouring from the altar boy's swinging pots. It was so thick you could cut it with a knife. The packed room had become very warm, with little ventilation. She thought if the prayers weren't over soon, she would either have to drop her head between her legs or simply pass out.

April watched the priest give Julianna a personal blessing. Mourners lined up to express their condolences and waited for the priest to leave. Like a chorus line, the men were in suits, and ladies wore similar felt hats and wool coats with padded shoulders and hose with seams down the backs of their legs. They looked anxious and uncertain of what to say as they approached Julianna.

April and Karl walked outside to the back parking lot to take a break as the crowd began to dwindle. There was a muffled cough. April became aware of someone behind her. Turning sharply, she spotted Uncle Andy. Everything in her line of vision became blurry as she focused on him in preparation for a diatribe. She bristled and attempted to fortify herself for what almost certainly promised to be an uncomfortable standoff. As soon as he saw her, he nodded absently and headed for the door.

Overwhelmed with anger, April crossed his path, reconnoitered the area, and blocked the doorway. Uncle Andy was trapped. She felt absolutely frigid. Under ordinary circumstances, she would have retreated, but she felt an air of confidence. She wasn't sure where this confrontation would take her, but the timing to set the record straight with this blasphemous family was opportune.

"How dare you and your family insinuate my father committed suicide!" she growled. "If anyone caused my father to commit suicide, it was Grandma! She's the reason he drank! She never gave him the love he longed for all his life. Instead of her moaning, 'What have they done to you, Josef?' She should do a mea culpa."

"You leave my mother out of this." Andy looked away and walked hesitantly toward her to get to the door. His piercing, sallow eyes widened as they circled the grounds, looking for an escape route.

Once again, she moved and blocked his exit. Now within inches of him, she stood with her face to his. Although he was the youngest son in the family, it was obvious from his heavily wrinkled face and yellow teeth that he was a lifelong smoker. She felt a knot tighten in her stomach, and a cold sweat broke across her forehead.

"You ought to be ashamed of yourself after what you did to my brother!" Andy lashed back.

"Wait just a damn minute, Andy," threatened Karl.

"What are you talking about?" interrupted April. "I've done nothing I need to defend myself for! Where have you been in the past? Why didn't you ever try to help him?"

Andy shook his head as he answered, "Let me by! There's nothing more we have to talk—"

Karl tried to stop the confrontation. "April! That's enough! You're upsetting yourself."

April took a quick breath, but she wouldn't budge. Veins pulsed in her temples. Anger extracted air from her lungs like a sump pump draining an overflowing basement. "You have no right to interfere in our lives," she shouted. "You were never there when any of us needed you. Where were you when Dad was thrown in jail for abusing us? Uncle Ted was the only one who ever tried to help." The cool air and tension sent a shiver through her body.

"Don't you talk to me like that, young lady!" Andy stopped abruptly. He kept opening and closing his hands, making a fist, as if to frighten her. "Let me by," he screamed. "My brother would be alive today if not for you—"

"That's enough Andy," interrupted Karl. "April, this needs to end." He began to pull on the sleeve of her coat.

The blood drained from her face. Her pulse quickened. Her body stiffened. She jerked herself away from his hold. "Karl, let me be. These people hurt my family."

By now, she was talking in rapid bursts. "I'll talk to you any way I want. I loved my father. You and your family never showed him any love. All any of you care about is Grandma's money. How can you stoop so low—calling the insurance company? Just remember karma. You've heard of that, haven't you? You'll reap what you sow. Your day will come too, and I only wish you the—"

"Shut up! Shut up! Let me by!" Andy's eyes searched for a means of escape, glancing at Karl.

April approached him, eyeball to eyeball, while Karl held onto her sleeve. "If you can't give respect to my family, you better stay out of our lives and leave us alone. I'm warning—"

"Your threats don't worry me—or anyone else in the family. Now move aside!"

She stared at him with stilted eyes, head leaning to one side. She dared him to take some kind of action. "Stay away from us. And tell that to the rest of the family!"

As soon as he left, she turned and started coughing uncontrollably, vomiting into the grass. She fell against Karl's chest. His arms clutched her shoulder to keep her from falling.

CHAPTER 9

An hour before the funeral, April sat alone in the kitchen, lost in thought. She smiled, thinking how she and Karl had made love last night. She felt guilty, but reveled being caressed in his arms that were so inviting and safe. His lovemaking helped soothe the aching she felt in her heart.

It was Good Friday. The sight of her father's body lying in the casket flashed in April's mind. She didn't know what to think anymore as she walked through the house. She felt watched and thought she heard his voice at times. Staring to her right at the landing to the back door, she heard a soft voice in her ears. She blinked a couple times to bring herself back to reality. She made a cup of coffee to clear her head and nibbled on a sweet roll as she stood at the kitchen sink and stared out the window, remembering her years growing up in this house.

Joe appeared in the archway. His head faced the floor, and his shoulders were slumped. He nervously rubbed his forehead. April noticed a glossy film across his eyes. Tears appeared. He tried to wipe them stealthily with his coat sleeves, probably hoping she wouldn't notice. He was dressed in a white cotton shirt and striped bow tie, gray wool slacks, and a navy blue blazer she had bought him for his YMCA basketball awards dinner. His auburn hair was freshly spiked with crew cut wax.

"If I'm supposed to be the man of the house, I shouldn't cry, should I?" He looked at her for approval with a wrinkled forehead, as if he was trying to puzzle it all out.

It was one of the first signs of emotion she had seen from him since the accident. "Joe, don't think that men don't cry. They do, and it's the strong ones who are able to show their feelings. There's nothing wrong with that. You look so handsome." She straightened the collar of his shirt that was left folded inside his blazer.

"But there must be something wrong. I don't even know if I loved Daddy. I know I should," he whispered imperceptibly. He nestled his face in her chest.

April hugged him. "Don't ever question your feelings. Feelings never lie. They can't be wrong, because they're yours. Naturally, we all feel sorry for Dad and sad his life had to end this way, but there was never anything we could do to help him."

When she let him go, she heard Karl announce that the limo had finally arrived. April was the last one to walk through the living room. She stopped for a moment on the way out to straighten a family picture that sat on top of the television. She felt vibrations as her hands slowly traced the picture's glass and frame. For a fleeting moment, all those childhood days and years of madness came rushing back to April. They seemed to spool out without any notion of when or how it was all going to end. Once her eyes came into focus, it was as if she saw the picture—really saw it—for the first time, attempting to bring to life the moment it was taken.

She lingered, hoping to connect one last time to the love and togetherness her family would never experience again. It would be their last family picture. She paused to remember Christmas Eve, when no one was really excited to pose, yet halfheartedly gathered in front of the tree. April's mom and dad stood with one arm on each other's shoulder and the other arm around Junior, who nestled between them. Josef wore a long printed shirt that fell well below his belly and hips. Julianna wore a white satin blouse and black bolero skirt. April and Karl sat on the floor in front. Josef's face was void of hope—much like a man who had gone astray, never to return. Yet there was another detail in the photograph that caught her eye. It was a glimmer of happiness in everyone else's face, except for Julianna, who revealed the strain of a marriage of unfulfilled dreams. Her eyes looked hollow and empty, as if she was far away and lost in another place. She betrayed a weariness that would linger into a nervous breakdown that occurred weeks later.

She paused for a few seconds to smooth her hand over the photograph one last time in a gesture to retain the happiness that filled the house that holiday evening, not knowing that weeks later, Josef would leave home to live alone at the shop. She tried to recapture other thoughts, but all she could remember now was her dad impatiently giving orders: "Let's get this picture over so we can dig into that Christmas turkey." But she knew this man by the twitch of hardened skin around his eyes—perhaps in his haste, he was feeling a reticent pulse of personal shame and disgrace. After a long moment, she straightened the picture one last time.

Tragedy alters everything. Now he was gone. His soul had departed, but his presence was everywhere—as real as the scent of his clothes in his closet. The time had come for his body to be laid to rest. She stepped out onto the patio and pulled her head down as the wind rushed past. Barely able to straighten Grandma's wreath on the way out, she locked the front door.

The sun broke through the gray March winter while the limo rolled through the neighborhood and down the streets canopied over with trees. A space of blue sky loomed over the road as they turned onto Poland Avenue, a busy street full of stores, service stations, and the funeral home. They extracted themselves from the car.

People had already begun to arrive. They talked quietly in the foyer, parlor, and viewing room. It would be the last time for them to see Josef once the casket was closed. The Straka family sat in the last row. Mourners, dressed in somber colors, streamed in and out, praying along with the priest. A woman with leathery, sallow skin and stringy hair moved toward a row of chairs in the back of the room. She was dressed in bright yellow. Mom said it was one of the barmaids who worked for Dad when he opened his first tavern.

Within the hour, cars with funeral flags on their hoods were positioned to begin the procession. Policemen sat at attention on motorcycles, waiting to accompany the motorcade to the church. The limo driver, with key in hand, maintained a somber look. Karl sat across from him in the front seat. The limo smelled strange—like baby powder and black tar. One by one, the family settled in. They watched six somber pallbearers dressed in dark overcoats slowly lift the coffin into the black hearse, which was positioned directly in front of their limousine. Aside from weddings or funerals, April could never remember attending church with her father. Tears streamed down her cheeks. Sliding her arm around Joe's shoulders, she filled her lungs with air to ease the heaviness in her chest. She held Julianna's hand. No one talked on the slow ride through traffic to the church.

When they arrived, the family waited for the procession to begin. Julianna stared into her lap with dry, weary-looking eyes; her lips moved, but nothing came out. The car filled with silence, except for the slow swishing of wipers clearing a light mist from the windshield. Church bells could be heard chiming in the distance.

Following the mass, the motorcade procession morphed into a slow-moving, elongated snake during the long drive to the cemetery. The limo coasted slowly down darker and more silent streets with staring spectators standing along the sidewalks. April peered out her window and was anxious to get the last part of the ceremony over. Although she had been staring out the window for a long time, she saw nothing of the view outside. Wisps of steam drifted up from manhole covers. She saw a lone woman wrapped in a long coat huddled in a doorway. She caught herself lost in a daydream, watching the blur of sunlight on the wet streets and grass.

The hearse led the caravan through the labyrinth of smoke-filled streets contaminated with coal and sulfur fumes. They crossed a gray bridge pocked with rust. There was a wide tower with two sets of smokestacks lined up, and four tall cylinders linked into a massive structure below. The hills along both sides of the river were brown. The limo was silent, except for the windshield wipers and Julianna's periodic whimpers. She looked exhausted. The skin around her mouth was drawn tight, and she stared out the window, seemingly lost in thought.

As the car entered the deserted cemetery, the limo driver turned off the lights and swerved around winding, narrow roads, which angled around a pond. A brown canopy had been set up as a temporary chapel. The priest entered the makeshift chapel first. Everyone lined up along the edges of the canopy. It was a damp cold—cold enough for snow. The ground was hard, and the sky was dangerously white. Candles in tall amber glass containers shimmered, throwing a warm glow around the inside perimeter of the chapel. The casket was placed amid the dark velvet rope stanchions.

People hurriedly returned to their cars the minute the priest concluded his prayers. With cheeks reddened by the March wind, Joe held his mother's hand. With Karl at her side, April choked on her sadness and stood motionless at the side of the casket, which was covered with the spray of flowers. She kissed the hard, shiny metal and leaned in to whisper to her dad that she wished she could sit on his lap one last time and tell him she loved him. Dabbing her nose with a tissue, she whispered, "Goodbye, Daddy."

She directed the driver to take them to the graveside. Hundreds of markers were neatly lined up. All types of headstones littered the plots, from large monuments to small markers laying flat on the ground. Some were decorated with flags or wilted flowers; some were bare. An old man sat on a nearby bench at the edge of a pond. He tossed seeds and breadcrumbs from a crumpled bag to a flock of pigeons circling the bench.

The limo stopped at the base of a tiny hill. The sun shone directly on a barren dogwood tree in the middle of the hill. Underneath the tree was a freshly dug grave waiting to be filled. Josef's grave would be the first one in the new section the cemetery had just opened. A spidery chill caused a shiver. April gathered her coat collar tightly around her neck.

"His grave faces east. He'll feel the warmth of the sun every morning." she said, squeezing Karl's hand. "We'll come back after Easter services."

"It's too bad your dad was surrounded by our love and yet never able to overcome whatever was troubling him," said Julianna.

"Who knows? Maybe it was feelings of unworthiness," answered April. "Whatever it was, it dominated his life and ours. He was never there for us when we needed him, Mom. Just think, other than Uncle Ted and Aunt Joy, we never have to see the Strakas again."

While the car slowly drove away, April stared out the window at the open grave and tree for as long as she could.

CHAPTER 10

Following Easter services, the family drove to the cemetery, stopping first to buy some gardenias for the grave. April held the bouquet and lifted them to her nose to revel in their sweet aroma along the way.

Soft, powdery snow covered the ground and tipped the flower buds on the trees. Once again, the car entered the cemetery's archway as the family motored to the gravesite. There were lots of cars and people honoring their loved ones, placing Easter flowers on graves. As the Straka family stepped out of the car, April's knees buckled. She slipped and fell, shivering in the damp, cold March air. Karl helped her up and hugged her tightly, holding on until she recovered her balance. He put his hand on her shoulder and drew her close. Joe and Julianna hurried to her side. "I'm fine. Just a little clumsy. "

April thought everything looked soft and pure. The car was unnaturally bright, with the sun reflecting off the snow. She saw the spray of red roses from the funeral home that lay on top of the fresh grave. There was a sprinkling of snow on the tips of the petals, which were beginning to wilt.

She gently laid the gardenias beside the roses. The wind cut through their spring coats while the family prayed in silence. April thought about Easter. Their lives would start over now. She wondered about the mysteries of death. Was it the end? Certainly when people die, they disappear forever—their voice, their laughter, their smile—and soon all memories slowly begin to fade. Maybe nothing really matters but being in the moment—being present for the here and now—because there might be no tomorrow. There were many questions left unanswered about the accident, and they were now buried with her father. She vowed she would not honor him by making pilgrimages to his grave, but instead would provide as much support as possible to her mother and brother.

On their way back to Julianna's, April asked Karl to take the long route through the park to the road, which led to the park entrance. Not more than three hundred feet from the entrance rose a massive oak tree situated on the edge of a small knoll.

As the distance between the car and the tree got closer and closer, April yelled, "Karl, stop the car! I want to get out and see the tree that killed my father." Julianna stayed put. April and Joe jumped out to get a closer look. They ran the palms of their hands up and down the huge trunk. The thick bark was hard and textured. There was a slight knot where a piece of bark was torn off. Joe tried to pull away at some of the loose pieces, but couldn't get them free.

"I don't believe it. My God, that's it? That's all it took to kill our father?" cried April, leaning her forehead against the huge trunk. "Will we ever really know what happened to you, Daddy?" Tears misted her eyes.

When they returned home, April went to Joe's room and asked to be alone for a few moments. She closed the door, sat on the bed, and took some deep breaths to reflect on the last several days that at least ended with good news from Mack. There was nothing suspicious about either the accident or autopsy reports. He would bring them over in the morning, along with the checks. It was over—all over. Now the family could go on with their lives.

She walked to the closet. There were notches of Joe's height markings along the doorframe. The bag of belongings brought from the hospital sat against the far corner of the closet wall. Sinking her hands deep inside the bag, she felt around for St. Michael. She grabbed the statue and held it against her heart, knowing it was hers to keep—that her father's hands clutched it from life into death. She wrapped her arms around his clothes that hung next to Junior's and held his clothes to her face inhaling the stale odor. She spent a long time in the closet, grabbing some of his shirts. She closed her eyes and cuddled them to her face. His energy was everywhere. She could feel his presence. She covered her body with his shirt. That night she lay in bed, grieving before falling deeply sleep.

Her mother and brother were crying. Everyone was at her parents' house. Daddy knew he was dying. He was getting dressed and preparing to go to the funeral home. He walked into the living room, dressed in his gray suit. April couldn't focus on his face, because it was hazy, as if it was covered with flesh-colored gauze. Mother and Joe wore black, but April wore a bright red dress and beautiful coral scarf. She begged her father to let her drive him to the funeral home. She cried when he refused.

Before they left, his hands started bleeding. He stopped to wash them in the kitchen sink. April continued to beg him to let her drive the car. Again, he rejected her. He asked Julianna to say his eulogy. It was nighttime. There was a full moon that was partially covered with clouds. Her face was wet with raindrops and tears as she tried to convince him to let her drive. He got into the car and wouldn't allow her in the car with them. She quickly jumped into another car and followed close behind. They kept passing each other on the road. Crying uncontrollably, she attempted to drive parallel to his car to get a glimpse of his face—to catch his eye. She sobbed, yearning to be at his side, but he would not look at her. A tornado loomed in the sky. There was a moat of rough and murky water around the funeral home. There were twelve strangers waiting for them inside. The dream ended when his face faded and he slowly lay down in the casket.

Tense, with every nerve on edge and teeth clenched, April woke to the sound of rain. She stared at the dark ceiling. The rain pelted against the house. She felt she could have a good cry without waking Karl. With her pillow saturated, she covered her mouth to muffle any sounds and gasped for breath. Erratic heartbeats brought on seismic coughs. Her chest ached. Her heart thumped, making her unable to breathe deeply. She lay still for a few minutes to regain control.

In the dark, she grabbed some paper in the drawer of the night table and scribbled everything she could remember about her dream.

She once read that a person loses half the content of a dream five minutes after it's over and 90 percent in ten minutes, so she scribbled hastily. Whenever she had bad dreams when she was little, Julianna told her to recite a short prayer before retiring, but prayers weren't in her repertoire. Not knowing where and whom to turn to, she was intent to bite the bullet and find a prayer—any prayer—because she had an uncanny feeling the dream might return if she didn't.

******

April and Karl finally returned home from Julianna's after three long days. They were quiet during dinner except for the rain teeming against the house and the hiss of the gas furnace in the background. April's face narrowed, and her eyebrows twitched, but she said nothing as she watched the rain against the windowpane. Karl excused himself the minute he finished his pasta, but hung around the kitchen that smelled of garlic and tomato sauce. They heard Pierre Salinger, JFK's press secretary, announce on the TV more news about the president's intention to establish a Peace Corps.

"Can I help with the dishes?" Karl asked as she filled the sink with water.

Without any warning, April began sobbing. She wiped her face with the dishtowel. Then she turned away and plunged her hands into the water. She stared at the window that was steamed from the hot water and boiling pasta. She tried to busy herself with the dishes, but was unsuccessful.

"Oh, Lord, what's wrong with me?" she cried. "I feel guilty that I'm at peace because Daddy's gone. How terrible is that?"

"Stop crucifying yourself. There's every reason for you to feel the way you do, but you have nothing to feel guilty about. Just think of the good things about your dad. Erase all the bad from the past. Be happy your mother and brother can finally live comfortably and in peace, which hasn't been the case the last few years. Isn't that a good thing?"

"Yes, but I wanted things to be different—as if I could somehow change them."

"Well, you couldn't." Karl dried her tears with the towel, then smothered her face with kisses. He wrapped his arms around her.

She felt his warm skin beneath his clothes—the smell of home, the dish soap, the sweat of his neck. She clung to him.

"One good thing we can say about the past is that it's not here anymore. We have a lot to look forward to," he said as he patted the little bump on her tummy that was beginning to bulge. "Let's go make love until dawn. That should take your mind off everything." Karl threw the towel on the kitchen countertop, took her hand, and nudged her firmly in the direction toward the hallway to the bedrooms.

"But it's only half past six," she said grudgingly, yet following with obedient slow steps.

"It's half past nine somewhere, silly. Who cares what time it is?"

"You know what I discovered about myself?"

"That you're madly in love with me, and I'm the most handsome man in the world?" he asked as he led her to the bedroom.

"No, I've always known that."

"Then what?"

"That I always had to be the strong one and take care of everyone in the family, but there never was anyone to take care of me."

"That's my job now, isn't it? Maybe that's why we both got married so young. We have each other to care for." When they reached the bedroom, Karl held her in his arms as if his embrace could erase her sad memories.

"What's it going to be then, eh? Dishes or lovemaking?" He wrapped his arms tightly around her.

"I guess lovemaking, since we're already in the bedroom, you silly goose. Forget the kitchen." She kicked off her shoes and looked at him in awe as he pulled her into an embrace which always brought her a feeling of total comfort. And then, unable to stop himself, he wrapped his arms around her waist, kissed the top of her head, and buried his sweat-streaked face in her neck, lifting her off the ground. His touch thrilled her and always sparked her passion. She removed his glasses and clung to him, smelling the warm skin beneath his clothes and the sweat of his neck.

April screamed, "Daddy, Daddy, Daddy!"

Karl shook her, but she wouldn't wake up. First he tapped her on the face—nothing. Then he nudged her harder—hard enough to sting—to startle and wake her up. "April," he shouted, "wake up!"

Finally, she tried to open her eyes, but they seemed to be pasted shut. Her head swam as she fought to wake up. The dream was so vivid, she had to take a few seconds to assure herself it didn't really happen. "What time is it?"

"It's only 2:00. You had a bad dream. What is it, April?"

"You don't want to know," she whispered.

"Then everything's okay; go back to sleep."

But she couldn't. Her throat constricted, and heart pounded from the same nightmare she had had the night before. It mystified her. The nightmares would persist, always leaving a troubling residue of desperation. She never realized how deep the shock waves would be with her father's absence, nor did she know what the haunting dreams meant. She wondered if she spent the first part of her life worshipping him and perhaps would spend the rest of it trying to put everything about him in the past.

CHAPTER 11

When the hospital staff whisked April out of the labor room, the last thing she saw was Karl's exhausted face and a flurry of nurses running around the halls. The labor rooms were abuzz with activity. April was finally on the last leg of her journey. The nurse put a mask on her face.

"Breathe hard, Mrs. Dunlap."

In an anesthetized stupor, the next things she was aware of were a symphony of strange voices, someone taking her blood pressure, an oxygen mask on her face, and a nurse saying, "Mrs. Dunlap, you had a beautiful, healthy, seven-pound, three-ounce baby boy. Wake up, it's all over."

April opened her eyes, sat straight up, and felt tears on her cheeks. She looked for her son, pulling off the mask. "Where is he?" she asked. "Is he okay?"

"He's fine. They just cleaned him up. They took him to the nursery. They'll bring him to your room after you get settled."

The world hadn't stopped on its axis. Everywhere, people were going about their business, babies were being born, and people were dying, but on September 26, 1961, Michael Dunlap entered the world and would take his rightful place. April felt disappointment after laboring all those hours and never getting to see the fruit of her labor—the blessed result of all her hard work. It took eleven long hours of pushing and groaning, and when the final moments were near, she willingly received the gas mask, took deep breaths to anesthetize the pains, and missed the best part. What a letdown that was.

Her next fully conscious moment was being wheeled out of the recovery room. She saw Julianna leaning against the wall with the widest Cheshire smile she had ever seen.

"I have a baby boy, Mom. Why didn't you tell me what all of this was gonna be like? Where's Karl?"

"That's something every woman has to find out for herself," Julianna said. "Karl saw the baby and then went home. He was exhausted and needed to get some sleep before going to work. He said he'd see you later today."

Shortly after April got settled in her room, a nurse arrived, holding a tiny package wrapped in a blue blanket. "I have a little bundle that wants to meet his mommy. He might even be hungry for his first feeding. Anyone here interested? "

April had her arms opened wide, ready to receive her little boy. She quickly unwrapped him and began to count each finger and toe. His eyes were shut tight. She was awestruck with the smallness of every feature—his toes, his nose, his nails. She laid his bare body on her chest—skin against skin. She held him close so he wouldn't miss the warmth of his blanket. He stirred in her arms and opened his mouth with an attempt to mewl, but nothing came out. He jerked both arms with clenched fists and next gave a tiny kick. She cuddled close to his head to feel the sweet, delicate breath on her neck. His head turned towards her as she sang a few bars of "You Are my Sunshine," but never opened his eyes.

"Mom," said April, "this is the most extraordinary moment of my life. I can't believe it. I wish Karl could have been here with Michael and me for our first moments together as a family. Can you believe it? I have a baby. He's mine." She looked at the dressing covering the stump of his umbilical cord that just a few minutes ago connected them as one—both part of the same—but she knew they would always be attached by an invisible cord. A feeling of overwhelming protection usurped her emotions.

"He's beautiful, honey. You're going to be a wonderful mother. I'll come back to see you both tomorrow."

April examined all parts of his warm, soft body, then immediately swaddled him. The smell of his skin was sweet. He had his grandpa's deep dimple in his chin. He was sleeping soundly. She whispered in his ear, "Welcome to the world, Michael, my little angel."

Michael was the Dunlap's first grandchild. April was happy that Karl's parents were so delighted that it was a boy to carry on the family name. They made several trips to the nursery to admire their new grandson. Uncle Ted and Aunt Joy's families came to the hospital bearing gifts. The remaining Straka family would remain estranged. They were relegated to the past. Grandma Straka's funeral would be the last time April, Karl, Joe, and Julianna would see the Straka clan. Later, April heard about the circus that ensued with the family fighting over her money.

Julianna and Joe had eased into living a peaceful life. April was pleased that Joe's two neighborhood friends, whose dads were attorneys, took him under their wings as surrogate fathers. It wasn't long before Joe's attitude and behavior began to change. His bullying stopped. He made the honor roll and became a YMCA basketball and summer league baseball star. April continued to play an active role in his life. She and Michael visited frequently, picking up goodies at the bakery. Joe loved cream-filled donuts. Julianna's friends encouraged her to join them dancing on the weekends, and before long, she began dating. Her spirit slowly began to come alive again.

In less than a year, Karl was out of work again. Sealtest had reformed their business plan. They sold the routes to individual milkmen. Karl couldn't afford to buy his route. It was an unsettling economy in the Midwest. The mills sustained a long strike. There were even hints of possible closings if the company and unions could not reconcile their differences.

This was the beginning of hard times for the young couple, which put an extraordinary strain on their marriage. Once again, college was out of the question until Karl could hold down a steady job. He bounced from job to job for the next few years. He took anything he could to supplement his unemployment compensation. He worked at a gas station, as a stock boy in a department store, played the drums in a country and western band, drove a truck making nighttime interstate grocery runs for a major food distributor, and helped a neighbor pave cement driveways. All those jobs in one year only earned him $5000.

Walter Cronkite called the 1960s "the most turbulent decade of the century". The 60s were bleak years: the Civil Rights Era, school desegregation, the Cuban Missile Crisis, President Kennedy and Martin Luther King assassinations, the Viet Nam War, urban riots and continued unemployment for Karl. Unable to afford medical care, April took Michael to the community Visiting Nurse Association clinic for his well-baby visits. They lived lean, sometimes buying milk and bread with the money received from cashing in bottles at the grocery store. Things got so bad, two men from St. Vincent DePaul arrived at the house one evening after they received a referral that the young couple, whose unemployment benefits were running out, needed assistance with utility bills.

Karl finally landed a job on a surveying crew that worked sixty miles from home. Shortly afterward, one of the big three auto manufacturing companies had selected a nearby town to build a robotic, state-of-the-art assembly plant. It was 1965, and a stroke of luck occurred one October morning. Karl overslept and missed his ride with the crew. Instead, he spent the day at the company's temporary headquarters to file an application and submit his resume.

He was notified before Christmas that he was hired to begin a two-month orientation training program as a Specifications Engineer beginning January, 1966. He returned to night classes at the local university. The six hard knock years since Karl and April left Virginia weren't pretty, but they taught the couple good lessons in endurance, survival, and triumph over tough times.

As months went by, the young couple in the little house on Selkirk Drive—which looked like every other house on the block—believed their good fortune would fabricate a new life and leave their old troubles behind. While some were gone, others remained, and a new crop appeared. Money was no longer an issue, since Karl worked every bit of overtime the company offered, and he returned to college. April's nightmares continued sporadically, and the in-laws—well, they remained the in-laws.

But a year after Karl started his new job, his father collapsed during a union meeting. He was lucid and briefly spoke to his wife shortly after arriving at the hospital via ambulance, then fell into a coma and died three days later. He had a long history of kidney problems.

Karl threw himself into work and school, leaving little time for his family. On weekends, he insisted April take Michael and visit Julianna and Joe to allow him quiet time to concentrate on his college studies. During the week, April spent many long hours editing, typing, and composing his papers. She and Michael spent their days on the floor in one of the unfurnished bedrooms. It was used as a playroom for him and a makeshift office for her. While Michael played with his toys, she sat on the hardwood floor, diligently working on Karl's college assignments.

One morning, while April was deeply engrossed on one of Karl's advertising term papers, Michael, who was two years old, walked into the room. He could barely balance an 8x10 glass picture of his grandfather, Josef, on his tiny hip. It was kept on the nightstand in the master bedroom. He teetered back and forth and almost dropped it on the floor. He proudly walked toward April, pointed to the picture, and yelled, "Me!"

"No, Michael, that's your grandpa, Josef."

He stamped his foot down, scowled, pointed, and stubbornly insisted, "Me!"

April jumped up, snatched the picture from his hip, and returned it to her bedroom.

He ran after her screaming, "Me! Me! Mine!" He threw himself on the floor and defiantly kicked his heels into the hardwood.

"Michael, settle down. That picture is your grandpa. It's not you." She could not stop him from screaming over and over and over, "Me! Me! Me!"

"Honey, that's not you. You're certainly defiant like your grandpa, but it's not you. That's Grandpa Josef. You cannot keep the picture."

It was impossible to control his tantrum. Only after April hid the picture and Michael spent a three-minute time out in the corner was his attention finally diverted enough for the remainder of the morning. When Karl returned home from work that evening, she told him about the incident. Josef's picture would be kept in the closet, permanently out of sight.

The more she worked on Karl's college papers, the more eager April became to rejoin the academic world. Abandoned in the suburbs without a car, she felt the increasing loss of personal freedom and independence, and she was lonely for companionship. She spent many evenings with her friend, Dorothy, whom she had worked with at Sears and lived three doors away. When Karl and Michael were in bed for the night, she'd sneak to Dorothy's to indulge in girl talk, TV, and snacks. Her life consisted of kids and college papers during the day, Dorothy in the evenings, and Julianna, Joe, and Michael on the weekends.

Dorothy's husband, Eddie, was a sheet metal worker. He and Karl were buddies. They were total opposites—as different as white and black—but good for each other. Eddie smoked cigarettes; was impulsive, carefree, and a risk-taker; and loved his beer, while Karl smoked a pipe; was serious, cautious, and premeditative; and always played it safe. They hunted and golfed together. Eddie's liberal lightheartedness helped to allay and loosen up Karl's conservative, serious side. Karl loved to come home and relate some of Eddie's antics on the golf course. One funny story he told was when Eddie got so furious at one of his wild golf strokes, he offered to sell Karl his club for a dollar. When Karl refused, certain that Eddie must have been kidding, Eddie slammed the club across his knees, broke it in two pieces, and threw it into the rough.

Eddie loved to goad Karl about wasting too much of his time and money studying and going to college. If he said it once, he said it a hundred times: "You know, Karl, after all the time and money you spend on college, what if you get hit by a car crossing the street on your way to graduation?"

Dorothy had begun cosmetology school to become a hairdresser. When the program ended, April spent her evenings drilling Dorothy with questions in preparation for her state board exam. It was fun quizzing her in the evenings, yet feeling good about helping her work towards a new vocation. There wasn't much else to do, being stuck in the suburbs without a car, since Karl was gone eighteen hours a day with work and college in the evenings. She ate to relieve her boredom and an absent husband, who was burning the candle at both ends.

She had always been a woman accustomed to independence—doing things on her own. Now, without a car and with no other friends who shared her interests beyond being a housewife, watching soap operas, reading cook books and Dr. Spock's latest advice on child care, playing Bridge, and decorating their homes, her depression intensified. In the early 60s, she had everything a modern woman was *supposed* to be satisfied with—a husband with a good job, a home in the 'burbs, and a child—but instead of happiness and contentment, she felt isolation, depression, and a lack of wholeness. It felt as if she had lost herself. She confided her problems to Julianna, who always tried to be positive with advice. "You need to be happy with what you have. Karl is a good man. It'll get better." But that didn't make her feel any better. In fact, the depression became worse. The house felt like a prison with iron bars and no means of escape.

April and Karl had fierce arguments that usually ended with a moratorium on communication. That was her punishment. He had a dominating mother, she had a dominating father, and each was determined not to be subjugated by the other. Karl could go days and even weeks without talking, but when he would lash out at her, sometimes his words would be so inconsiderate and biting, they could cut into her soul. He seemed to be unaware of the effect his words had on her. In anger, he once said, "What you do for me, I can hire any woman off the street to do." That string of words hurt her deeply.

She divided her time as best she could between Michael and Joe. She attended Joe's baseball and basketball games and YMCA award banquets or just spent time talking on the phone with Julianna into the wee hours of the night. Somehow, that wasn't enough. Days of quiet desperation increased. Nothing seemed to be going right. She felt trapped—painted into a corner, with no hope of getting out.

In the evenings, April began to mix barbiturates with Southern Comfort for an escape valve. Depression eventually progressed into thoughts of suicide. At the end of one of her severe arguments with Karl, she ran into the bathroom, locked the door, stared at her face in the mirror above the sink, and wondered what the hell had happened to her life and all her expectations. She felt she had failed. She went to the medicine chest, flipped open the bottle, and dug deep to grab a handful of pills. She emptied them into her mouth and washed them down with Southern Comfort. The house was quiet. Karl and Michael were sound asleep.

Desperate and wanting to scream at the top of her lungs, she tiptoed through the darkened hall, swallowed more Southern Comfort straight from the bottle, and slipped into their parked car in the attached garage. No one could hear the motor running from the locked car or her uncontrollable sobs and cries into the palms of her hands. She sounded like a wounded animal. She was at the end of her rope. This would be a good way to end it. There was nowhere else to turn.

She put her hands to her face and wailed, "I just want to die ... then all my pain'll be gone ... then I won't have to think anymore. He'll be happy and better off without me when I'm gone. I want to die. I want to die. I want to die ..." April coughed, cleared her throat, and choked for a while on her sadness; the heavy barbiturates and alcohol burned in her throat. She began to feel drowsy and became frightened. Almost losing consciousness, thoughts turned to her mother, Joe, and Michael. She couldn't do that to them. As soon as she snapped back, it took everything she had to shut off the motor, open the garage door, and contemplate what she had almost done. She took some deep breaths and lay across the front seat of the car until her coughing and crying stopped.

She wished she could have talked to someone about it. She thought maybe she could confide in Dorothy, but she was too ashamed to let her know how depressed and at the end of her rope she had become. Besides, Dorothy was busy working as a hairdresser. Maybe she could talk to Julianna, but she couldn't put that burden on her either, for all that she had gone through with Daddy. She decided it was best to work through the depression herself.

Minutes after she drifted back into full consciousness, she quietly tiptoed into Michael's room. She crawled into bed and snuggled next to her little cherub—her little boy who was so lovable. As usual, he was curled up with the stuffed Mother Bunny he named Minnie Mom. Minnie had a zipper across her abdomen that encased two baby bunnies.

She stared at his angelic face, cuddled close to his warm body, and wondered which treasures he was dreaming about—his erector set, vroom bike, building blocks, books, or bunnies?

She lay there for hours to ponder what she had almost done to herself. She ruminated over what choices she had to dig herself out of this depression and change her life. She remembered a poster her father had hanging in his electric shop when she was a little girl. It read, "Some people make things happen, some people watch things happen, while others sit around and wonder what happened."

How long am I gonna sit around and wonder what happened? How the hell did I let myself get to this point? How long am I gonna let this go on? I need to think about my choices. Am I gonna drink myself to oblivion like my father? Maybe I could have an affair. I already tried suicide and chickened out. What's left? After lingering moments of no answers, it finally hit her—learning. Of course—why didn't I think of this sooner? What a dummy I am. I always loved to learn. I need to take control of my life. No one's going to change it for me but me.

It was this "a-ha!" moment that would finally set her on a path to a whole new world. It had been ten long years since she left college. April began to research books that could help get her back on track—to provide the insight, understanding, and solutions to dig herself out of this hole.

It seemed that things were going nowhere until she stumbled upon the book *Passages by Gail Sheehy.* It had messages that hit a chord with her; opportunity for change and growth toward a person's potential only come with life crises. Sheehy said that each decade in life has challenges and expected adult crises. April saw a fit with her personal crisis on one of the chapters concerning "the trying twenties." It helped her discover that what she was going through was not unique, but common to her peer group of other twenty-something married women. Like her counterparts, she had been catapulted into adulthood long before she was ready. It made sense. She married Karl before she even knew who she was. She couldn't fall into the trap of thinking that men had more value than women.

She realized that she and Karl were on different growth paths. Her growth spurts didn't coincide with his. She was jealous that he seemed to be rising while she was slipping. How could she expect that they would grow in tandem? Given the described patriarchal 1960s, she began to recognize that he would never be able to understand that she didn't represent the average housewife. Although she had heard a few distant drums beating a message of frustrations through an organization called NOW (the National Organization for Women) and a book, *The Feminine Mystique,* those drums weren't very loud. She had yet to meet other women who shared her restlessness, and she didn't feel comfortable revealing her thoughts and depression with others. She concluded that she needed to return to college. That would be the answer to elevate her to a new level. Little did she know that women's liberation and the birth control pill were right around the corner.

Next she stumbled across *Erroneous Zones* by Wayne Dyer, which also helped give her an understanding of her depression. Dyer made a point that resonated loud and clear: "Don't let anyone should on you." Everyone seemed to be "shoulding" on April, especially herself. She had temporarily lost who she was and wanted to be. Dyer clearly explained that in order to be happy, a person needs to be internally controlled, not externally controlled. What an epiphany that was! She began to see her situation in a new light. *Why didn't I think of that? Who else would be in charge of my emotions but me? My happiness—or lack of—can't be what Karl, or my in-laws, or anyone else did or didn't do. My happiness has to be up to me. I can't blame it on anyone else. How I see and react to life is internal, not external. It's so simple. Why has it taken me this long to wake up? Living my life for someone else would never pay off.*

Everything came together when later she read an article in the newspaper that the local university had plans to establish a two-year, accredited associate degree nursing program. The article encouraged interested people to sign a waiting list. April made plans to submit her name, complete the requirements, and be ready to return to college by the time Michael would start first grade. Now she had a real goal—a personal goal. That's exactly what she had been lacking—a goal that could lead to a path of independence.

Everything seemed right—but how was she ever going to convince

Karl? Anxious thoughts of him and how he'd react to the idea preoccupied her plan of attack. Since he could have bouts of moodiness, she had to play her cards skillfully. The idea she had to sell would have to be presented at just the right time and in just the right way. She knew a lot about the importance of timing and waiting for the right sweet moment to bring up the subject, given the experience she had with her father.

She sweetened the pot by taking Michael out of the house for the entire day on the weekend to leave plenty of quiet time so Karl could study, since he was scheduled to leave for Detroit on business in a couple days. Next, she made his favorite Italian meal. It was now or never. *Even if it isn't the right moment, I'm goin' for it, and nothing he says will change my mind. After all, I've been the dutiful wife and mother. It's my turn.*

After dinner, she took the plunge. "Honey, I know we've settled into a pretty comfortable life. We're finally getting on our feet financially, and you're back in school. I have an idea that I've given serious thought to. Hear me out before you jump to any conclusions. I want to go back to school. There's a two-year university nursing program that's just been developed. I already have one year of pre-med courses, so the expense shouldn't be that bad, since my grades will transfer. I won't even have to take that many classes. I could be done in two short years." *Phew! There! It's finally out in the open.*

Karl laughed. "You can't go."

"Why not?"

"Because I'm in school. We both can't go."

"You go in the evenings. I can go during the day."

"Well, we both can't go, and that's that!" Karl ended vehemently.

"So, why can't we both go? Don't be so selfish."

"Because we don't have the money, we don't have a second car, and we don't have a babysitter."

"Karl, I wouldn't start until Michael begins first grade, so that takes care of the babysitter. And we could save up enough money the next couple years to have the extra tuition when I need it. Besides, maybe I could borrow from Mom if things get too tight."

"That still leaves the car. We only have one. Remember?"

"Of course I remember. I'm the one stuck all day without one. I know. Listen … " April's back stiffened up as she continued. "Don't you think being in the car production business, you could rustle up a deal sometime between now and two years from now?"

"April, why can't you just be happy like other women in the neighborhood? I finally have a good job. We have a nice house. What more do you want? What's the matter with you?"

April simply replied to his comment with a nod and a smile, waiting for an explosion. Since it didn't occur, she answered, "I don't know, but I'm not happy talking to friends about the latest cookie recipe and decorating my house. And by the way, what makes you think these women in the neighborhood are so damn happy? You knew when you married me I was in college and loved it. My life's dream wasn't to be a wife and mother. I didn't go to college to get an MRS degree. You knew I always wanted a career."

There was silence in the air for what seemed like minutes before he finally responded, gritting his teeth—a habit that April hated. He ran his hand through his hair in an agitated manner. "If you insist on doing this, April, I'll have to leave you. You're so stubborn once you get an idea in your head! Why don't you dissolve into tears like other women?"

In silence, she stared back at him, transfixed by the uncertainty glimmering in his face. "Because I'm not like other women, and why are you giving me ultimatums and threats? You know I love you and don't want you to leave, but this is something I need to do for myself. It'll benefit you and Michael too. I'm going!" She remained obstinate. "You need to think about this while you're gone. I'm not backing down." She sat staring at him, her face set hard. She held herself rigid.

She felt she had to stand her ground. For the first time she could remember, she felt a sense of peace, freedom, and confidence, even though she was crossing the line into the unknown. Her resistance couldn't be squelched—even at the threat of her marriage. She couldn't get to the edge of no return again. She just could not do that to those she cherished—especially Karl and Michael, who were her world. She loved them deeply, but was unable to deny her longing to return to the world of learning. The thought of losing Karl and destroying her marriage loomed heavy. She didn't want that to happen, but knew if she relented, her soul would be obliterated. It was a choice between him and her, and she won out.

The die had been cast. She had crossed the Rubicon. Her uncharted journey had begun. There was no turning back. It had taken months to finally discover where the guidepost wanted to lead her and where her happiness would lie. She knew she had to give a voice to her soul. She could not surrender to silence. However it would turn out between her and Karl, he was a kind and loving husband, father, and responsible breadwinner. She knew he loved her, and he didn't want his comfortable life to change.

The women's movement had just begun to unearth all the old mores and values long before men had a chance to finally catch up to all the new changes. April was glad the paradigm was beginning to shift. It yelled out to her to wake up, and she finally had. Feminism was merely the totality of being equal. Men didn't understand yet that women's gains did not equal their losses. It would take time for their resistance to subside, and with some, it would never happen. She hoped Karl would not be counted in that group.

Women were schooled in their limitations, but the truth is that most of the limitations they imposed upon themselves existed not in reality, but in their minds and beliefs. Josef taught his daughter that she had no limitations—that she had the power to do whatever she wanted. She remembered the story about the baby elephant that tried to break free while chained to a tree, but soon learned the effort was futile and gave up. But when the elephant was full-grown and able to easily escape, it believed it could not. April was not going to be chained forever. It was her time to break free.

Neither Karl nor April said a word for the remainder of the evening, yet more was spoken during their silence than ever before. There was no body contact. They stayed clear of each other. He pouted. The moratorium had begun. April could never be dissuaded once she made up her mind. They slept under one roof, but in separate rooms.

Karl was picked up the next morning to make an early flight to Michigan and wouldn't return for two weeks. April called the hotel that evening and left a message, but he never responded. She was willing to hold her ground for however long it would take. She knew it would be a long time before the uncertainty of where her marriage was going would be resolved.

Five days later, she received an emergency call that he had been taken to a hospital with chest pain and was flying home after being treated. He had been diagnosed with pleurisy—an inflammation of the lining of the lungs. She picked him up at the airport and nursed him back to health before they ever broached the subject again.

"Honey, I didn't mean to be so stubborn about the whole situation, but the way you came at me the night before I was to leave didn't give me a chance to think about it, let alone discuss it rationally. What with me out of town for the next few months, we'll both be under a strain with my new schedule ..."

"I know. I know," she interrupted. "When they told me you were in the hospital with chest pain, I couldn't believe it was your heart. Thank God it wasn't. That's probably why you got so sick. That's all the more reason we need to be together on this. I've been supportive of you going to school, and now I need you to support me. You'll see—it won't take me that long. I know it's hard for you to understand, but this is something I have to do—not only for me, but for us."

After much patience on April's behalf, Karl struggled, but eventually learned to support her and accept their new way of life. They both worked hard at crafting their new relationship and undoing the old. She learned a lesson long ago that significant emotional events always lead to change, and this one was a major shift in their marriage. She had temporarily lost her way, but was beginning to find her way back—she was awakening to who she was meant to be. The question was, would Karl adjust to this new arrangement?

Things didn't happen overnight. With patience and persistence, April and Karl worked together to slowly unlearn the old marriage and relearn a new one. Karl's work assignment in Michigan helped to foster the changes—his job, and his and April's dependencies, which began to shift from a patriarchal relationship to a more egalitarian one. It seemed to take forever—waking every morning with an element of uncertainty as to how their lives would evolve, or even last—but surprisingly, Karl slowly accepted the changes.

In the time that ensued before returning to college, April threw herself into as much as she could, since her life would be on hold for the next two years. She had time to accomplish a list of activities before reentry into the halls of ivy. She was elected PTA President, joined a bowling league, took swimming lessons with Michael, continued to play Bridge with the ladies, and spent as much time as possible with Julianna and Joe. Meanwhile, Karl continued working out of town.

April was proud of Michael. He was doing well in school. The principal stopped her at one of the PTA meetings to tell her that he wouldn't mind having three sons "if they could be just like your Michael. He is a good student and a fine young boy."

Even though Michael was tall for his age, he was not a ruffian. Although he enjoyed wrestling on the floor with Karl, he was more a lover than a fighter. Three brothers next door loved to bully him. It was hardly a fair fight—three against one. Michael would come home crying. He'd run home and climb into April's lap to be consoled. April talked to the boys' mother to reason with her that her sons needed to be disciplined, but it didn't do much good. "Michael, there's other boys in the neighborhood for you to play with; stay away from those boys next door."

"That's okay, Mommy. I want to stay home and play with you."

April and Michael enjoyed playing together on the floor with his building blocks or erector set or just reading books; otherwise, they could while away hours working puzzles. His favorite game was Monopoly. He relished making money, buying properties and houses, and breaking the bank.

"Michael, you're pretty smart. How would you like to learn how to play chess? If you think so, there's a game in my bedroom closet. It's in a brown box. Go get it, and I'll teach you a new game we could play."

He came running into the living room with the chess set and a picture frame under his arm. "Mommy, I remember this man. Isn't he my grandfather?"

"Yes, he is, but how did you know who he was? You never met him. He died before you were born."

"But I do know him. I remember him. I used to talk to him in my dreams, and sometimes, he'd come into my room to talk to me before

I'd fall asleep. Why do you have his picture all wrapped up in your closet? Don't you like him? He told me he loved you and me. Can I have it in my room?"

"If you want Grandpa's picture in your room, you can have it." April was aghast at what she was hearing from her son.

Two weeks before their wedding anniversary, Karl surprised April with their second car. That fall, Joe entered college on a basketball scholarship, and April started college. Everything was on schedule—just as she had planned. Julianna continued to enjoy dating and dancing. She was in her element. She dated frequently, but was determined to stay single and fancy free.

CHAPTER 12

More than a hundred women and three men between the ages of eighteen and thirty-five crowded together in a room, waiting to hear the Nursing Department Chairwoman begin the orientation. Dr. Gilda Capote impressed on the new students at the conclusion of the orientation, "You must never forget who you are here for. You are here for the patient, first and foremost. You are not here for the doctor or the hospital, but the patient. You will hear this from all your professors and instructors during your education here. You do not rise to give your chair to the doctor. Those days are over. You will need to continue with your education, complete your bachelor degree, and function as an equal."

Following the orientation, the gathering of the new students sounded like a gaggle of geese while they laughed, introduced themselves, and got acquainted. Traditional nursing schools included three- and four-year programs. This radically accelerated university curriculum was only two years. Gossip on the street was that hospital staff disparaged these students. They called them "instant nurses: add water and shake."

Aside from all the giggly young girls was an older woman, Judie Bartley, who was to become April's best friend for years. She was a Licensed Practical Nurse, worked the night shift in the emergency room at an Osteopathic hospital, was eight years older than April, was married with two children, and had a great sense of humor. She was a feminist who supported the women's movement for equal rights, volunteered at Planned Parenthood, believed in astrology and reincarnation, and indulged in pot. There was nothing in particular about Judie that delighted April, but it was simply her eccentricities that April loved. She was just the type of friend April longed for—someone not afraid to step out of the norm. Judie cast a glow around her person—like a bright light bulb. April got a kick out of everything Judie said and did.

April and Judie were like Frick and Frack. They sat side-by-side in most classes, and while they lived thirty miles apart, they always studied together. Since Judie worked full-time, April outlined every subject and lecture to hit the salient facts necessary to instill into Judie's brain. They had fun studying together. While April helped Judie study, Judie helped April with the practical stuff on the nursing floor. Whenever April got into a pinch in the hospital and didn't know exactly how to perform a procedure with precision, she ran to find Judie, who after years of practical nursing experience, could do many of the procedures with her eyes closed.

One evening, while they were studying at Judie's house, April revealed, "We're gonna start giving shots next week, and practicing on an orange just doesn't do it for me."

"You want to give me a shot?" Judie asked.

"What do you have that I can use to give you a shot?"

Judie went to the refrigerator and returned with a vial of liquid labeled caffeine, an alcohol swab, and a syringe. "I keep this handy, because sometimes my husband gets headaches from caffeine withdrawal when he hasn't had enough coffee." She dropped her drawers, exposed her hips, and laid down on the sofa. "Draw it up and give me a shot."

April washed her hands, drew up the liquid, and wiped Judie's hip with alcohol. As soon as she jabbed the needle into the hip, she got scared and immediately pulled the needle out without injecting the caffeine.

Judie roared with laughter and said, "Well, you found the right spot and cleaned the area, but you'll never pass nursing if you don't inject the medicine. Now do it again—and this time, dummy, inject the caffeine." From that day on, April's nickname was "dummy".

The second time was the charm, even if it was done with a shaky, sweaty hand. They broke the mold when Judie was born. She was a friend like no other.

Judie would rush to college every morning after working the hospital night shift. She and April attended an Anatomy and Physiology class Monday through Friday every afternoon after lunch. About 150 students filled the A&P lecture hall. Judie and April sat in the front row of the balcony. Invariably, Judie would nod off. The instructor would stop the lecture and yell into the microphone, "Dunlap, wake up Bartley!" Judie would bolt upright after feeling April's elbow wedged into her side.

It was 1970, and April was heading into the home stretch of becoming a nurse. With April and Karl both in college, money was tight. April had a problem coming up with tuition for one of the semesters. When April mentioned it to Judie, she pulled out her checkbook and said, "How much do you need? Don't worry. I know you'll pay it back. If not, I'll haunt you till the day you die."

Emotionally detaching from the past, April had reached into an unknown future that hadn't yet come into clear focus. This new life had fueled a sense of liberation and independence that she had dreamed about for years.

On a break from her Microbiology Class, news spread like wildfire about a campus not more than seventy miles away. Members of the Ohio National Guard had fired into a crowd of unarmed Kent State University Viet Nam War protestors, killing four students and wounding nine others. It was a year when America was polarized on many levels—social, legal, and political. College campuses were hotbeds of unrest.

One morning, when April arrived at the local psychiatric receiving hospital to begin her psych experience, the nursing students were caught by surprise when greeted at the door with music blasting from the Woodstock Festival album: "F-U-C-K, F-U-C-K!" The adolescent psych patients laughed hysterically at the rise they produced from the student nurses in their starched uniforms and white caps. April felt exhilarated from stumbling into this new life of people and experiences. It was everything she had hoped for. No one even knew or cared how old she was, or that she was married with a child. They accepted her as just another young nursing student. That felt awfully good. A smile of delighted surprise crept onto her face. She was back in the world and full of verve.

April was assigned to a forty-five-year-old woman who was severely depressed following the death of her husband. She was scheduled for electroconvulsive therapy—a shock treatment. April spent time counseling the patient before the treatment, attempting to allay her anxiety. The woman showed multiple signs of depression—sunken eyes, slumped shoulders, shaky hands, and inability to make eye contact. April accompanied her into the treatment room to observe the overall procedure. First, a nurse injected a muscle relaxant; then electrodes were attached to her scalp. It was like watching a scene from *Snakepit*. April was stationed at the patient's side to protect her from injury as her body jerked into spastic motions. April stayed with her until she regained full consciousness, helping her recover, then returning her to her room.

Michael always asked about April's patients—who they were and what their illnesses were—but Karl never really showed any interest, given his busy work and school schedules. As graduation neared, Karl presented another ultimatum. "So, what are you gonna do when you graduate?"

"Get a part-time job. I might even get one sooner. Why?"

"Because we need to talk about it."

"What's there to talk about?"

"Because I don't want you to go to work. I make enough money. You don't need to work. Don't you think you need to be at home with Michael and me?"

"Here we go again. You must be kidding! You know your threats don't become you. I'm not getting a job just to make money. Besides, what makes you think I'd spend all this time, effort, and money to learn and not get a job to start building my career? If you're concerned about my schedule, I plan on working part-time nights and weekends. I'll be home when you and Michael need me. I won't interfere with anyone's schedule."

"I don't care what your schedule is. Don't you ever stop pushing? I don't want you to work! If you do, I'm gonna leave."

"For God's sake, Karl, I love you and don't want you to leave, but I'm gonna get a job. If I don't use the skills I've just learned and studied for, it'll be even harder for me to get a job later. Don't you see that?" April stormed out of the room.

97

During the last quarter of school, April got a part-time job on the night shift as a nursing temp at the hospital with Judie. Karl never left. The evening after April finished her senior nursing final, she was assigned as a graduate nurse in charge of a fifty-bed medical unit, managing nurse aids, an orderly, and three LPNs.

Karl and April had made their peace with her returning to college, but life hadn't changed that much. It wasn't until she started making money that he finally realized this transition wasn't so bad after all. Once Karl got a taste of the additional income and their lives had begun to ease into a new schedule with little disruption, the walls of opposition quickly melted away. The old marriage had begun to morph into a new one built on an even more balanced, egalitarian relationship.

Karl and April put their house on the market before April got the results of her Nursing Boards. It sold the following week to one of Karl's fellow workers at the plant. The family moved into a newly constructed large colonial house in an upscale community fifteen miles away. Karl immediately hired a carpenter to completely refashion the basement into a cozy nightclub setting with paneled walls, a well-stocked circular bar, strobe lights, and a sound system for disco dancing. While Karl had music blaring at deafening decibels in the basement, Michael had his sound system pumping out music from his bedroom on the second floor. April could be found on the first floor in the middle of the house with earplugs.

Two years later, April and Karl purchased a summer cottage on Lake Erie that served as a family gathering spot during summer weekends and holidays. Everyone in the family still lived in Milltown, except for Joe. After college, he worked for an oil company in Houston, then was promoted to vice president, and later transferred to Pittsburgh. Joe brought many girlfriends to the cottage, but the latest one, Nata, seemed to be his favorite. She was Croatian. Nata came to America to teach folk dancing and had only been in the country a few years. Her English was impeccable. She was athletic, beautiful, dark-haired, and was studying for a fashion design degree at the University of Pittsburgh. She fit right in with the family, and she and Joe eventually married.

Julianna enjoyed family summer holidays, especially the badminton and volleyball tournaments behind the cottage. In the evenings, the family bunked together in two small bedrooms, the living room, and the porch. It took forever to say goodnight. They sounded like the Waltons from the television show. They'd laugh and call out to each person from their beds: "Good night, Joe; good night, April; good night, Michael," and on and on, until each person was recognized.

******

Early one morning, Dorothy called with bad news. Eddie was driving home after a night out drinking with the guys and was hit head-on while making a hairpin turn. He was in critical condition in the hospital. There were no empty beds in the intensive care unit. April offered to do private duty nursing until an ICU bed became available. Karl's buddy died from complications five days later. He was only thirty-five. Karl was one of the pall bearers. Dorothy had a successful beauty shop in her basement, and within a couple years following his death, she remarried and began a family.

******

April returned to college to complete her bachelor's degree and was hired as a head nurse in a hospital system with four unions. Karl had been promoted to Personnel Administrator, heading up labor relations at the automobile complex. He was April's management and union affairs mentor. Whenever she got into a tight union situation at the hospital, she'd call Karl for advice. She oversaw an important building program that supported the hospital's pediatric residency program and quadrupled patient population. In three short years, she was asked to consider interviewing for a new corporate director position over all three hospitals.

She was seduced by the offer. It fed her ambition. April desperately wanted to pursue the job, but had serious misgivings. How could she continue to fulfill perfection at home—the perfect wife, perfect mother, perfect daughter, perfect sister—and take on more challenges at work? As much as she wanted the position, she felt there was no other recourse but to decline the offer. She fell into a depression that was the beginning of a midlife crisis. April's nightmares about her father were long gone, but had been replaced with a new disturbing recurring dream about Karl.

Darkness closed over her like a blanket as she finally sank to the final depths of sleep. Many people gathered for a celebration at the house. Karl was asleep in the bedroom. Some of the guests came to tell April that Karl was dying. April was happy when she heard the news. She talked to Dorothy about how she was adjusting to Eddie's death. Dorothy went to see Karl in the bedroom and told April that he wasn't dead. He was alive. April ran to Karl's bed and happily told Dorothy that Karl just had residual air in his lungs—that was normal when someone died—but he was dead. She wanted him to be dead. April was deeply troubled by this dream. She loved Karl and never wished anything would ever happen to him. Her depression deepened. She confided her dream to one of her social worker friends at the hospital.

"I don't think you need to see a psychiatrist or anything so serious that you need to get into any long, drawn-out therapy sessions. April, you're having an identity crisis." The social worker gave April a pamphlet about the Gestalt Institute in Cleveland and recommended she register to spend a weekend there. "They can help what ails you. They're known for dream therapy. That's what you need."

The pamphlet detailed the Institute's mission. They used an experiential form of psychotherapy to emphasize personal responsibility. They offered education and training to professionals and lay persons to help them learn about themselves and their relationships with others. Gestalt therapy focused more on process (what is happening) than content (what is being discussed). The Institute emphasized things that are being done, thought, and felt at the moment, rather than on what was, might be, could be, or should be.

Judie was also aware of April's depression. April confided that she was giving serious consideration to leaving Karl. Judie offered April the use of a house her father left to her when he died. "It'll give you enough distance for a while to clear your mind and decide what you want to do. In the meantime, let's take a bus trip to Washington to march in support of women's rights. By the time we get back home, I'll bet you'll know exactly what you want to do."

That weekend, they took a bus and marched along with some notable women. Gloria Steinem and New York Congresswoman Bella Abzug were among them.

Judie was right. When they returned, April didn't leave Karl, but registered to attend the Institute. The class included eleven participants—male and female. Two males facilitated group dynamics. The only information the participants were allowed to reveal to each other were their first names. Later, during evening dinners, they began to share their backgrounds. The group included university professors, a politician, two lawyers, and a couple CEOs.

April told the facilitators that she had an important dream that she wanted to relate to the group to understand its message. The morning of the last day, they finally relented. As best she could, April summarized her sketchy dream as she remembered it.

One of the facilitators took the lead with April. "Now I want you to stand in front of the group. Close your eyes."

April stood up with her eyes closed.

"Now, I want you to cast *death* first."

April opened her eyes. "How can I cast *death?* It's not a person."

"But if it was, who would play the part?" he asked. "Close your eyes, and who do you see?"

With her eyes closed, it took a while, but all of a sudden, a tall, commanding man, standing erect, appeared in her mind's eye. It was Yul Brynner as the King of Siam. "Death is Yul Brynner."

"Why Yul Brynner?" he asked.

"Like in the movie, the *King and I*—he's standing so tall, so imposing, and so dominant. Death is like that—so final. No arguments—it just is."

"Now, I want you to keep your eyes closed, April, and tell us about your dream when you're ready."

As in a theater, the curtains began to rise, and April saw her dream in detail—the setting and the people. "My God, the celebration is for my son, Michael. Everyone is at his party to celebrate his high school graduation. I'm sitting next to my friend, who is a widow. I'm talking to her about losing Karl, because I know she'd understand what I must be going through." All of a sudden, April stopped talking.

"Go on," the facilitator encouraged. "Why did you stop?"

"Oh, my God! I walked into the bedroom, and it's not Karl who's dying—it's me!"

When she finished her detailed description, the facilitator said, "Now, I want you to open your eyes and talk directly to me as if I'm Karl. Tell me what you want. Tell me why you want to be dead."

April began a long soliloquy. "Karl, I've helped you with school and waited for my time. I've done all the right things, made a good home, been a good wife and mother, raised a fine family, worked hard for my education. I'm beginning to excel in my career." The more she talked, the more she cried. "Now they want me to take on more responsibilities and have asked me to consider applying for a high-level corporate director position, but I can't do it and still be the perfect wife, the perfect mother, the perfect daughter, the perfect sister, the perfect housekeeper and cook, and do all that's required if I take this job. It's my dream, Karl. I've been waiting, and now it's my time, Karl. It's unfair. I can't go back to when I was unhappy, okay?"

The facilitator looked deep into April's eyes and said, "Did you hear what you just said? April, you're still asking for approval. You said, "Okay?" You're not going to get any approval from your loved ones, so don't expect it. They don't want you to change. They love you the way you are. They want you to stay the way you are. They want the world as they know it with you to stay the same, but it's time for you to be happy, and you won't be happy unless *you* change. You're the only one who doesn't like who you are. The celebration that you said is Michael's graduation party is merely a metaphor for *your* graduation to the *new you*. You want to graduate too, but it's going to take you some time to adjust to this newness. Your new self wants to emerge. The death of Karl is your death, not his. You want the *old you* to die so the struggling *new you* can finally be born. Do you understand?

"Whenever death shows up in a dream, it indicates some type of transformation. Remember one thing. The answer to a dream is never *in* the dream. The truth is always *outside* the dream. You have been indoctrinated to be the pleaser—the performer for everyone. This new life wants to emerge from its cocoon.

"When you go home, you need to gather your son and husband and declare what the changes will be—the changes that will make *you* happy. They won't be happy, but it needs to happen for you. You will not get their approval. You will not even get approval from your parents or siblings, either, because again, they love you the way you are—but give them time. Be patient; accept their resistance—they'll adjust. But go on quietly becoming your new self."

When April returned home, she did as she was instructed. She gathered Michael and Karl to explain that things would be different. "We all need to share in some of the daily things that are taken for granted. For example, each of us needs to take turns making dinner."

Michael spoke first. "I can't make dinner. I go to school."

"So do I," said April.

"But I work."

"So do I."

"But I don't know how to cook."

"It doesn't have to be a meal. You can open up a can of soup and heat it for the family dinner one night. You can make us peanut butter sandwiches, but everyone will take their turn during the week. I'm not asking for much, but I don't ever want to come home anymore from college at 10:30 at night after having worked all day to have you both tell me that we're out of milk. If you see we're out of milk, someone needs to take the responsibility to go to the store and buy some. Don't wait for me to do it. Those are some of the things I'm talking about."

Karl was quiet. He and Michael listened intently and agreed, but it was a bitter pill to swallow for the people April loved the most in the world. April had imposed all these requirements on herself—it was no one's fault but hers. She was the one who felt she *should* be the perfect mother and wife, go happily about her housework—cleaning, laundry, cooking—to please her husband and son, and kill them with kindness. Now there was a whole world out there that was beginning to show itself as she stood on the shifting ground called midlife. The dream was the turbulence that summoned and forced her to a transformation from one identity to another. She would finally be able to answer the question, *Who is this person inside of me that I almost lost?*

CHAPTER 13

Michael decided to pursue engineering. After reviewing various types—civil, mechanical, electrical, etc.—nuclear was his favorite. He chose the University of Cincinnati, an excellent engineering school in southern Ohio almost six hours from home. Most engineering programs lasted four years. This one, however, was a five-year program. It combined classroom-based education with practical work experience, commonly known as co-op.

April dreaded the thought of Michael leaving home for the first time. She woke up in the middle of the night to write him a poem entitled, "My Son."

> Youth becomes so clouded with survival needs
> that the worth of life's true gifts sometimes
> are reserved for later maturity.
> It is only through years of growth and eventual wisdom
> that enlightenment has surfaced the meaning of its
> profound anchor, tightly wrapping
> my soul's silver cord to my son,
> who was conceived on Christ's birthday.
> As I gaze at you, years later, my eyes well up with
> pride, fulfillment, and wonder.
> Whatever have I done to be bestowed such a
> spectacular gift from Spirit as my son?
> So loving, so beautiful, with such deep, dark,
> expressive pools from his soul's windows,

seeking warmth and always reaching and
risking life's wonders for new adventures.
Whenever I gaze at my son, his soul and mine are one,
and he becomes the tiny pink infant I saw
for the first time when disconnected from my being.
It is through him that I have truly learned the meaning
of love and the mysteries of life.

April was despondent throughout the six-hour trip to the University of Cincinnati. The college had a full weekend orientation planned for the students and parents, which included fraternity/sorority parties, a President's tea, and many other activities, ending with a Sunday brunch. First on the agenda was getting Michael moved into his dorm. Once Michael was settled in, April and Karl spent their first meeting together with the incoming nuclear engineering students, their parents, and the professors. Next, parents and students went separate ways for their respective meetings, then planned to meet later for dinner.

April and Karl attended a two-hour parent orientation, which concluded with a movie of campus life and college activities. A Beatles song played in the background. The strains of the music that permeated throughout the auditorium grabbed April's heartstrings and wouldn't let go. It had omniscient power over her. From the first few notes and pictures, which showed the gaiety of campus life, April finally realized her baby was leaving and that things would never be the same. Before this moment, she had never given Michael's departure much thought other than happiness that he had embarked on an important goal for his future. But now, she began to feel the golden life-chord connecting her to Michael slowly begin to detach. There was no denial. It was happening. She was even jealous that he was leaving Milltown, but she had to return.

Karl and April planned to meet Michael for dinner, then stay overnight at a motel. April knew she couldn't bear to stay another night for the final parent-child events. Karl agreed they would leave after dinner. They picked up Michael following his orientation to campus rules and policies. By the time they arrived at the restaurant, April was one minute away from tears and remained in that state throughout dinner. She had a tight knot in her stomach and no appetite. To Karl's surprise, she held back her tears.

Michael talked like a magpie about all the exciting and overwhelming activities the school had planned for incoming freshmen. "This weekend's gonna be so much fun. I've met a lot of neat kids and pretty girls. The President's tea will kick off your trip back to Milltown. I know it's gonna be tough getting acclimated to everything, and …"Michael continued ad infinitum while Karl and April remained a captive audience, watching his expressive eyes. When he finally finished, Michael asked, "So what do you guys think?"

Karl took the lead. "Sounds like you made a good choice picking UC. Mom and I like the school too. Just remember to keep up with your studies, and don't get too crazy with either the girls or drinking. Nuclear Engineering's no piece of cake—nose to the grindstone, son. Make the best of it. This time in your life will never be repeated. Remember, Michael, it's *showtime!*"

"You always say that, Dad. What does it mean?"

"You're on stage. Do your best."

April's eyes widened. She took a deep breath, slowly exhaled, and looked down at her plate of food that was barely eaten. "Michael, Dad and I won't be staying for the President's tea or Sunday brunch. It's just too hard for me to stay, knowing that we'll be leaving you here. I hope you understand, honey." Her voice was strained and stressed.

"You don't want your 'rents to stay here and curb your fun, anyway, do you?" Karl asked, trying to add some levity to the heavy conversation.

Michael picked up on it right away. "I understand."

Not much was said in the car on the way back to Michael's dorm. All three of them knew in their hearts they were entering a new place— one where their lives would change again forever. They were in a kind of limbo. Their baby was entering a new stage, marching into adulthood and independence. Things would never be the same again.

When they dropped him off at the dormitory, April and Karl hugged him tightly for the last time. As he turned and walked away from the car to the dorm—his new home—April saw his entire life flash before her swollen, tear-filled eyes. The tears she had suppressed all day had finally broken through. She cried throughout the long drive home. As soon as they arrived back in Milltown, they threw some clothes and food in a satchel and headed for their cottage at the lake. The following weekend, they returned to the university to be with their son.

******

Michael loved his major. He researched possible nuclear plants, developed a resume, and interviewed for his internship. At the conclusion of his freshman year, he procured a co-op job with Duke Power, a nuclear power plant in Charlotte, North Carolina. He would spend two quarters there every year for four years. Karl bought him a new compact car. Michael earned a good salary each quarter. Karl joked that Michael earned $10,000 in one quarter for his internship, yet spent $12,000 and needed money to tie him over. Michael rented a nice apartment and bought fine clothes and a sound system. Like his grandfather, he liked to live the high life.

April and Karl visited him the first quarter he worked at Duke. He took them on an extended tour of the power plant and offices. He explained everything in great detail—nuclear energy, its operation, the infinite quality programs, and government regulations and requirements. Michael's parents were impressed with his range of industry knowledge.

The following year, during one of his co-op sessions, April and Julianna flew to Charlotte to spend a week with him. It was the first time Julianna had ever flown. She always said she was afraid to fly, but she would do anything for Michael. Michael picked them up at the airport and took them on a tour of the city. He had a special relationship with his grandmother. He surprised her the evening before they were to return home and gave her a beautiful amethyst pinky ring.

"Gram, you're my sweetheart. I want you to wear this ring and remember how much I love you." Even when he was little, Michael and his grandmother were always hugging and kissing each other like sweethearts.

After a couple quarters of practical co-op experience, Michael decided he didn't want to crunch numbers all his life. He took business classes to pursue a double major. He had a habit of making calls home and explaining ideas he had to start some new type of business. Those calls usually ended with the words, "If I only had …" He'd name an amount of money and say, "I could put this deal together and make it happen." There were times he would also try to hit up Uncle Joe, who by that time, was a successful oil man. He'd ask for money or just bounce off ideas for his latest business deals. His pleas, however, produced no additional funds, but that didn't make him quit trying.

Michael was considered a ladies' man. If he told April once, he told her a hundred times with each girlfriend, "Mom, she's the one. I think I'm gonna marry her."

One Mother's Day morning, April received a call. "Happy Mother's Day, Mom. I have some news. Are you sitting down?"

April swallowed hard. Thoughts rushed through her brain. *Did he get some girl pregnant? Did he get expelled? Did he flunk out?* It took a while before she finally broke the silence. "I'm sitting down. What happened?"

"Mom, I went out for cheerleading, and I made it!"

"Well, that's great news. Congratulations!"

"But how do we tell Dad?"

Since Karl was such a macho guy, Michael was concerned about his dad's reaction to his news. He had played high school football *only* because Karl wanted him to. That was what every strapping young boy should do in high school—or so Karl thought. But Michael was a lover, not a fighter. All things considered, Karl took the information well, and he and April were headed to all Michael's home games to film and watch him cheer. It was no effort for him to bounce and hold any one of the cute little cheerleaders, given his strapping six foot three stature.

It began to look like five years of school would be stretching into six or seven. Finally, Michael and April had a come-to-Jesus meeting one holiday when he was home. "Michael, you know you started with engineering, added cheerleading, added business, and now recently, added ballet classes. You've got to focus on finishing what you started. I'm gonna give you an end date, and if you're not finished with engineering, you're on your own. The money from us will cease. You will have another two years to finish, and that's it."

"Since you and Dad are making more money, don't you think I should get more?"

"It doesn't work that way, kiddo. You need to learn to live within your means—the same as we do."

Karl thought she jumped the gun on declaring a specific date, but it was too late. The gauntlet had been thrown down. Now he and April would hold their breath and hope Michael could make it. He was headstrong, but this was an important lesson he needed to learn.

There was no word from him for months. Finally, he called. "Can I come home next weekend?

"Of course you can," April encouraged. "This is your home too, and always will be. Dad and I really miss you. We'd love to spend the weekend with you. I probably won't be home, though, by the time you get here, because I have tickets at the playhouse. That'll give you and Dad some alone time together."

******

Before April had a chance to stop the car and turn the headlights off, Michael came running at breakneck speed down the driveway. His face was pale and limp, and his eyes opened wide, as if he had just witnessed a train wreck. She hit the brakes. As soon as the car came to a skidding stop, he jumped in. He was out of breath and gasping for air. "Dad was in a bad accident. The hospital just called. He's in the emergency room."

April gunned the engine. They took off down the street. "What did the hospital say?"

"Just that he was in a bad car accident and was in the emergency room."

"It's a damn good thing you were here to take the call, honey." For an instant, April was back in the hospital grieving room, feeling the long-forgotten despair and hearing her mother say, "He's gone." *This can't be happening to my father and husband, for God's sake!* But the thought only lasted for an instant. She had to put it out of her mind.

When April and Michael arrived at the hospital emergency room, they were escorted to Karl's gurney. Karl's face and clothes were bloody. He had a deep, angular laceration across his nose. He was unconscious. The minute Michael saw his father, he immediately turned and walked away, with tears in his eyes. "I'll be in the waiting room."

The policeman who discovered the accident was still in the hospital. The nurse notified him that the victim's wife wanted to talk to him.

"Mrs. Dunlap, I got the call about 7:30 p.m. that there was a bad accident on Kirk Road. I arrived minutes later. Your husband's car was completely totaled. Based on the tire tracks, he hit a tree and rolled over. I immediately called the ambulance and wreckers and told them that I expected the victim to be dead. To my surprise, I found your husband lying across the floor. I can only surmise that he must've fallen on the floor before the car rolled over. All I can say is that he's lucky to be alive. Obviously, he had had a few drinks too many, because his alcohol level was 0.2—well above the normal limit. He'll have to appear in court and may lose his driver's license."

The nurse reported, "Mrs. Dunlap, we sutured the laceration on his nose. We'll get him admitted as soon as there's a bed available to observe him overnight and rule out any internal or head injuries. Call Information in the morning to find out if he can be discharged."

The next morning, April arrived with clean clothes. Karl's eyes and nose were badly bruised. She received the discharge orders to take him home.

"How are you feeling? You know you're lucky to be alive, don't you?"

"I'm all right—just a little sore. I have a headache."

"It's a good thing that's all you have after what the policeman who found you told me." She related the information to him. "So, what happened after you left work?"

"I went out with the guys for a few drinks. You know how it is on a Friday night. You want to start the weekend winding down. The accident happened on my way home."

"Well, it looks like you did wind down enough, didn't you? How did it happen? How'd you lose control? It rained a little, but the weather wasn't bad. Do you have any idea how scared Michael and I were? He was home alone when the call came that you were in the hospital."

"I don't know what happened. I don't remember anything. I don't even remember being brought to the hospital. The first thing I remember was when they brought me up to this room."

Regardless of the fact that Karl had no recall of either the moments before or during the crash, he returned to work on Monday. It would take months for him to psychologically and emotionally recover from the accident. He didn't lose his license, thanks to some of his legal cronies, but he did attend safety driving classes.

******

The year was 1981. When April backed out of pursuing the Corporate Ambulatory Director position, she scheduled a meeting with her boss, the VP of Nursing, Miss Jane Damone, who had hired her. April and Miss Damone had a good relationship.

"So, what brings you here this morning, April?"

"As you know, for personal reasons, I was unable to pursue the ambulatory position last year, but I'm getting restless and ready to move on. I thought we could discuss other nursing administration positions that might be coming up in the near future that I would qualify for."

Miss Damone proceeded to list some of the opportunities. April settled on the Corporate Director of Quality Assurance. The accrediting body for hospitals had just developed a new set of quality standards that all hospitals would need to comply with. The position would develop, implement, and educate the nursing staff to the new quality policies and procedures. April completed her due diligence, attended the accrediting body conferences in Chicago, and then went to work on developing the hospital nursing program. April and a nursing supervisor collaborated on developing a new quality tool to be implemented throughout the three hospitals. Later they published the development and implementation of this tool in a national hospital quality journal.

Life seemed to be going well when suddenly, everything changed. A new President and CEO, James Thomas, who had the reputation of a being hatchet man and was not fond of strong women in high places, was hired. The Board of Directors invited everyone to a tea to meet the new guy in the corner office. There was a lot of publicity in the local newspapers about bringing him in from a major medical center in Boston. April attended the tea with Miss Damone. April extended her hand. "Glad to meet you, James. I'm April Dunlap, Nursing Quality Assurance."

"Hello, Miss Nursing Quality Assurance. What's that pin on your lab coat?"

"That's my NOW pin."

"And what does NOW stand for, Miss Nursing Quality Assurance?"

"It stands for the National Organization for Women."

"I think I've heard about that organization." He grinned and walked on.

Obviously, April didn't think she made a good impression on the new guy in the corner office.

It wasn't long before major policy, building renovation, and production consultants roamed the halls like hospital drones. Major reorganization of most departments was underway. Staff morale took a nosedive. Nursing was first on the chopping block, since it was the largest and mostly populated with women. Miss Damone was demoted. She was stripped of some of her positions. April retained her position; however, she and the new CEO were like oil and water. She knew things probably weren't going to get any better. She decided to pursue a graduate degree to firm up her credentials and job security. She was accepted into a two-year weekend executive MBA program which the hospital and Women's Board funded. It could be her ticket out of Milltown if she could ever convince Karl to move, but he was firmly entrenched with his job.

Instead of attending her graduation, April and Judie traveled to Denver for the twentieth anniversary celebration of NOW. Although the Equal Rights Amendment had been defeated, the attendees took to the streets to march for women's rights. Oprah Winfrey was featured as the guest speaker. NOW was honoring her for the strong woman's role she played in the movie *The Color Purple*. It was the eve of the syndication of the new Oprah talk show. April scoured the convention rooms in hopes of taking her picture. The minute she spotted Oprah, she made her request. Oprah snatched the camera from April's hand and gave it to her assistant. She put her arm around April and hugged her tightly. "Come here, honey!" she said. "We're gonna take a picture together." She was quite a dynamic woman. At the conclusion of her forceful, inspirational speech, everyone was on their feet to give her a standing ovation.

CHAPTER 14

The winters in Ohio had become brutal, with arctic freezes and enough snow to make igloos in the front yard. It was if those long winter seasons would never end, and when they did, they were followed by overcast, dreary days. April was in a state of constant yearning, planning for a future in which she and Karl could escape the winters temporarily for brief respites until they retired. She tossed around the idea of finding a little spot of paradise. April had a yearning to be anywhere but Milltown, so when her friend at the hospital, Terry, invited her and Karl to join her and her husband on vacation to a small island in the Bahamas, April gave it serious consideration.

"Have you ever heard of Treasure Cay?" asked Terry. "It's very quaint. There are no televisions, telephones, or holiday commercialism. How does that sound to you?"

"Like paradise. Let me clear it with Karl, and I'll let you know."

When April broached the subject with Karl, he replied with a question and an answer. "Remember when we returned from the boat show at the Cleveland IX Center, and the streets were covered with slush and dirty, grayish snow? When do we pack and get the hell out of here?"

The adventure began when the two couples got to their connection in the West Palm, Florida airport and the attendant asked for their weight—not the baggage weight, but each person's personal weight. It turned out their puddle-jumper carried nine passengers. The flight took less than one hour air time. The Treasure Cay airport wasn't any bigger than April and Karl's triple-car garage at home. Customs was a joke. As the couples piled their luggage on the massive table, the jovial, well-fed, tall officer asked, "How long you here, Mon?"

"One week."

Next, he asked, "Business or pleasure?" The travelers flashed their passports, and that was the extent of customs. There was no opening or examination of luggage.

It was love at first sight when they caught their initial glimpse of the beautiful Sea of Abaco. A brilliant cloudless blue stretched from horizon to horizon. The travel brochure described it with the words, "stunning is the word for this 3.5-mile stretch of powdery, white sand, matched only in brilliance by the turquoise water colors lapping at its shore." They were right. It was stunning. The sea was even voted one of the Caribbean's ten best in the *Caribbean Travel & Life* magazine.

April and Karl had previously visited Nassau, but Treasure Cay was vastly different. It was one of the places people dream about—unforgettable sunsets, peaceful solitude, no crowds, and all the Goombay Smashes and conch chowder a visitor could want. The resident Bahamians and Haitians were very personable and colorful. People from various other countries bought second homes and condos there, adding to the island's charm.

One night, when April and Karl were eating dinner in their rental, they heard on the radio that President Reagan had just been shot by John Hinkley, a young man trying to impress and garner the attention of Jodie Foster, the movie star.

A few days after April and Karl arrived, they bumped into a couple they knew from their neighborhood who had a second home on Brigantine Bay in Treasure Cay. While having drinks on their patio one evening, April and Karl lamented having to leave their newfound paradise and head home to a cold and rainy Ohio spring. Conversations led to their interest in purchasing vacation property, whereupon the couple introduced them to their next door neighbor, a spirited woman in her seventies from California who lived permanently on the island, only leaving every six months to renew her visa, visit her doctor, and shop for clothes.

Thelma Lovelace was a widow of three husbands. She had property on the Bay and a condo on the marina for sale. She was a tiny, rather frail, bent over woman about four foot eleven who had traveled the world. She had short, thin hair—a mix of blonde and gray—and a brown cigarillo with a quarter inch of ash, which perpetually dangled from her mouth. She was always dressed tastefully in colorful island cropped tops and bottoms.

She named her canary-yellow house Eureka (I found it). It was beautifully decorated in California furnishings. The large leather recliner, telephone (which probably was only one of six on the entire island), and 30-inch television set were situated against a ten-foot wall covered with a mounted zebra skin. Everything Thelma did, she did with verve. She had a twenty-five-foot white Mako boat, loved to snorkel, and offered to teach the skill to the two couples.

"When can we go?" asked April. "We only have a couple days left before we return to the Snowbelt."

"Honey, if you're ready, I'm ready. Get your snorkeling glad rags on, and let's go!"

Within the hour, the two couples met Thelma on her dock to prepare for their first snorkeling lesson. They loaded the cooler with ice water. Thelma had the motor warming up. Karl took the bow and stern lines from the dock, boarded the boat, and headed down Brigantine Bay. April went up to the bow of the boat and watched it slice through the water. They motored to the other side of the island, then set their sights on Don't Rock, which was Thelma's favorite snorkeling area. Thelma said, "There's always an abundant supply of starfish, conch, yellow tail, sea fans, sponges, and parrot fish." Everyone received a lesson on proper application of snorkeling equipment.

When Karl mentioned he had problems with the mask because of his gag reflex, Thelma spouted, "Don't be such a pussy. Just keep it in. You know how to do that, don't you now?" She laughed. Thelma enjoyed her own jokes as much as everyone else. She had a great sense of humor. Whenever she thought she said something funny, she'd throw her head back, hold her breath, and belly-laugh heartily.

April and Karl took to her right away. "Can we call you our Bahama Mama, Thelma?" April asked.

"You can call me anything you want, honey, except a dumb bitch."

The day before April and Karl were to leave the island, they spent the day with Thelma. Over lunch, they discussed the condo and property she had for sale. The property was directly across Brigantine Bay from her dock, and the condo was in Mariner's Cove in the heart of the island's marina. Thelma's prices were fair, and Karl and April considered purchasing both.

The couple sold the cottage on Lake Erie, put a second mortgage on their house, and took the plunge in buying Thelma's condo and property on Brigantine Bay. The planned to make the condo the annual Dunlap family vacation home, and the property was earmarked for their retirement home. It provided a temporary escape from the cold and gloomy Midwest. April and Karl promised each other that as soon as they retired, they would move. The day they made their purchase was their twenty-fifth wedding anniversary. It was their gift to themselves. Karl kneeled at April's feet and sang Stevie Wonder's new hit, "I Just Called To Say I Love You."

Treasure Cay had become the annual family respite every Christmas and New Year's. These vacations altered their lives in unexpected ways they hadn't foreseen. The vacations were uplifting and helped to allay the rest of the time they spent in the gloomy Midwest. It was peaceful to escape the cold winter weather and incessant holiday commercialism. Michael would fly from college to join his parents for the holiday celebrations. Naturally, the family spent their holidays with Thelma.

Many families from the States, Canada, and Germany also had second homes in Treasure Cay. Some flew their private planes, as they were also vacationing with their college children during the holidays. The kids enjoyed their annual reunions. They played beach volleyball for drinks with reggae music blaring in the background, threw darts at the Tipsy Seagull, and danced at the Junkanoo, which was a Bahamian festival reminiscent of New Orleans' Mardi Gras and Rio's Carnivale. Everyone on the island danced at the Junkanoo throughout New Year's Eve before the first hours of light on New Year's Day. Dressed in brightly colored clothes, people danced to the rhythmic accompaniment of cowbells, drums, and whistles. The dancing had a way of lifting one's spirit beyond the flesh.

Thelma loved good-looking men. The more time she could spend with Michael, the better, as far as she was concerned. Michael could do no wrong. She loved getting hugs from him.

It had become a tradition every New Year's Eve for each person to decorate and wear some outlandish head covering—the more outlandish, the more likely the person was to win. Everyone would take pictures, and whoever won the contest would have the honor of carving the prime rib roast for dinner. Thelma always voted for Michael, and she'd insist on helping him carve the roast.

"Do you wear those silk shorts to attract the girlies?" Thelma asked. "If I was fifty years younger, I'd pinch that butt of yours."

Karl eventually bought a boat so the family could venture out on their own to snorkel and island-hop at will. He named the boat MIAPKA, taking two letters from each of their names. It was a tongue-twister, but it worked for them.

There were continued suspicions about drug-running on the island. One early morning at sunrise, Karl, with coffee cup in hand, walked the beach in search of unique shells. He spotted a bale wrapped in black plastic which had washed up on shore. He opened a corner and saw it was packed with marijuana. He continued walking as if he hadn't seen anything. There was an unwritten rule on the island that if you saw anything suspicious, you were to forget about it and walk on, because someone might be hidden in the trees or bushes, waiting for a pickup.

Cigar boats would drop bales of drugs into the bay from time to time. During one of the trips, Karl and April spotted Coast Guard helicopters and Bahamian police helicopters. The helicopters circled the bay. Men armed with machine guns climbed down ropes. They suspected a major marijuana drop. That was the excitement for that day.

Michael was befriended by a young Haitian, Lymon, whose livelihood depended on the money he earned from fishing and lobster-catching in his boat, the *Hummingbird,* for the island hotel and tourists. After a storm or any kind of inclement weather, Lymon and Michael would leave early in the morning with snorkel equipment, dive to the bottom of the ocean, and catch lobsters one by one with a Hawaiian sling, which was a device used in spear fishing. The sling operated much like a bow and arrow on land, but with the sling, the energy was stored in rubber tubing rather than a wooden or fiberglass shaft. Bahamian law did not allow spears to be used. Michael and Lymon would stuff each lobster into a bag as it was caught.

April had recipes for lobster stew, steamed lobster, lobster Newburg, and lobster salad. If you could name it, she made it, similar to Forrest Gump's sidekick, who cooked shrimp twenty different ways.

CHAPTER 15

Michael missed his parents' deadline for finishing college. They held their breath that he'd come through, and he did. He got a student loan, worked a couple jobs on campus, and that money plus two semesters at Duke Power got him to graduation. He and April both graduated in 1986 and ventured off into different directions, leaving Karl behind in Milltown. Michael left for the Naval Officer Candidate School in Rhode Island, while April took an administrator position in a Cleveland health maintenance organization eighty miles from home.

April rented a furnished high-rise apartment on Lake Erie and traveled back to Milltown to be with Karl on the weekends. Ultimatums had become a thing of the past. Karl went along with the flow, even though he was left behind. Both Karl and April survived their midlife crises, and their bond had morphed into its strongest incarnation yet. Their marriage seemed to be going through stages every few years; yet they managed to ride it out. That was all that was necessary. Now Karl even offered to help with her move.

Together they packed both cars and took off for her apartment. He spent the entire day helping her get moved and settled. When it was time for him to leave and return to Milltown, she followed him to the parking lot to see him off. She fell into his arms in a passionate embrace, placing her lips firmly upon his. He squeezed her tightly. They kissed longingly. He winked at her as he drove away. She stood there, eyeing him with a slight frown, watching his car grow smaller and smaller until it was out of sight. She cried to herself, knowing she would miss him terribly. *What's wrong with me? Why do I keep pushing and pushing? Why the hell can't I be happy in Milltown? I wish I could click my heels like Dorothy and make all my sadness go away.*

Within two years of living apart with April returning to Milltown to be with Karl on the weekends, both April and Karl agreed the time had come to finally leave their jobs and move to the South.

There were too many career changes to spend the holidays in Treasure Cay that year. They decided to stay home. A blustery rain melted the snow that was blanketed on all the rooftops. Everything looked gray and dirty. The days became shorter and colder. April cherished the early morning hours before sunrise. She did her best thinking when everything was quiet, and the world was asleep. Her favorite place to drink her morning coffee was on the window seat in the loft that overlooked the frozen lake that stretched for miles behind the golf course. She could hear the clock ticking in the background. Michael was home for the holidays.

"Why are you sitting in the dark, Mom?"

Startled, April turned and switched on the low beam of the floor lamp.

When she looked up, for a fleeting moment, Michael's gesture and expression bore a striking resemblance to her father's—the dimple in his chin, dark brown hair, and captivating brown eyes. Michael was a veritable carbon copy of his grandfather in his youth—not only in looks, but in many other ways. Michael was a risk-taker—an idea man who was always looking for something different. He was stationed in Tacoma, Washington on a nuclear submarine. The Navy had made a difference in him. He stood ramrod straight, as if he had Harrison rods inserted into his spine. He walked with a mature confidence April was attracted to when she first met Karl. Michael's short scramble of hair was matted; it stuck straight up in the back, like Dennis the Menace. April stared at her beautiful son with pride.

"I didn't expect to see you up so early." She wet her fingers with saliva and attempted to pat down his hair. "Sit down and join me. We can watch the sun come up together. We only have a short time before you leave again. You know Dad and I are pretty proud of you and your promotion to Lieutenant." They sat together in silence for several

121

minutes. The grandfather clock ticked in the background. The rain made syncopated sounds on the tile roof. April watched the steam rise from Michael's hot coffee. It masked a clear outline of a troubled profile. Worry seemed to tighten the muscles in his jaw.

"Since this is the first time we've had a chance to be alone, there's something I've been wanting to talk to you about, Mom—something that's been haunting me for some time."

"Go ahead. I'm listening."

He drew in a breath. "You're gonna think I'm crazy, but I've had some strange feelings."

"Like?"

"You're never gonna believe this, but like I was your father in another life. There, I said it. I don't even know how to explain it, but—but sometimes, I have these funny sensations. I told you this would sound ridiculous, but hear me out. I have these feelings about split-second impulses of wanting to drive off a bridge or head into a cement wall. It's like something or someone is pulling at me to see how easy it would be to lose control and crash."

As Michael spoke, April tried to contain her surprise. She nodded in a reassuring gesture. She reached for his arm and shoulder. She stroked his face with her soft hands while he spoke. This disclosure unleashed a whirl of emotion—it was startling, daunting, and baffling. *How could this happen to my son?*

"I know you said your dad was an alcoholic. I think maybe I had a problem with alcohol in another life. I don't know if I was your Dad this time around or years ago, but I have a real appreciation for it that I can't explain. I don't know anything about reincarnation, but sometimes these fleeting sensations drive me crazy. They wash over me like a wave that I can't control. I just needed to tell you—to tell someone. It even sounds weird as I hear myself repeating this, but it's been on my mind to talk to you about it. I don't want you to say anything to Dad."

"There's something I need to show you that might shed some light on this." April left and returned with the St. Michael statue wrapped in tissue paper, along with newspaper articles and pictures of Josef's accident. She handed them to Michael. She watched him closely for his reaction as he read and studied the pictures in one hand while he held the statue in the other hand. For half a minute, he was unresponsive. The only sound in the room was the rain that pelted against the patio doors. Minutes later, his face turned white. He put everything on his lap and covered his face with outstretched hands for a few moments to shield his emotions.

She understood quite clearly in that moment how truly troubled he was. "Well," she asked, breaking the silence, "what do you think? How did it feel? How do you feel?"

He turned and looked at her with a tightened jaw. "I'd appreciate it if we never bring up this subject again." He shook his head back and forth a couple times and handed the items back without further comment.

"I promise," she said. "It's between you and me. I can't tell you I understand it, but I'm here for you if you want to talk about it again."

April felt Michael's arms wrap around her back. She turned and hugged him hard. She wanted to comfort him enough to dispel the strain and agony he must have been feeling. Her life was truly blessed, but she felt helpless, as she could not provide the insight he needed to ease his disclosure. She wondered if this mysterious story had a bead of truth. She knew nothing much about reincarnation, so she was unable to help or say anything that might allay his anxiety. She hadn't thought of her father for a long time. It had been almost thirty years since his death, and the nightmares had ceased long ago. Suddenly she remembered the incident when he was a toddler—how he held his grandfather's picture, screaming, "Me! Me! Me!" Later, he told her that he knew his grandfather—that they talked in his bedroom.

She changed the subject and tucked the articles under her afghan. "Michael, Dad and I have been making plans to leave our jobs and move south. We were going to tell you last night after we rang in the New Year. We feel it's time to make changes for the future—to move where there will be lots of sunshine and no snow. We'll be making connections in Florida to find jobs. We decided whoever lands the job first will move and leave the other one behind to sell the condo here. You know eventually we wanted to live somewhere that's sunny and warm. It was never an option for us to wait until we retired. We stayed here because of Dad's job and to get you and me through college. That's over now. There's no reason to stay. The time is right. We're ready."

"It's time you guys enjoyed yourselves. You've worked so hard these last few years. Do you have any contacts in Florida?"

"Well, I'm on an Ohio Hospital Association Committee, so I plan to call my colleagues there to get some contact names they may have with those in the Florida Hospital Association Committee. That's how I'll get started."

"Wow, things are really gonna change for you guys. Does Gram know?"

"No, this is pretty new. I haven't said anything to anyone. You're the first. Dad and I just decided before you got home. I'll let the family know in due time. Have you thought about what you're gonna do when you're finished with the Navy?"

"I want to go to grad school—probably get an MBA, like you. Who knows from there where life will take me?"

"If there's anything I want you to remember, it's that you must always follow your dreams. Goodness knows, there will always be roadblocks along the way, but if you listen to your inner voice, you'll never regret the results. I have an idea. You'll be gone in a couple days. Let's celebrate a new beginning when Dad gets home tonight. We'll break open another bottle of champagne and have a party—just the three of us."

CHAPTER 16

Networking began with a call to the Hospital Association. By day's end, April had talked to eighteen people in four different cities in Florida. Networking was exhausting! That evening, she received a call from one of the regional medical directors at the largest insurance company in Florida. By the end of the week, she had scheduled interviews with two insurance companies—one in Orlando and one in Tampa.

******

After running to make her flight connection in Atlanta, April sat aboard a DC10 bound for Orlando. The passenger seated next to her was polite and friendly. She couldn't take her eyes off the woman's gaudy necklace, which caught a blinding reflection from the sun's glare that streamed through the window. April hoped the woman wouldn't notice her fascination with the necklace. It was a round, gold, antique medallion the size of a half dollar with a knight in armor on a horse, holding a flag. When the woman's long, white, well-manicured fingers weren't fidgeting with the medallion, sliding it up and down the chain at her throat, or twisting her opal ring, they seemed to be shaking with a slight tremor.

The woman introduced herself as Rachel Ripley Blackburn, born and raised in Orlando. She held out her hand. "Do y'all live in Orlando?" she asked while she adjusted her seat belt.

"Not yet, but I hope to real soon. I live here in the Midwest. I'm interviewing for a couple jobs."

"Who with?"

"Two different healthcare insurance companies."

"What a coincidence. I'm in healthcare, too. I work for a large cardiology practice in Orlando. Which companies are you interviewing with?"

"Call it superstition, if you must, but I'd rather not say just yet. Bad luck, you know." April observed the woman's strange expression. She looked rather anxious and gave her a sideways glance as soon as her question was rebuffed. April didn't have much experience with southerners and thought perhaps getting personal so quickly was part of their culture.

When the flight attendant approached, April offered to buy Rachel a drink, but she declined. She said she didn't drink anything harder than a diet soda. As the jet passed over the Florida coastline, April was lost in thought, wondering if this would be the new home for her and Karl. When the plane touched down, she was enveloped with a warm sensation. This was not the first time she had been in Orlando. She and Karl had vacationed here with Michael years ago. She woke out of a daze when she heard, "We're here, sweetie."

Together, April and Rachel rode the airport monorail and walked through the terminal. Orlando was truly a cosmopolitan city. April felt as if she had been transported to a foreign land as she listened to all the dialects and languages from passengers dressed in colorful ethnic clothes. The atmosphere and energy were uplifting—why wouldn't they be? Orlando was the vacation capital of the world. April had to move quickly to keep up with Rachel. This woman took long, quick strides.

The trip through the airport was a sight to behold. A huge glass cylindrical fish tank in the main concourse was filled with gallons of saltwater and hundreds of beautiful tropical fish. Departing hordes of tanned children dressed in colorful Disney and Sea World t-shirts, wearing Mickey Mouse ears, and carrying stuffed Shamus were followed by exhausted parents dragging slowly behind. In contrast, crowds of arriving people flashed bare, alabaster arms with pale-faced, happy children. The newcomers walked arm-in-arm with their parents in an energetic, uplifting pace, anticipating their fantasy vacations.

Rachel wrote her home phone number on the back of a business card and gave it to April. "Give me a call if everything goes well and you come here to live. We could meet for dinner. I'd love to show you around town." Once Rachel retrieved her luggage, she waved and said, "Ta-ta, sweetie. Wish you luck!"

April admired the tall, well-endowed, and manicured southern belle. Rachel had a firm, springy saunter in trim stilettos that added more than three inches to her tall stature. She walked briskly through the crowd with an air of classy sophistication and flamboyance, fluttering her long black eyelashes at male passers-by. Her thick auburn hair framed a widow's peak on her forehead. April wanted to get to know her. She could even turn out to be a good business contact. With a touch of ambivalence, April questioned her sincerity, southern charm, and hospitality. Everything about Rachel instantly screamed superlatives, which seemed to be a façade. April put thoughts of Rachel out of her mind. There were too many other things to think about now. Getting a job monopolized her concentration. Feelings of anxiety crept into her thoughts as she realized the importance of nailing her interviews. If everything worked out, her job could be the foothold to the future for her and Karl.

April sat in the silver-gray Chevy Caprice rental car long enough to read the map and get her bearings for directions to the downtown Helmsley Hotel. The streets had begun to dry following a spring downpour. Once April was outside the confines of the airport, she was amazed at the beautiful blue ice-cream-cone-shaped cumulus and cirrus clouds, bright sun, and big rainbow overhead. She was exhilarated and energized, landing in her new environment, and considered the possibilities the magical city could offer.

CHAPTER 17

April couldn't shake the cobwebs from her head. It seemed impossible that within only one week after arriving back from Florida, she had received an offer. She and Karl had completed a trip to Orlando to check out the corporate suite the company had rented for her. Only a week remained before she would embark on her departure to Orlando. Julianna planned a farewell family celebration for a sendoff to her new life.

Karl had already left for work as she slid off the side of the bed, sinking her bare toes into the deep, lush shag carpet. She walked into the shower. The initial pelts of hot water over her head and body were as exhilarating as a Swedish massage.

By midmorning, it was time to make a trip to the cemetery to say her final goodbyes. The only stop along the way was to buy some gardenias. Now that April was finally leaving Milltown, she noticed for the first time how quiet and deserted the empty, chewed-up buildings were, the lack of any bustling traffic near the mills, and the crumbling smoke stacks. The steel mills had been silenced. Their thriving prosperity had ceased when they closed on the morning of September 19, 1977, much to everyone's surprise. It would be remembered as "Black Monday" in Milltown. Although it had been more than a decade since the last furnace cooled down, people continued to think it was coming back, but the industry was decimated. It was sad how the change enveloped the town and its people. The closing of the steel mills would go down in history, and the place would be remembered and referred to as the Rust Belt, symbolic as the end of a major American industry.

As April's car merged into the road to the seven-foot, stonewalled cemetery, she felt the place emit a warm and inviting aura, even though the cold March air was thick with fog and dew—one could almost reach out and grab it. The rolling terrain of some green brush unfurled before her. Although this was her first venture in a couple years to visit her dad, the car seemed to know the direction of that peaceful hill. The cemetery hadn't changed much, but now the hill was densely populated with headstones. She made her way around the winding road and gazed up at the rows of mausoleums framed against the fog-darkened sky. The only sound and movement was the wind, which howled over the trees, and a cool breeze that drifted through the sunroof of her Oldsmobile Toronado. A tiny space of blue sky loomed eerily over the road. She made a sharp left turn and shut off the motor. Straight ahead was the marker.

Josef Straka
1913-1961
Rest in Peace

April carefully placed the flowers on the grave and felt a chill as she knelt down next to the headstone. The remembrance of that spring day in 1961, mottled with light snow, presented a never-ending memory that still made her shoulders knit with overwhelming sadness. She leaned back and coughed into her fist, hiding a frown. She tucked her cold hands under her armpits for warmth. Private memories returned— taking her father's shoes off when he came home after a hard day's work, making his highball, and watching his face light up whenever he read her report card. She pulled her head down as the wind rushed past. *Goodbye, Daddy. I pray you're finally at peace. I hope we'll meet again someday.* She hopped into her car and closed the sunroof. The sun broke through the gray of an Ohio spring. With eyes closed, April's head turned toward the sun, and she felt its healing rays against her face. She turned her head back and craned her neck to look out the rearview mirror to catch the last glimpse of his grave as she drove off.

******

Shortly after everyone's arrival, Julianna, the family's finest cook and hostess, entered the room with a tray full of hors d'oeuvres— cheese puffs, pate, miniature buttery, croissants filled with chicken and mushrooms—and placed it on the oak coffee table.

"Now this is what I call a real family get-together," said Joe, "great food, good company, a gathering to send my sister off on a new adventure."

"Anyone care for a drink?" asked Julianna. "Help yourselves."

"I would say so," said Karl. "I'll make a Manhattan."

April stirred her martini with a toothpick, which was loaded with two huge olives. She stared at her mother and admired her optimism. Julianna didn't look or act the part of a woman approaching her mid-seventies. Years of suffering from nervous breakdowns were not evident in her youthful face. Her life was peaceful following Josef's death. There still was plenty of spunk and energy left in the old girl, who used to never reveal herself for fear people wouldn't approve.

"I'm always saying goodbye at these family get-togethers," Julianna said as she pointed a blaming finger first towards Joe, then Michael, and finally April. With tears in her eyes, Julianna held her highball in the air for a toast. "Let me be the one to start this off. April, you've always made the best of opportunities that came your way. To a daughter who means so much to me. I hope you know how lucky I've always felt to have your strength. I'm going to miss you." Julianna rocked her chair so far back everyone worried she was about to tip over, but instead, she rose up and fought back her tears.

Julianna linked arms with April. With a sad expression, she held her glass high, nervously rattling the ice cubes in her drink. She started over. "I know a woman of strength and beauty ..." She looked down at her hands to collect herself and regain composure enough to continue. Joe inched over to his mother. He wrapped his arm around her shoulders to give her added support.

Julianna cleared her throat and continued, "I-I know a woman of strength and beauty." I've watched her for years. She's my daughter. She's given me much love, happiness, and a shoulder I could always lean on. I love you, and I'm sad that another one in our family is leaving.

May God bless you in this new job and life. You've worked hard for it, honey. You deserve it—to April!"

Everyone raised their glass and joined together in the toast. "To April," they echoed.

April kissed her mother.

Joe was next. "April, I just want to tell you that your words of inspiration helped guide me in the right direction, and it's really your fault I have so many worries—"

"And money," laughed Karl.

"And money, yes—and for that, I will be eternally grateful—to the new Floridian! Here—"

"Wait!" April cut in. "Before we toast, what were my words of inspiration? It's not often I'm profound. Please remind me when I am."

"Don't you remember the day Dad died, you told me I was the man of the house? Believe it or not, those words turned me around, sis," said Joe. "I took it seriously after that—too seriously. As hard as it was, I tried to become the model son and brother. I felt it was up to me to make major personal achievements to bring pride to our family after all we had suffered while Dad was alive."

"And achievements you've certainly made, Senior Vice President of an oil company at twenty-eight. I'm so proud of both you and your accomplishments. Daddy would be so proud of you too—his namesake." April was moved to tears and dizzied by all the warm and loving gestures. Peace had come to the family.

Joe raised his glass once more. "To my sister, the new Floridian! Here! Here!"

"I'll second that," said Nata, Joe's new wife. Everyone toasted in unison.

"We wish you luck," said Karl, with his hand raised and clenched around his Manhattan. "Don't change too much and get too comfortable with being alone."

"Let's eat," said Julianna. "I'm starved."

"Wait," said Michael. "It's my turn. Before we eat, I want to make a toast to my mother and my family."

All eyes were in Michael's direction. The family waited for him to continue.

"Even though our lives may spread us miles apart, our love will keep us together in our hearts—to us!"

"To us!" they all cheered.

Julianna outdid herself. She prepared an Italian feast fit for kings. Everyone worked away at the food—Italian wedding soup, lasagna, salad, and cannolis for dessert.

April was aware how unusually quiet Karl remained throughout the meal. It wouldn't be long before they would be separated in two very distant cities, not knowing how long the separation would last.

******

April watched Karl as he walked out of the bathroom after performing his usual rituals—removing his watch, hanging his clothes on the dresser drawer, setting the clock one last time, and spooning up to her in bed.

Those marital signs of familiarity brought swells of aching emotion. Her body was hungry as she waited for his touch.

He grabbed her longingly, kissing her neck, ears, and eyes, smothering her with deep kisses.

On their last night together, April was eager to surrender everything to him. His touch and passion thrilled her. They made love for what seemed like hours. His body was warm and brought her deep contentment. He wasn't a man of words, but he knew how to consummate beautiful and magical lovemaking. Their bodies were so well known to each other, they became one. It was impossible to know the difference between what each was feeling. She felt a twinge of regret that tomorrow she would embark on a life without him, but hoped it wouldn't be for long.

"Do you think that'll hold us for a while?" he asked.

"Don't worry. Remember, I'll be flying home every month," she laughed. "Hopefully, it won't take you long to sell the condo and join me."

They had an Amaretto nightcap and kissed one last time before retiring. Karl pulled the silk quilt to his chin and was asleep in minutes. April tossed and turned, unable to relax. She had difficulty sleeping soundly that night. She was wildly keyed up. She and Karl would be living separate lives again. About 5:00 a.m., she carefully wriggled out of bed. Karl was twisted into such a tight fetal position that except for a few inches, it looked as if his head would touch his knees.

April made herself a scalding hot cup of cocoa, walked to the patio door, and opened it for a minute. A blast of cold spring air blew open the vertical blinds. Sweeping the hair off her forehead, she wondered what new adventures lay ahead in the city more than a thousand miles away. Lost in thought, she stared out over the golf course and listened to the soft rhythm of rain on the rooftop. She sat on the chair next to the door for what seemed like minutes strung out, a silhouette against a rectangle of moonlight. Her fingers traced an endless circular path along her smooth gold ring before finally returning to bed.

The bed squeaked when she jumped up at the sound of the alarm. Her head swam as she fought to wake up. She moaned as she swung her feet onto the warm plush carpeting. Karl sat up and squinted as he shut off the clock. He put his arm under his head and stared intently at her. "It's sure gonna be hard to wake up in the morning without you next to me." He yawned and blew a kiss her way. "I'm gonna miss you big time, honey." He scooted off the bed and walked to the bathroom. "You better be careful and call me when you get there." He jumped into the shower.

Not one for sentiments, Karl had been sweet and loving the past few days. April knew he was as deeply affected by their imminent separation as she was. She cuddled up behind him as he stood in front of the bathroom mirror. Smells of coffee brewing in the kitchen wafted into the bedroom. Tiny bits of gray that she had never noticed before shone through his dark brown hair. After being married for almost thirty years, she couldn't help but admire his good looks. Like every other morning, she handed him his wake-up mug of espresso. He smelled clean and fresh. She buried her head in the back of his neck with thoughts that in a couple hours, she'd finally be off by herself.

Karl turned, wrapped his arms around April's waist, and kissed her forehead. "Do you think you have everything you'll need?"

"Everything but you. Seriously, I think so. I've checked everything twice. My Toronado and I are ready for Florida, but I don't know if Florida's ready for me."

April could tell he was worried. The muscles in his jaw were tight when he said, "Just remember, you're my girl."

"Aren't you going to eat anything before you go?"

"Not today, honey. I'm still satiated from last night." He winked and turned toward the back door.

"One last hug?"

Karl's arms were strong. April felt secure, feeling his warmth and rubbing her cheek against his clean-shaven face. She turned away, choked back tears, and yelled, "I love you" as he started the car and backed out the drive.

"I love you too."

April stood at the back door and watched his car slowly round the bend and drive out of sight. It was time to get ready. She had a long trip ahead. She wrapped Karl's gray terry cloth bath towel around her waist. It reeked of Poco Robanne. She basked briefly in the tenderness of their lovemaking last night. The towel was still warm from his shower. Wearing it made her feel better about leaving him and incredibly lucky for all her good fortune. She decided to roll it into a tube and use it as a pillow for her head so she could inhale his aroma throughout the long drive.

April stared at her face in the bathroom mirror and smiled. *Not too bad for an old, late-blooming career woman, soon to hit the half century mark, huh? It's not every woman who would venture out alone to a strange city. Why shouldn't I? Daddy always said, "Columbus took a chance, so why can't you?" I didn't exactly plan on leaving town alone, but I'll make the best of it—I always do. It's finally time to spread my wings, meet new people, and experience a new culture. Oh, how ready I am!*

Water dripping from the shower was a reminder she better get a move on. Time marches on, and it was April's time to march out. She organized the car and stacked books, her briefcase, water bottles, a coffee thermos, maps, and her purse on the passenger seat and floor. A metal pipe loaded with clothes hung across the back seat of the car. Anthony

Robbins' *Personal Power* tapes and a tape recorder were on the floor in the back seat. The trunk carried the remainder of her items: clocks, radio, luggage, and tape recorder. Shoes and socks were tucked into all the small crevices. She lovingly placed a portfolio of family pictures on the passenger seat so she could look at them throughout the trip.

When she packed the last of her gear into the car, a feeling of finality swept over her. She smiled, hummed the theme song from *The Mary Tyler Moore Show,* and checked her list to assure herself that everything was complete. She ran back into the house for one last item—the St. Michael statue. She hunted everywhere, but couldn't find it. She left a note for Karl to look for it and send it ASAP.

She straightened the rearview mirror, checked the passenger side mirror, and with her key in the ignition, she put the car in gear and congratulated herself again. It would be the first time ever driving alone on such a long trip. She tucked Karl's bath towel behind her head for support and comfort. His smell was still strongly evident. She kicked off her tennis shoes and pressed the gas pedal with her bare toes. As she backed out the drive, she had the sense that she had been living in a city under siege, and the gates had finally opened. The journey she had always prayed for had finally begun.

PART TWO

SALVATION

Don't follow where the
path may lead,
Go where there is no path
and leave a trail.
—From a truck sign

CHAPTER 18

A sudden flash of light hit the windshield as the sun began to rise east of Interstate 4 heading toward Orlando. The morning sun had burned through, and the breeze smelled of jasmine that lined the Florida highway. The temperature on the instrument panel registered a comfortable seventy-six degrees. April was on the last leg of her trip. The farther south she drove, the more beautiful the spring sky became, and the more her demeanor was uplifted. The trees and grass alongside the road were plush green. April drove with an open sunroof and windows to absorb as much of the atmosphere as she could. Her restless eyes glanced lightly off the city streets and incoming highways, which were peppered with digital billboards that changed messages every eight seconds.

It was early Sunday morning when she arrived at the corporate apartment complex where she would live rent-free for the next three months. It gave her a sense of freedom—a heady feeling, like she had just won the lottery. She had no misgivings the instant she turned her car into the development that this new temporary home would begin the start of an exciting new phase in her life. She was confident Florida had the charisma and essential powers to accomplish her dreams. If she looked upon her whole life, this would be the first time she had no one and nothing to worry about except herself, her new job, and new adventures. She could not think of another time when she felt more comfortable—no fears or desires, just an overwhelming feeling of peace and possibilities. April delighted in the anonymity of big city life, being liberated, and being totally consumed with the importance of *me*. With not an ounce of trepidation, she was ready and eager to begin her new journey.

The apartment buildings in the complex were pale yellow stucco with rust-colored Spanish tile roofs and shutters. A grove of gnarled oak and crepe myrtle trees surrounded the perimeter. There were approximately forty-eight units arranged in a geographic configuration similar to the capital letter E, with the vertical part of the letter facing Kirkman Road. There was a circular turret over the clubhouse. Parking conveniently outlined the apartments at each of the three horizontal legs of the E. The cars in the lots had a panoply of license plates from states around the country. This city was truly a melting pot. April's eyes traced the office, mailboxes, swimming pool, and tennis courts, which stretched horizontally across the top of the E. Between the street and April's unit was a circular pool with a fountain that lit up in all the colors of the rainbow. This was a development of multiple hues.

The starkly furnished, 850-square-foot corporate suite with plain vanilla walls and linoleum floors consisted of a bathroom, living room, and kitchen, separated by a bar and three stools. April was pleased with the temporary accommodations her new company had made for her. It only took two hours to unpack the car, make the bed, and put everything in order. She threw on some shorts, a t-shirt, and a baseball cap to shade the hot sun. The rest of the day would be spent grocery shopping, exploring the city, and tracing her steps in the car to her office to assure herself she wouldn't get lost during the height of rush hour traffic on Monday morning. First, she needed to decide where to eat, since her stomach had begun to growl like a bear that had just awakened from a long hibernation.

The flat soles of her sandals smacked the pavement as she walked across the street to a cute restaurant called *LePeep*. She bought a copy of the *Orlando Sentinel*. April figured the food here must be quite delicious, since a group of about twenty people were lined up in a queue outside the door and halfway down the sidewalk, waiting to get in for brunch. It took fifteen minutes before she was finally seated. Her scrumptious veggie omelet arrived with a side order of grits, a Southern dish she was unfamiliar with. Eating alone at a restaurant was another new challenge to add to her repertoire.

"Y'all enjoying your breakfast?" asked the waitress.

"Everything's great, but I could use more coffee."

"Comin' right up." She bustled around the booth in a perky trot to fetch the coffee. "Are you fixin' to live here, or are you on vacation?"

"I arrived this morning. I just moved into that apartment complex across the street." April pointed to her new home. "What's all that construction down the road?"

"It's the new Universal Studios theme park. It's supposed to be ready in another year or so. Did you notice that house sittin' on top of the hill when you drove in?"

"Yeah, I sure did. It looked familiar."

"That's because it's the haunted house from *Psycho*—you know, that Alfred Hitchcock movie. The park will really add to the traffic congestion when it's done. So what else is new? This town can't stop growin'! It's bustin' at the seams. Honey, you're in for some excitin' times here." The waitress turned on one heel and headed for the kitchen.

April grabbed the paper and scanned the latest news. After breakfast, she went next door to the grocery store to stock up on some staples to get her through the week. Friends had warned her not to forget to buy a can of bug spray. Cockroaches were the state pet. Even in the best of places, somehow they found a way to get in. April wasn't well schooled in the way of cockroaches, snakes, and gators. With two heavy shopping bags held tightly under each arm, she managed to fight six lanes of traffic crossing to her apartment. She kicked off her sandals the minute she walked in the door, set the groceries down, and opened the living room windows to listen to the calming sound of the fountain about a hundred feet from her front door. As she unloaded the groceries, she saw her first Florida cockroach, dead inside the kitchen cupboard.

The complex was a cacophony of sounds: water running, toilets flushing, music blaring, and cars coming and going. This was a good time to fish around for the business card from the woman April had met on the plane to announce her arrival in town. "Rachel, it's me, April. Remember me on the plane? I'm here in Orlando."

"April, hello. Y'all made it. You got the job?"

"I sure did—to both your questions."

"Congratulations! When did you get in, and what was the lucky company?"

"About five hours ago, and First Coast Insurance."

"What're ya fixin' to do for the rest of the day?"

"The only thing I planned was to explore the city a little—particularly the directions from my apartment to the office. I've been reading the map to familiarize myself for the drive to and from."

"Why don't you wait another hour, sweetie? I'll come by. We can go together, grab some early dinner, and get better acquainted."

"I'd love that, Rachel, but I don't want to impose on any plans you might already have made for the day."

"Don't you worry about that. My daughters have their own plans today. I'm free for the pickin'."

Next, April called Karl. "Honey, it's me—safe and sound."

"Jesus, I've been waiting for your call all morning. I've been worried sick."

"Um … I didn't want to call you until your golf game was over."

"There's no golf today. It's cold and raining."

"Warm and sunny? Did you say it's warm and sunny?" She held the phone a distance from her ear, laughing and waiting for the backlash.

"No, cold and raining. C–O–L–D and R–A–I–N–I–N–G. Don't rub it in."

April filled Karl in on the final leg of her trip, her first morning in Orlando, and her plans for the afternoon with Rachel.

"Just be careful whom you befriend; you're all alone in the big city."

"No kidding. Yes, dear," she said perfunctorily. "I think at this age, I better be able to take care of myself. By the way, have you had any luck with your Florida job search? Any bites on the condo? Have you heard from Michael lately?"

"No to all your questions, but I've got a busy day planned next week to make some important connections. I hope it turns into something promising. I'll keep you posted. Have not heard from Michael. By the way, I got your message about the statue. I haven't found it yet, but I'll keep looking."

About the time April finished putting the groceries away, there was a knock on the door. April stood inside the screen, sizing up her new friend. Rachel walked into the middle of the living room like she owned the place. She stood there with her dark hair and tall, slender body in all her southern grandeur. She shucked off her full-length linen coat as she entered the room, and laid it over the kitchen bar stool. She wore a matching bone-colored sheath dress and brown patent leather knee-high boots. A ray of blinding sunlight, which filtered through the front door, masked her facial features and altered her outfit to shades of winter white. Once again, her medallion caught April's eye. April glanced at the glistening piece of jewelry that peeked slightly above the neckline of Rachel's boat-necked dress.

Rachel looked taller than April had remembered. She was quite shapely, like a middle-aged Lauren Hutton model. April had struggled with her weight in midlife and admired anyone who could pull off such svelte, clean lines.

"Boy, am I happy to see you! I haven't had a real conversation since I left my husband two days ago. I really appreciate that you've taken the time away from your family to come over."

"My pleasure. We already did our Sunday ritual—church, brunch with Mother—and now the girls are out with their friends. The rest of the day is mine and yours now. I know you've been in your car for the last few days, so let's take mine. It'll be easier to tour the city if I drive. Come on, sweetie. Lock up. Let's go. My company car is that blue Buick Skylark out by your front door. Jump in. I'm gonna take you on a little tour of my world. Then we'll stop off at Mother's for some tea. She wants to meet you. You know, you're in a hot area here. You've got a new Universal theme park across the street. Disney World and Sea World are about five miles to the south, and two miles to the East-West Expressway exit will take you to your office. You're in a perfect location."

April and Rachel toured the city. Their first stop was Church Street Station, a complex that offered live entertainment, fine dining, and lots of downtown shopping. It was constructed around Orlando's original train station. They stopped to examine Old Duke, a steam locomotive that was in the John Wayne movie *Wings of Eagles*.

Next was the Station's original bar, Rosie O'Grady's Good Time Emporium. They indulged in a refreshing drink and popcorn—April a cold brew; Rachel a soda. While they listened to the honky-tonk music and chatted about the hot spots to visit, Rachel picked out dozens of local travel brochures from a curbside rack outside the Emporium entrance. The stands, filled with travel brochures and entertainment news for the week, were located along street corners throughout the area. April and Rachel drove down the notoriously busy Interstate 4 and International Drive, known as I-Drive. It was an unending strip of restaurants, t-shirt and souvenir shops, putt-putt, boutiques, cafes, and everything a tourist could want and imagine. Tourists reading maps while driving rental cars twenty miles per hour drove the hometown folks crazy. Rachel explained that most major cities in Florida were crowded with snow birds in the winter, which eased up in the summer when they returned home to their northern and Midwestern cities. Orlando was different. Its population was inflated 365 days a year.

April marveled at the city's hustle and bustle. It was the only major landlocked city in Florida. It was eclectic, with an assortment of international visitors, transient residents, and nothing but new construction everywhere April looked. The cluster of buildings looked no more than a few years old—as if the entire city was born the day Walt Disney came to town.

"You see those construction cranes all over the city?" Rachel asked. "We call those cranes our state bird."

"It feels great to be in the midst of all this prosperity and positive energy," laughed April. "I've spent my entire life in a relatively small town whose claim to fame was the Mafia, political corruption, and the steel mills, which have since closed and economically devastated the city."

"Not here. Our problems are with growth. As you can imagine, Florida's been in a continuous struggle to maintain an adequate infrastructure. It's been tough keeping pace with a burgeoning population since the advent of air conditioning. Believe it or not, almost a thousand new residents migrate to this state every month."

Rachel's mother's house was the next stop on their trip. It was a beautiful, southern-style two-story white stucco building. The house had forest green shutters, three large staghorns, and moss draping from branches of huge oak trees. A narrow walkway led to the massive oak front double doors, which were framed by black wrought iron filigree. Rachel's mother, Dinah, greeted them in a pink flowered billowy dress that fanned out in whirls like a parachute ready to open as she walked. Her silver hair was tied back with a slender gold clip in a French twist. She had rings on four of her fingers. She left a hint of Chantilly fragrance as she walked.

The three women walked through a room lined with book shelves and pictures of the old South on the way to the parlor. Dinah's manners were impeccable. She served refreshing sweet tea and round shortbread cookies layered on an ornate silver platter with tiny, pink-rosebud-embroidered linen napkins. April felt she had been transported into another time and place. Dinah's house reminded April of Tara from *Gone with the Wind*. She expected to see Scarlett O'Hara walk through the door any minute. The furniture was circa 1920—antiques, hanging needlepoint pictures of antebellum mansions, and a display of family pictures in silver frames on the piano. A heavily tufted sofa and wing chairs were covered with colorful fringed shawls. April could feel Dinah looking her over, sizing her up, and probably categorizing her as a real northerner, sans southern manners. In no time at all, Dinah began to drill her with questions.

"Rachel's told me a little bit about you and why you're here. She said you've made a major life change. I admire you young women today and the freedom you've had chasing after your careers."

"That wasn't the case for me. I married young and had a child by the time I was twenty-one. Remember, I'm from the generation of women who were *supposed* to be satisfied as stay-at-home moms."

"And you weren't?"

"No. I wasn't among the bra-burning feminists that emerged in the middle sixties. I was a Johnny come lately who marched the Washington streets in support of equal rights in the 1980s. I didn't complete my education until I was forty-six. It took me over seventeen years, off and on, to finish while raising my family."

145

"So, you're still married?"

"Yes, and to the same man."

"You're fortunate," chimed Rachel. "My husband abandoned me after the twins were born."

"I was the dutiful wife, but I finally shed my Stepford image when I got my first full-time job at thirty-eight," continued April. "Until then, I focused on raising my son, lending a hand with my mother and younger brother, and helping my husband with his career. My father died when my brother was little, and I tried to be as much a part of his life as I could."

"Sounds like you were a pioneer and a late bloomer. Where's the rest of your family?" questioned Dinah.

"Most of them live in Ohio."

"How'd your father die? What happened to him?"

"He died in an auto accident."

"Would you like to contact him?"

April choked on her tea and quickly put down her cup to wipe what she had spilled on her shorts. She was shocked and didn't know how to respond. She was caught off guard in a swell of intense confusion. "Excuse me?" she asked.

"Mother, don't start," said Rachel.

"April, you'll have to pardon my daughter. She embarrasses easily. You see, I'm a psychic. If you're interested, I'd be more than happy to see what we could dig up—no pun intended," Dinah tittered.

"No, Mother, I think you're more of a *psycho* than a *psychic,*" answered Rachel.

"Don't mind my daughter," Dinah continued. "April, you need to come see me at Cassadega. I work there occasionally."

"What's Cassadega?"

"It's a spiritualist community a few miles north of here. I have a sense that you're on the cusp of a spiritual odyssey. Several of us offer psychic readings. I'd be interested in doing one for you. Have you ever had one?"

April nodded in agreement with a pasted smile. All she could think of was cognitive dissonance from her psychology background.

Something just didn't seem to fit. Dinah's proper and demure appearance was starkly incompatible with her behavior and unusual vocation.

"I read a book about Edgar Cayce and went with a friend once to have my Tarot cards read," April answered, "but this sounds quite different, and a lot more fun …"

Before April finished her sentence, Rachel turned her face down to avoid looking at her mother. She emoted a feeling of disgust and jumped up. "We really do need to go and finish our tour, Mother. Maybe some other time."

When they got to the car, Rachel apologized. "I'm sorry about my mother. She's different, if you know what I mean. I didn't think she'd get into this stuff so quickly. Since we were going this way, I thought it would've been nice to stop off and have you meet her. I didn't know she'd bring her psychobabble into our conversation."

"You don't need to apologize. I like her. I think she's adorable. She's got a unique sense of humor. I'd be interested in taking her up on her offer. I'm always open to something new."

April immediately thought of Michael and his recent revelation. *Who knows? Maybe this delightful woman can help me understand what's going on with him. God, I can't believe in less than one short day, all this has already happened to me.*

April and Rachel left to clock the number of miles from April's office to her apartment. They stopped for an early dinner at a Village Inn restaurant. The smell of freshly baked bread permeated the dining room. They passed a refrigerated three-tiered glass display cases filled with shelves of delicious homemade pies and a room full of empty booths. There were two other people seated, and they were completely absorbed with each other. The restaurant was conducive to superb service and quiet conversation.

Rachel started flipping hastily through the menu with one hand while she nervously slid her medallion up and down the chain with the other.

The waitress brought their water and stood over them with pad and pencil in hand, poised to take their order.

"Could you give us some time to look over the menu?" Rachel

smiled at her, sweetly unfolding her napkin in her lap, and nervously ordered. "Just bring me some decaf now, and make this on one check." She looked at April. "Now, don't argue with me, sweetie. It's a southern thing. You must let me pay for the first dinner in your new hometown. I insist! So, tell me about your new job."

"Well, I'm sure you're familiar with the health insurance business. I'll be managing the medical staff. The medical director and I are responsible for the cost and care that's provided to our policyholders."

"Then you might be the person who can help me. I've been able to obtain pretty good contracts for our cardiologists with every other insurance company here except yours, and you're the big player."

"Rachel, I haven't even started yet. If you don't mind, I'd rather we didn't talk business tonight. I'd just like to get to know you and thank you for a lovely afternoon. You've gone out of your way to make this such a pleasant first day for me. Thank you so much."

Rachel tilted her head to the right, letting out a small sigh, and gave a shrug of her shoulders. "I'm sorry. Sometimes I get so involved with my job, I lose all sense of reason. Sweetie, you're my guest. Whatever you say. Have you made any plans yet on how to get acclimated to our town? Being a single mother, I don't have much free time, but I do attend an interesting group that might be fun for you to try. Would you like to join me tomorrow night? I could pick you up at seven. Sessions are held in a furniture store on Sunday mornings and Monday and Thursday evenings. I usually go on Monday evenings."

"What do you do in this group?"

"It's kind of a spiritual thing, but not religious. It's hard to explain. Give it a try, and see what you think. The people who attend are great." Rachel spoke passionately, although in monotone.

"Sure, I'd love to go. I'll give it a shot. I have nothing else to do when I get home from work." April smiled and thanked her for a lovely day.

As April walked to her apartment, a beautiful orange- and red-streaked sunset had begun. She pondered the day with her new friend. Something in her gut told her things didn't seem to compute, and she was a little unsettled. Her new friend reprimanded her mother's psychic remarks, yet she attended a spiritual group in the evenings.

Before preparing for a soothing bath, April called Karl and babbled nonstop about her day with Rachel. Then she grabbed the phone book to look up the addresses and phone numbers for the nearest library and the NOW office—books and new friends would be next on her list of things to explore. She'd have a great deal of time on the weekends, since she had no ties or responsibilities and didn't know anyone yet. She was beginning her new life from ground zero.

April played one of Anthony Robbins tapes—*How to Shape Your Destiny Now*. She prepared for a soothing bath and poured cobalt blue bubble bath into the tub as it filled with warm water. Bubbles foamed to the surface, filling the bathroom with the scent of flowers. She slipped off her clothes and sunk low into the tub to luxuriate in the soothing water. Tiredness came over her. Dizzied by all that had happened since she left Karl, she rested the back of her head on *his* bath towel. She closed her eyes to sustain the alpha moments while her brain relaxed, devoid of thoughts.

CHAPTER 19

April woke up disoriented, unable to quickly recognize where she was. The sparsely decorated room, ceiling, and small double bed didn't seem at all familiar. Then she remembered this was her new life alone without Karl to cuddle up to. Strange noises emanated from outside her apartment. She opened the blinds behind the bed to see lights in some of the units across from her. Somewhere, a car drove by with its radio blaring. The fountain outside splashed rainbow colors in the dark. Its trickling sounds made her stay in bed a little while longer to adjust and integrate all the new sounds, smells, and thoughts. This morning would be imprinted in her mind forever.

Once the first hint of daylight seeped in, April edged along the foot of the bed and through the hallway. There wasn't much space between the bed and dresser. As she made her way to the tiny bathroom, she felt like the giant Alice in *Through the Looking Glass*. Bubbles in the tub from the night before had dissipated. Karl's bath towel hung on the back of the door. She inhaled it, but his scent was gone.

Driving to her first day at work on this beautiful, sunny morning brought mixed feelings. April was excited to meet new people, yet cautious that initial impressions would be critically important. She took a deep breath before she walked into the double glass doors marked "First Coast Insurance Company—Central Region." She thought how all her hard work had paid off. This was what it was all about. She had arrived.

A receptionist, who looked busy, turned away from her electric typewriter, pulled off her glasses, and greeted April. "May I help you?"

"Hi, I'm April Dunlap, the new Medical Services Director. Would you please call Dr. Peters for me?"

Within seconds, a red-haired, petite woman in her early forties who was dressed to the nines in a navy wool suit and white long-sleeve blouse with scalloped cuffs greeted April. The woman had an exaggerated spring in her step. She warmly replied, "I'm Toni." She extended her hand for a friendly shake. "We've been expecting you. We talked on the phone. I was on vacation when you came for your interview. I'm glad to finally meet you. Dr. Peters told me all about you. Welcome. It's about time we finally got a female director in this office. I'm Dr. Peters's secretary, and yours too, now."

April's new office was adjacent to Dr. Peters office. It was spacious but bland, with plain white walls and hardwood floors. There was a stack of manuals on her desk.

"This is your light reading for the week," Toni jokingly said. "I gathered our medical policies, standard operating procedures, maps of the eight counties, a list of the medical department employees, and a multitude of other materials I thought you might need."

She took April on a tour of the building and introduced her to the Central Region directors of four other departments—finance, customer service/operations, and marketing—as well as Dr. Peters. Pete Barnett was the new regional vice president.

******

As April drove home that afternoon, it seemed impossible the day was already over. There was much to learn and many improvements to make, but she was up for the challenge. She barely arrived home in time to drop off her homework and change clothes before she expected to be picked up for her evening group session with Rachel. She sat on a bench outside her apartment and began to shift uneasily, glancing at her watch every two minutes. She hated being late for anything. It was 7:15, and Rachel wasn't there. Finally, the Buick rounded the corner.

"What happened? I didn't know if you were coming."

"Got tied up with teenager problems. Don't worry, starting time depends on how quickly everyone shows up. We'll be fine. You're in the South now, sweetie. Take it easy. Relax. 7:00 here means around seven—maybe 7:15, 7:30, or 7:45."

Rachel parked the car next to a white coquina one-story building. His-and-her cement steps lined with a white iron railing led to double doors. A sign at the entrance read "Winter Park Furniture." As the two women walked from the warm night air into the cool, air-conditioned store, Rachel explained, "It's comfy after a long day at work to pick out a comfortable seat and relax. The wife of the guy who conducts the group owns the store. Just a suggestion for tonight: listen and take it all in."

The smell of freshly brewed coffee penetrated the room. While some people were filing into the store, holding dark blue notebooks, others were streaming in and out of a small backroom carrying Styrofoam cups. During all this activity, people greeted each other with hugs, smiles, and lots of talking. It was more like one big, happy family arriving for a reunion than a study group meeting. An elderly man with a shaved head, bad teeth, and a gray goatee headed toward April with outstretched arms. "Nice to meet you, I'm George."

"Nice to meet you too, George," she said as she backed away from his arms, satisfied to shake his hand. "I'm April."

George moved on to Rachel. He held her for a moment and then embraced a man.

"Does everyone know each other here?" April asked.

"People come and go. If you attend enough sessions, the faces become familiar, but they change from time to time. We believe hugs transfer loving energy and bring us together. It helps to erase the separateness we seem to have otherwise. It's something we do when we arrive and when we leave. You don't need to participate if you're uncomfortable with it. Just do what suits you. It's not structured. You'll see. Relax, sweetie. Just take it all in. The instructor is an architect who took a one-year sabbatical to put this study group together. His name is Breau." Rachel pointed him out. He was slightly built, blonde, in his forties and was soft-spoken. He wore a sky blue Izod golf shirt with khaki slacks.

April spotted a comfortable leather La-Z-Boy chair. She sat down and waited for all the kumbaya to cease. She crossed and uncrossed her legs, wondering if anyone noticed her nervousness. There were about twenty-two people, including Breau. People slowly began to take their seats. The room became very quiet.

"Good evening, everyone. For those of you I haven't met, my name is Breau. Are there any new members here this evening?" Two men, a woman, and April raised their hands. "Please introduce yourselves by your first name only and how you came to join us tonight."

When the introductions were complete, Breau began with a short prayer. He introduced the lesson for the evening and asked the group members to turn to a page in their handbooks. People took turns reading a paragraph from the chapter. Sometimes there would be a pause and discussion; sometimes not. Breau usually lent his interpretation to the discussion.

April grew concerned when she heard words that sounded too much like religion: spiritual psychotherapy, judgment of the Holy Spirit, Jesus, God, and ego. Breau led the group in a guided fifteen-minute meditation at the conclusion of the readings and discussions. He closed with a prayer about God's blessings and protection through the Divine light. Rachel took April to meet him at the conclusion of the meeting.

"I'm so glad you could join us this evening, April. What'd you think?" Breau asked.

"I'm still not sure what this is all about, but if I may be so blunt, I have my doubts. This sounds too much like religion to me—maybe even something that might border on being a cult. I'm not a religious person. I believe in God, but have never been one for institutional religion. The metaphysical is very new to me. I don't understand much about it."

Breau closed his book, tucked it under his arm, and looked into April's eyes. "I sensed you felt very uneasy tonight. That's not unusual for someone here for the first time. Let me assure you, our group is not a cult. It's also not an organized religion. It's just a different kind of thought system—a training to eliminate our fears and open ourselves more to love. It simply focuses on two emotions: love and fear. Fear becomes the emotion when there's a lack of love. The only purpose for our group is to provide a way in which people can find their own internal teacher. We're not here to dictate what they should think. The most important objective is for each of us to find peace in our lives. There's no dogma, no rituals, no statues, no icons. It's merely a self-study program. You've probably been exposed to enough tonight. Please come back. Give yourself time to process all this. It's a lot without any preparation. We have extra notebooks if you'd like to borrow one. We'd love to see you again. Thank you for coming."

April invited Rachel in for some coffee. They kicked off their shoes the minute they stepped into the living room.

"Tell me a little about yourself," April asked.

"There's not much to tell. Born and raised here. There's nothing I don't know or haven't seen through the pre- and post-Disney growth." Rachel took a long drink, sinking low into the sofa. "I'm an only child. I've been supporting myself and my kids—pretty boring stuff, huh?"

"Not at all. I enjoyed meeting your mom yesterday. Is your dad still living?"

Rachel tried to ignore the question, mumbled "No," and quickly changed the subject. She began talking about her job and started fidgeting with her medallion. "The last four years, I've been working with fifteen prima donnas—I mean, cardiologists. It's not the best job, but it pays well. I'm always in the market for better opportunities—looking for more and more challenges. Does that sound familiar?" she asked.

April's new friend could not seem to endure any conversation for long. Little beads of perspiration began to form on her upper lip. April walked across the room to turn on the overhead fan. "Should I put the temperature down on the air conditioner?" she asked.

"No, I'm fine." Rachel's expressive, deep brown eyes matched her animated body movements when she talked.

"Are your daughters in high school?"

"Yeah, and I told them they need to go out on their own the minute they graduate. So, enough about me, tell me about yourself and your family."

While April talked, Rachel seemed to intently study her and the contents of her apartment—almost like an exhibit in a museum. Rachel jumped up, passed her hands along the plantation shutters, and fluffed and propped up the pillows on each corner of the sofa before she sat down again.

"You know, this furnished apartment isn't too bad."

"It'll do for now. I only plan to be here until I either buy or rent a house. Then I'll move my furniture from Ohio."

"It's getting late. I need to go and let you get some sleep. Give me a call, and we can plan something for the weekend. There's a good movie in town called *Dead Poets Society*. Robin Williams plays an inspirational English professor in a private boys' prep school. It must be funny, with him as the main character. I promised to take my girls to see it. I'd love for you to meet them. Let's plan on Friday evening. Have a great week! If you need me for anything, I'm a phone call away."

As soon as Rachel left, it was too late to call Karl. He was always in bed by 9:30, so April dove into her company manuals to digest some of the standard operating procedures—a practice that would consume her evenings for weeks. However, she was sidetracked with thoughts of Breau and the spiritual group. *What's all this stuff about? Am I tripping too far down a rabbit hole? Be open, April. Just take it one day at a time.* She turned the lights off and went to bed.

CHAPTER 20

April lay across the bed in the dark, listening to Anthony Robbins tape entitled *How to Get What You Really Want* when the phone rang. It startled her and pulled her out of some-thought provoking ideas. It was almost 10:00—much later than anyone would call, unless it was an emergency. She scrambled to stop the tape, turned on the lights, and threw off the afghan to reach the phone.

It was a friend from Pennsylvania. They talked for a few minutes about April's new job and relocation. "You'll never believe it, but on the third day, when I got off the elevator at the office, an unusual feeling swept over me. You know, it felt like I was home—like I was truly meant to be there. This has never happened to me so quickly on any other job I ever had in the past. I'd love for you to come visit me the first chance you get."

After a few minutes of small talk, her friend revealed some terrible news. "Martha was discovered dead on a cot in the basement of her townhouse."

Martha, a mutual friend, was a quality assurance consultant April had hired to assist in the preparation of their hospital's accreditation. Martha and April had hit it off and became good friends. They visited each other and attended medical conferences together.

April's friend continued, "Martha's brother was notified that she hadn't reported to work and was mysteriously absent. He discovered her body. She took an overdose of sleeping pills, prepaid her funeral, left instructions for her cremation, and left a note that her brother could have her horse and dog. According to her friends and family, there were absolutely no clues she was depressed or had planned to do something like this. Her last evening was spent with a girlfriend. They met for dinner at a favorite Japanese restaurant. They talked about work. Everything seemed normal. She was in good spirits. The only thing different was that she usually took home the leftover sushi, but on that night, she threw the doggie bag into the dumpster before leaving in her car."

After the end of this alarming call, April turned off the light. She lay in bed in the dark, stared at the ceiling, and wondered what would have caused her friend to take such drastic action. *A single woman with everything to live for—what makes people end their lives? That could've been me.* She was shaken, thinking how close she had once come to ending her own life. Her emotions became overwhelming. She started crying and played a tape of soothing music to help lull her to sleep, but instead, she lay awake for hours, thinking of the things she admired about her friend: her smile, sense of humor, knowledge, and cosmopolitanism. All of that was gone—except for memories.

******

April's eyes burned from lack of sleep. Birds chirped outside. The fountain in the pond wasn't working. She readied herself for work. It was Friday, the dress-down day. Her grief burdened her throughout the day. She was happy her date at the movies might help dilute her sorrow. She waited for Rachel on a bench outside the movie theater, excited to meet her daughters. A warm spring breeze blew against her face, which helped ease the humidity. It was a telltale sign summer was close behind.

Once again, Rachel was late. A pattern had begun to develop with her new friend. April bought her ticket and was about to hurry into the theater alone when she turned to see a woman running with long, fluid strides. She was dressed casually in a dark brown cotton jumpsuit with a beige Irish sweater over her shoulders and long, dangling silver earrings. It was Rachel, running to the ticket office. She apologized for being late again. She had an argument with her daughters. They were grounded for the rest of the weekend.

The movie, *Dead Poets Society,* had many compelling messages about life, adventure, following dreams—everything April was living. She was captivated until the story focused on a young student who was unable to follow his passions because of a controlling father. Suicide was his only escape. It came as such a surprise, she had no opportunity to anticipate or prepare for the scene. Visceral body changes occurred. Blood thudded in her temples. It was as if her friend's suicide was being played on the big screen in front of her eyes. She began to cry uncontrollably. She was having a meltdown.

It wasn't until the movie credits began and the theater lights came on that April's reaction to the movie became evident to Rachel. "Are you all right? What's the matter?"

Unable to talk or move, April sat there, sobbing into her tissues. Finally, in a cracked voice, she eked out a few words. "I-I-I got a call last night about a dear friend of mine who committed suicide last weekend."

Rachel wrapped her arm around April's shoulder and waited for her to collect herself. "Oh, sweetie, I'm so sorry. I had no idea—either about your news or this movie's disaster."

"Of course you didn't. I haven't talked to anyone about it. I thought a movie would help me forget. All it did was open up a fresh wound from last night. I don't know how I'm gonna get through this weekend."

"Let's get out of here. We can stop on the way home for some dessert."

April dried her eyes. She stood up in slow motion. The theater was empty. All the lights were on. A young man in a red and blue theater uniform began to clean up the trash left in the aisles in preparation for the next showing.

"If it's all the same to you, I'd rather go home. I haven't had much sleep. I need to be by myself. I won't be very good company."

Rachel persisted. "Ah, come on, sweetie. A sugary dessert with a friend will do you good. It's what y'all need!"

"I wish you were right, but not tonight, Rachel. Please understand."

Within seconds, Rachel's body and face completely changed like some stranger quite different from the woman April thought she was getting to know. April hoped it was her imagination, but then she noticed Rachel's body stiffen as if she was being rejected.

Through the shield of her glasses, Rachel's restless eyes and scowl were quite noticeably unsympathetic. "Suit yourself," she said abruptly. "I guess that's what I get for tryin' to help."

April's brow furrowed in apparent confusion. She didn't understand Rachel's impertinence and rather mean looks. "I appreciate your help, but now isn't the time. Please understand. I need to be alone and sort things out. Maybe I'll join up with the group next Monday and see if Breau has any words that could help me through this ..."

"You can go by yourself. I can't make it, but you don't need me anyway, do you?" Rachel said icily as she turned and walked away.

"Don't be angry, Rachel. Please call me this weekend." April was puzzled that her new friend obviously doesn't seem to practice Breau's preaching. She wondered what the heck was going on with her.

As April unlocked the door to her apartment, she shed her jacket and sat in the dark by the window. She watched the flickering colors from the fountain. It was working again. She thought she spotted Rachel's Buick and a woman's silhouette in the driver's seat. The car quickly turned into the complex with only parking lights on, swept past her apartment, and then vanished.

April would call Karl tomorrow. She put on some music and lay on the bed with the evening's images spinning before her. She felt spent as if she had taken a hypnotic drug as she reflected on the first week's profound events.

CHAPTER 21

The night was humid from an evening rain. Sweat ran down April's back and between her breasts. She fanned her hair away from her face with a napkin. Cicadas were going crazy, their loud buzzing and clicking noises amplified into an overpowering hum. The love bugs were out in full force. April sat on the front step of the furniture store, sipping iced tea. She was early, and she waited for someone to open the door.

"Looks like someone's anxious to get started this evening," laughed a beautiful young woman who looked as if she had just stepped out of *Harper's Bazaar*. She made a ninety-degree vertical turn, climbed up the steps, and unlocked the door.

The woman introduced herself. "I'm Trent, Breau's wife. I own this store. I don't think we've met." Trent stood at the edge of the light over the building, and her face was masked in a shadow. Her body seemed to float out of the darkness of the night. As she and April stepped in from the heat of the evening, the air conditioning swept across April's face like a blast of cold winter wind that steamed her glasses. When the lights came on, April marveled at the likeness and movements Trent had, which were similar to the shape of a graceful Greek statue. Captivated with Trent's long golden hair and ethereal qualities, April carefully studied the outline of her body.

"I'm new in town and attended the group last week for the first time."

Suddenly, it was as if a bus had stopped outside. People quickly invaded the room. They began their hugging ritual. April spotted her La-Z-Boy chair from last week and dropped into it. She ran her fingertips along the dark oiled spine of the blue notebook she borrowed and cradled it on her lap to avoid the hugs. Slowly, she let her eyes trace the outline of the room and the seating arrangement. She hadn't paid much attention during her first visit, but now she began to take all the extraneous details into account for the first time. There was a random array of chairs, sofas, and tables. Beautiful artwork lined the walls. Obviously, this was an upscale store that catered to affluent Winter Park customers.

Breau led off with a short prayer and then began his discussion. "If life is not working, it means we're out of alignment with the truth." He directed everyone to turn to page 200. The silence in the room demanded a pious anticipation of profundity. People began to take turns reading aloud, paragraph by paragraph.

When it was April's turn, she felt hollow as she began her paragraph. "Fear is a symptom of your own deep sense of loss. Fear and love are the only emotions of which you are capable. By interpreting fear correctly ..." She read on to the end of the paragraph. "I really don't know what all that means," she said to Breau.

He began to explain, "Fear is merely a call for love and is simply an appeal for help. All emotions except for love are based in fear. Fear manifests when there is a lack of love. You can live a life of peace if you are willing to let go of limits that you place upon love. There's nothing more important than love. With love, we are powerful and can overcome anything."

April continued, "I've been troubled, and I need some help. I learned last week that a dear friend committed suicide. Later, I went to the movies to forget my grief, but instead, one of the most poignant scenes was about a young man who commits suicide. It was a double whammy. It reminded me of my father's accidental death years ago. How can I get over these feelings of grief?"

"It's certainly natural for you to be sad, but just think of death as a gentle letting go of the body—like removing a suit of clothes. There is no such thing as the finality of our perception of death. Anything that's been created by the Divine cannot be destroyed. Even Einstein said energy can neither be created nor destroyed; thus, birth is not the beginning of life, nor is death the end. Suicide is merely doing away with the medium, which was perfect for the lessons we are here on earth to learn.

"People who kill themselves see death as an escape from intractable, psychological pain of their guilt and suffering. But their unconscious guilt will remain intact. They end up reincarnating, which keeps the problem unresolved. They need to learn that death is not a way out and that forgiveness is the only true answer."

"So how can I feel at peace and begin to reconcile these tragedies?" April's thoughts were interrupted by the sight of Rachel tiptoeing into the room, trying to unobtrusively slip into a vacant chair.

When she glanced back at April, they momentarily made eye contact. Rachel shifted uneasily and quickly looked away, shooting glances in every direction but April's.

"You have the power to fill yourself with light and love," continued Breau. "The power is within you to erase your sorrow. You can surrender from past tragedies and ask for loving thoughts. We even have power over disease …"

April hung on every word as Breau continued. Her thoughts raced as she tried to process the implications of what this all meant and how it related to her life experiences. She had a hundred more questions but knew she shouldn't monopolize the discussion. Her brows knitted together in intense concentration. She hung on to every word he spoke. She wished she could have recorded them to play them back over and over until she was able to fully comprehend his interpretations.

A weepy voice from across the room spoke up. "We just buried my mother last week. Are you telling me she had the power over her disease?"

Breau continued, "We are responsible for what we see. We choose the feelings we experience and make decisions upon the goals we want to achieve—be it conscious or subconscious. The power is in us. We can receive what we ask for."

"If the power is in each of us, does that mean we can then make our own destiny? Does that mean it wasn't a coincidence I went to a movie that involved suicide?" April asked.

"That's right—but keep in mind, we still do have free will. Have you ever heard of the word *synchronicity?*"

"I'm not sure."

"You always hear stories about someone deciding at the last minute to board a plane that later crashes. This is not a coincidence. That person was meant to be on that plane, just as you were meant to see that movie. We do have free will, but there are no accidents. There must've been some takeaway messages for you in that movie to help you deal with your pain. If you didn't get them that night, you need to reflect on the messages that were there to help you. There's a spiritual energy within us that we must connect with. We believe our intimacy with the Divine charges us to be co-creators in every aspect of our lives.

"When a coincidence occurs, always try to understand the reason. Look for new information or learning that's attempting to lead you forward in your life. We're able to take control of our pain and reclaim power over our emotions. Now, let's go on to the next paragraph."

The more Breau talked, the more April was convinced that these thoughts had begun to make sense. She might be on the right track, but there was much more for her to learn.

Everyone stood up to leave when the meditation was over. George approached April and extended his arms again. This time, she accepted his hug. It felt good. The energy in the room was warm and loving. She ran to catch up with Rachel. When April tapped her on the shoulder, Rachel turned, smiled faintly, and acted amazingly surprised to see her.

"Oh, hi. I didn't know you were still here."

Like hell you didn't, April thought. "Do you have time to stop somewhere before going home? We need to talk."

Rachel took a deep breath and stared directly into April's eyes, answering, "Sure." She said cryptically, "Follow me. There's a great coffee shop around the corner."

They drove past a Dairy Queen, a Wal-mart, and Florida Hospital and into the Coffee Cup parking lot. The building was shaped like a round white coffee cup with a brown-and-yellow-striped handle. To enter the restaurant, they had to climb a set of steps into the cup. As soon as they were seated, April began, "I asked you here for a reason. Are you upset with me?"

"Why, sweetie, whatever gave you that idea?"

"Well, it seemed like you left in a tiff from the movie last weekend, and I haven't heard from you since. I thought you would've called me this week. You never did. Is something wrong?"

"I just wanted to give you time to grieve over your friend's death." Rachel quickly changed the subject and started talking about the subject of synchronicity. "You know, if everything happens for a reason, like Breau said, and there are no accidents, then I wonder what the purpose was for you and me to meet on the plane. I wonder if we'll ever find out."

Rachel dug into her purse, yanked out a leaflet, and handed it to April. "There's a two-day past life regression weekend coming up that looks fascinating. If you're interested, I'll send in our money to reserve our seats. It costs $100. It's being held southeast of Orlando at the Reese School of Massage Therapy. Have you ever done anything with past life work?"

"Heavens, no, but I've always been intrigued with things like Tarot cards, reincarnation, dream therapy, astrology—all that kind of stuff. I'm always open to learning new things." April stared at the last line on the leaflet. *What is the importance of life in your past? Find out what happened when you've lived before.* Her thoughts immediately turned to Michael.

"I'll make our reservations. We can go together. I'll pick you up."

"You don't need to pick me up. I can find it, I'm sure."

Rachel insisted. "It's no bother. I'll call you with the details. So, how are you enjoying your new job? I've been calling your provider contractor, but he hasn't returned my calls. I wanted to schedule a meeting with him." She started fidgeting with her necklace.

"Let me see what I can find out, and I'll get back to you. You know, I've been attracted to your necklace ever since we first met on the plane. It is so unique. I've never seen anything like it." April paused, as if she expected to hear Rachel respond, but she remained speechless.

Rachel's hand immediately dropped from the medallion. Her face transformed from pleasant to annoyed in an instant. She stared at April with angry, piercing eyes, as if she was looking straight through her. Then, with unnatural intensity, her eyes looked above April's head.

"I hope I didn't upset you by asking about it. It's so unusual, I was interested in its meaning."

Rachel hesitated getting the words out, pursing up her lips as if she had just sucked on a lemon that tightened the edges of her mouth. Her voice became sharp. "It was a gift," she said abruptly, never responding further about it.

April noticed a two-inch thin scar that extended from Rachel's right eyebrow halfway to her ear—an area that was usually covered by her hair. April didn't break eye contact and continued to stare at her. She noticed Rachel's inability to hold a normal gaze or even carry on a conversation for any length of time.

"Excuse me. I need to go to the restroom." Without hesitation, Rachel quickly left the booth and hurried toward the back of the restaurant. Moments later, she returned. "I think I'm getting a migraine. I need to leave." She shot out words in staccato rhythm, like they were being released from a machine gun. "I'll call you in the morning."

April finished her coffee and wondered what the hell was going on with Rachel. Usually detached and cool during stress, April was upset with herself for feeling so emotionally intimidated. She questioned why she seemed to transform into an obedient child in this woman's presence. Their friendship had slowly transformed into parent-child. April felt paranoid that the least little thing she might say or do could be the catalyst to cause her friend to come undone. She had compassion for Rachel but wondered about her life as a single mom, the scar, and her purpose for attending a spiritual group.

Quietly, April left the coffee shop and eased out into the crisp spring air and moonlight. A serene peace swept over her as she stepped into the warm air and beautiful, star-studded sky. Before she entered the car for the drive home, she paused to admire the full moon that rose above the trees. She wished Karl could be there with her to enjoy the evening. His absence was like a hole in her heart. Part of her was missing. She longed to hear his voice and feel his arms around her. Her heart ached for him. The night would have been a beautiful one to share with him.

She promised herself she would call when she got home to find out if he had any luck selling their condo.

She needed to take Breau's advice and reflect on the movie to discover what messages were there to help her through her pain. She closed her eyes and attempted to bring back its details, but as much as she struggled, nothing came forth. She promised herself she'd see it again.

She remembered what Breau said about coincidences. "When a coincidence occurs, try to reflect and understand the reason. New information will lead you forward in your life."

CHAPTER 22

April turned on the lights in her office at 7:00 a.m. She loved to arrive before everyone else to tie up loose ends before beginning the string of daily back-to-back meetings. She unpacked her briefcase with papers she had read and worked on the night before. Her appointment book lay unobstructed in the middle of her desk with a note from Toni: "T.G.I. Friday, you have a busy day. Call Rachel Blackburn! She left three urgent messages after you left last night!"

Toni kept April organized with an efficient system. Everything was stacked into neat piles in her three-tiered mail bin. It sometimes looked like it would collapse from the weight of work that needed her attention—new incoming memos on the bottom, papers that needed to be signed in the middle, and outgoing papers that were completed and ready for filing on the top.

April's phone was glued to her shoulder as she began to respond to voice messages while she signed memos. Multitasking was the only way to keep on top of things. It was 8:30 by the time she finished her dictation. It was a decent hour to reach Rachel at home before she left for the office.

"Hope I didn't catch you at a bad time," April said in a bubbly tone. "Toni left me a note that sounded like I needed to get in touch with you ASAP. Since my day's filled with meetings, this was the only free time I had. What's up?"

"Since your provider contractor hasn't responded to my calls, I was hoping I could get an answer from you. I'm still waiting," mumbled

Rachel, "and the president of our group continues to press me for answers."

"Actually, I thought we could talk about it sometime this weekend at our Regression Work—"

"I can't wait." Rachel cut her off, demanding, "I need an answer now. Do we have a chance, or don't we? I don't want to talk business this weekend!"

"Okay. Okay." Feeling as if she had just been reprimanded, April tried to placate her ire. "I did speak to our medical director about your group, but apparently, an exclusive contract was made with another cardiology group long before I arrived. There's no reason or interest to make any changes at this time."

"Is Dr. Peters your boss?"

"No, he isn't, but if this group is performing according to our agreement, there's no reason to cancel their contract. I'm sorry. Maybe things could change in the future. Who knows?"

"Who knows won't cut it for me! My head may be on the block if I can't get to first base. I guess I was mistaken. I thought you were the boss, and I thought you were my friend."

"I am the boss, and I am your friend, but as a fellow businesswoman, a true friend wouldn't ask me to do something unethical." Rachel gave no answer. April was angry at herself for being bullied and unnerved. Her friend had become unhinged over this.

"I need to get going. I'm late already. I'll pick you up tomorrow morning at 8:00 for our workshop. Thanks for nothing!" Rachel screamed in a shrill pitch.

That's it, April thought. *This so-called friendship needs to come to an end this weekend—once and for all.*

******

April awoke to the squeal of brakes from the parking lot and the simultaneous shrill of her phone ringing. "Hello," she answered sleepily in a raspy voice, clearing her throat. Her head was still foggy.

It was Joe. "I'm coming to Orlando on business soon. Maybe you could pick me up at the airport and we could spend a couple days together."

April was overjoyed at the sound of his voice. "Great! I'd love to see you. Just let me know the days and times. I don't want to brush you off, but I need to run. I'm getting ready to attend a *Past Life Regression Workshop*. Give me a call later in the week so we can make final plans."

"Sis, are you getting into some kind of cult?"

"Of course not, silly; this is all for fun. It's a way to meet more new people."

"But are they the type you want to be friends with? Do you believe in that past life stuff?"

"I don't know enough about it yet. You worry too much. Anyway, aren't you the one who returned from California with a beard and long hair swearing that Maharishi Mahesh Yogi and Transcendental Meditation were the cat's meow? Look who's talking!"

They both laughed.

"By the way, did Mom tell you she heard Uncle Andy committed suicide? Although she really doesn't hear much from the Straka family anymore, she did find out about it. The family kept it from the newspapers, telling everybody he had a heart attack. The truth is, he hanged himself in the cellar of his home."

"You're kidding! Well, isn't that ironic. It's the law of karma—responsibility for unpleasant actions borne by the person who committed them. What you give out will always come back to you."

"You lost me. I don't understand. What does that have to do with Uncle Andy?"

"It's a long story, and you were too young to know what happened when Daddy died. I'll tell you all the sordid details when you get here. I need to run now. Someone's picking me up in less than an hour, and I'm still in bed. I'll call you next week. Love you."

"Love you back."

April jumped in the shower. She began to think about all the suicides in her life—her friend, the character in the movie, and now her uncle. Then thoughts quickly turned to Rachel, and she wondered how the day ahead would play out. In the beginning, April enjoyed their friendship, but now it was getting her down. She even began to feel some reactions to Rachel that she hadn't felt for a long time. She was mad at herself for trying to be so obliging.

The event was a BYOL (bring your own lunch) weekend, so April hurriedly threw a sandwich and some snacks together. Dressed in a loose-fitting sweatshirt, shorts, and sandals, she waited outside on the bench. A UPS truck pulled up to her. "I have a delivery for an April Dunlap."

"Then you're in the right place. I'm April. I can't imagine anyone sending something to me."

The delivery man climbed into the back of the truck and came out with a pink beach cruiser and a small wrapped package. April signed the invoice while he wheeled the bike into the apartment. She opened the package. It was a pink sports watch with a card that said "Happy 50th birthday to a sporty woman. I love you, Michael."

Oh my God, I forgot that my birthday's next week. April hurried back outside, knowing that Rachel would be there any minute. She hoped Rachel would be on time for once. By 8:30, she ran into the apartment to call, but there was no answer. She decided not to wait any longer, left, and arrived at the Reese Institute fifteen minutes late. That was it! She was determined to end this friendship.

It was unseasonably hot and muggy for an early spring morning. The country grounds were peppered with Magnolia trees, rhododendrons, and wildflowers of pink, violet, white, and blue. A fresh breeze from the pond that overlooked the entrance carried the scent of a meadow lined with palmetto bushes and oak trees.

April pulled into a parking space adjacent to some pine trees and entered the building. Luckily, the start of the workshop was delayed. The two educators were late. About thirty-five men and women were in attendance. Some were scattered on chairs, while some sat on the floor. Anatomical charts hung along the walls. April spotted three women and a man sitting on the floor in a corner at the front of the room, close to the podium. She asked to join them and nervously looked around to see if Rachel had arrived. There was no sign of her.

"Cup of coffee?" the older woman politely asked. She extended her hand, which held a cup with steam rising from it. The steam shrouded her angelic face like a veil. She sat in a beam of sunlight that made her eyes appear so clear it seemed you could see right through her. Her words bent around a western, muted accent. "I'm Jill, and these are my friends."

Jill introduced Vickie, a matronly, well-fed woman close to April's age; Mary, the youngest of the group; and A. J., a soft-spoken young gentleman.

"Come join us, please," said A. J.

April stood there, distractedly fumbling with her purse. She pulled out a crumpled workshop pamphlet from the pocket in her shorts. She carefully lowered herself to the floor. "I didn't think I was ever gonna find this place."

"Have you ever been out this way?" Jill asked.

"Heck, no; I've only been in Orlando a few weeks. I moved from Ohio."

"What brought you here?" asked Vickie.

"Sunny Florida and a new job with a health insurance company."

"Welcome to the Sunshine State," said Vickie. "Technically, I'm in healthcare too. I'm a medical sales rep for nursing homes."

"So am I," said A. J. "I'm a dentist."

"I hope you're a good dentist, because I'm gonna need one," said April.

"You're darn right I am." He handed her his business card.

"I guess I'm the only one in this group that doesn't fit in," said Mary. "I own a gift shop in Maitland. How'd you hear about this workshop, April?"

"A new acquaintance invited me. She was supposed to pick me up, but something must've happened. She never showed."

"Who's your new acquaintance?" asked Vickie. "Maybe we know her."

"Rachel Blackburn ..."

"We know Rachel," Jill, Vickie, and A. J. quickly answered, almost in unison. All three rolled their eyes. They looked at each other inquisitively.

"I thought I saw you at Breau's the other night," said Jill. "Didn't you talk about recently losing a friend to suicide?"

"That was me. I've only gone to a couple sessions, but the more I go, the more I learn. That spiritual study group gets into a lot of good issues and is fascinating. The discussions are so deep, yet so simple. I even bought the notebook. I know nothing about past life regression, though, so these two days should be interesting. If Einstein said there's no such thing as time and space, then there should be no such thing as past lives, right?"

"Just have fun with it," said Jill. "Don't get hung up with the past. The importance of life is not in the past, but today, in the moment."

The facilitator began, "I want you to relax. Lie down on the floor in a comfortable position. I'm going to guide you into a setting that will take you back in time." His voice was deep and captivating. He talked slowly. "With closed mouth, inhale deeply, hold it for a few seconds, and slowly exhale through your open mouth. Let's do this together. Breathe in, hold, and slowly release; allow your higher self to show you more of what you have inherited in your soul's memory. Let it take you back in time. Acknowledge your past."

Soft music played in the background as he talked through the meditation. The entire exercise took about twenty minutes. When the participants opened their eyes, they began to share their experiences. While April enjoyed the relaxation, music, and new friends, she didn't get in touch with any past lives. As the workshop was in full swing, she noticed someone in the group that looked like Rachel. It reminded her of the quandary she was in with this woman, and she wondered how it was going to play out. She put it out of her mind for the time being to concentrate on the workshop, trying to stay in the moment and enjoy her new experience and friends. The group took a ten-minute restroom and coffee break.

"Are you okay? You look kinda startled."

April turned to see Jill approaching. Jill walked toward her with long strides, like she was floating about an inch above the floor. Dressed casually in an indigo pant outfit, her salt-and-pepper hair fell unstyled around her neck, framing the face of an angel. There was an aura that radiated around her entire body as she moved with a confidence and holiness that April found surreal.

"Oh, I'm okay. I saw someone who looked like Rachel, and for a moment, it must've rattled me."

"Let's go outside. We still have ten minutes before the session resumes."

April followed the unembellished, sinewy beauty. "So, what do you do, Jill?"

Jill handed her a business card that read *Contextual Empowerment Coach.* "What's a Contextual Empowerment Coach? That sounds awfully complicated."

"It's not. It's simple. I teach people how to take their power back from various things. My clients either have health, business, or personal problems which need to be resolved."

"Say more."

"By regaining your power, you can overcome anything or anyone you've relinquished it to, like addictions, allergies, smoking, any number of health problems, unhealthy relationships. You'd be surprised how easily people surrender their power. For instance, I had a client whose family was dominated by negative conversations that heart problems had run in their family for generations, and she thought there was nothing she could do about it. I helped my client refuse to buy into this thinking. She wasn't willing to have that happen to her. She took her power back and was successful in breaking the family cycle of disease.

"That's exactly what Breau talked about. He said people have the ability to contribute to their own healing process and that it's important to balance the mind, body, and spirit, which work together. He said we can do that by taking control and reclaiming our power," replied April.

"You'd be surprised at how much power the thoughts we hold and the words we use have with our life and experiences. I've been able to help many people regain a belief that all they need to do when they want something is to simply ask for it, because Spirit is in each of us. We are Spirit. I just provide the training to help them recognize and regain the power they always had. This is just another tool to add to our spiritual tool box."

"You know, I haven't gotten anything out of this past life stuff yet," said April. "They've guided us through three meditations, and nothing's come up for me. Maybe I'm trying too hard. I can't seem to focus and clear my head. Either I'm too left-brained, or I don't have any past lives. I don't really understand it much."

"That's okay. I haven't been able to tap into much today, either. Don't worry about it. Just remember some of the simple messages from today, like that our soul lives lifetime after lifetime, that we're the result of everything we ever learned, that we can't lose it even if we're not conscious of it, and that everything we ever learned was here on earth, because it's our schoolroom. Regression is just supposed to help us understand who we are and our purpose in this present life. It's largely focused on forgiveness and healing the hurts of the past so they can be avoided in the future."

"Boy, it seems that everything distills down to forgiveness, doesn't it? I hear that at Breau's group, and now here."

"The brochure states that our past lives hold the key to unlocking our future, and by healing our past, we'll heal our present emotional and physical problems," replied Jill.

"Then I guess I won't be able to heal my emotional and physical problems—if I have any, that is," said April. "I get nothing with these meditations. Maybe something will resonate tomorrow."

During the long drive home that evening, April had many thoughts—not only from the workshop, but also from everything else she had experienced in such a short timeframe. As soon as she arrived, she lay on the sofa and played a tape by Anthony Robbins called *How to Create a Compelling Future*. She called Karl after listening to the tape. It was late, but she wanted to hear his voice. She missed him terribly—his sweet smell, his warmth, and mainly his strong arms and hugs. "Hi, honey, I'm sorry I woke you up, but I just had to call."

"Is everything all right?" he asked in a scratchy tone.

She could tell he was half asleep. "I'm fine. I just missed you and needed to hear your voice. I can't wait until I fly in on Friday. You'll pick me up, right?"

"Of course I will."

"By the way, I just wanted to let you know I've been scouting around, looking for a rental house so we can move our furniture down here. I have to make all these changes while the company will still pay for them. Before you know it, my three months of free rent will be up. I think I found a new rental house in Metrowest. It's only a few miles from the apartment. I really like this area, and I'm familiar with it. It's even in a golfing community. You'll love that. The house was just built. I'll be the first renter. It's three bedrooms, two baths, family room, and patio—would work for us until you get down here and we find something to buy. What do you think?"

"Hard for me to give an opinion. You know what you need to do. Just let me know what you decide."

"Well, you said you were gonna fly down for the Christmas holidays. I should be settled by then. I know we just talked a few days ago—any news on the condo or job front?"

"Yes to both your answers. I'll tell you all about it this weekend. Nothing earth-shattering yet, but we've had some showings. This area's not doing well. The rust belt is getting rustier. I can't wait to get out of here. Talked to some timeshare companies about a human resource job. We'll see what happens. You stay safe. I'll pick you up on Friday. I love you."

"I love you too, honey. I really miss you. When you come down, I'll introduce you to my new friends. Work's going well. See you soon. Now, go back to sleep. Sweet dreams. See you in a few days."

Suddenly, April awoke from a light sleep. She heard footsteps outside her door and then heard them stop. The doorknob jiggled back and forth. Thankfully, she had slid the deadbolt into its socket before falling asleep. Moments later, shadows moved along the shutters in front of the apartment.

She panicked in the darkness. She breathed so hard, her heart pounded. It felt as if it was in her throat. April grabbed her stun gun and then the phone, and she dialed fast with shaky hands to reach the apartment security office. She whispered, "Help, there's someone trying to get into my apartment. This is 109. Hurry!"

"I can't hear you. Can you speak up?" the voice answered.

In a stronger plea, April started over, "Someone's trying to get into Apartment 109. Hurry!"

The doorknob stopped moving. April remained in the dark, waiting for the night security manager. Within minutes, there was a knock. A voice asked if she was okay. She fearfully walked to the door and flipped on the outdoor light. In her right fist, she held tightly to the stun gun Karl had bought her for safety when she was living alone in Cleveland. Her palms were so sweaty, she had difficulty turning the lock and doorknob. Cautiously alert for any further sound or movement, she warily opened the door. The assistant manager assured her that he saw nothing suspicious. Since all the apartments were similar, he said someone might have mistaken her apartment for theirs and that he'd take another look around.

She reported the suspicious car driving the other night with parking lights on and circling the lot. She kept the outdoor lights on when he left and made sure the drapes, shutters, and blinds remained tightly closed. She crawled into bed with her clothes on and stun gun close by on the nightstand.

That night, the haunting nightmare of April's father returned after more than twenty years. She was deeply troubled and couldn't understand why she was transported to memories of the past. Somehow, after leaving Milltown, she came to believe that by making a new life, all the unhappy remnants of her old life would be left behind. Obviously, she was wrong. She shook her head in an attempt to extricate her ghosts. She was determined to do everything she could to detach emotionally from past haunts.

******

Before leaving to attend the past life group for the second day, April called Michael, who was stationed in Norfolk, the city where she and Karl began their marriage. She hadn't talked to him since arriving in Florida and wanted to thank him for the pink bike and sports watch. It was early Sunday morning, so she figured she'd be able to catch him at home. He was happy to finally be transferred from Washington State to Virginia and in his own apartment rather than on a submarine, crowded into smothering, small compartments. He was excited his naval squad would be making two-week excursions on a destroyer soon.

Excited to reunite with her new friends, April reached the Institute well ahead of schedule. She saved space on the floor for them. She and Vickie enjoyed lunch together on a picnic table behind the building. They sat with their backs to the marsh under the cool shade of an oak tree with drooping Spanish moss that almost touched their heads. Pampas grass swayed with the morning breeze. Hanging pots of bright coral bougainvilleas were scattered around the building. The air was sweet with flowers.

"So, tell me how you landed here in Orlando from Ohio," said Vickie.

After April finished giving Vickie the abbreviated version of her background, she asked, "What about you? Have you always lived in Orlando? Most everyone I talk to is from somewhere else. We all seem to be transplants."

"Well, you've finally met someone born and raised in Orlando. I'm divorced. I have three grown children and live with my mother." As she talked on, April realized she really liked Vickie. She seemed to tap into April's loneliness, endearing herself in a motherly way. She was the most affable person April had met since arriving in Florida. They spent their breaks together, and by the end of the workshop, April felt she had a new best friend.

Vickie, Jill, April, A. J., and Mary had become fast friends by the end of the weekend after sharing their meditation experiences and coffee breaks. "Let's plan to get together soon," said Vickie. "Memorial Day's right around the corner, and I'm planning a barbecue. I'd sure like the four of you to come and meet my family." Mary had other plans, but everyone else gladly accepted the invitation.

Although disappointed that the regression meditations provided no insight into her past lives or Michael's issues related to her father, April felt the workshop served two important purposes. First, she met four wonderful new friends. Next, she experienced a profound insight that only by bringing up negative experiences and beliefs from her past that had poisoned her thinking would she ever be able to understand and finally resolve them. She couldn't change what she didn't acknowledge—that was one of the instructor's preambles. He urged everyone to reach out to their lost child in an effort to finally give them love and embrace the glory within themselves.

Vickie and April walked together to their cars. "Do you have to hurry home? It's still early," Vickie said.

"Heavens, no. Remember, I'm alone here in this town. There's no one waiting for me at home. My time's my own. What'd you have in mind?"

"There's a neat store I want to take you to that's on the way to both our homes. Then maybe we could catch some dinner. Follow me. It's located on Colonial Drive, not far from your office."

"Sounds like a plan to me. See you there," replied April.

The Spiral Circle was a spiritual store off Colonial Drive. It was a quaint store with an open attached garage set up with folding chairs. "So, why the chairs in the garage?" asked April.

"They have Saturday morning spiritual classes similar to what Breau teaches us, but the classes are for children. They obviously haven't put the chairs away, nor closed the garage door. Let me show you around inside."

Most of the rooms had shelves of books with comfortable chairs to sit and read. One room had a large display case filled with crystals, candles, greeting cards, signs, incense, and lots of pretty trinkets. Two rooms were set up for private psychic readings, and a large room for yoga classes.

"Come here, April, there's one book that you must see. I know you'll love it."

It was a powerful book that packed a punch in its eighty-three pages—*Heal Your Body* by Louise Hay. It was exceptionally thought-provoking. It identified mental causes for physical illnesses and metaphysical ways to overcome them. The book's foreword read, "This little book does not 'heal' anyone. It does awaken within you the ability to contribute to your own healing process. For us to become whole and healthy, we must balance the body, mind, and spirit."

April first looked up *ulcers.*

"***Probable cause***: fear. A strong belief that you are not good enough. What is eating away at you? ***New thought pattern***: I love and approve of myself. I am at peace. I am calm. All is well." *Well, that certainly fits Mom to a T.*

Next, April flipped the pages to *alcoholism.*

"***Probable Cause***: what's the use? Feeling of futility, guilt, inadequacy. Self-rejection. ***New thought pattern***: I live in the now. Each moment is new. I choose to see my self-worth. I love and approve of myself." *Given these descriptions, it's no wonder Daddy was an alcoholic. His self-worth was decimated by Grandma's constant rejection.*

She flipped through the pages. *Too bad nightmares* and *dreams aren't listed—but then, they wouldn't be; they're not physical illnesses.* April pored over every page, hoping to get to the core of how all the spiritual bits and pieces fit together. It sure made more sense than the traditional, religious hocus-pocus. The connection between mind and body— the psyche soma similar to all she had learned about psychosomatic illnesses in nursing—is powerful. The medical community labeled hypochondriacs "the worried well." Thanks to Rachel and her new friends, April's spiritual awakening was beginning to emerge.

"Are you hungry yet? I'm starving. Now that you know where this store is, are you ready for some Thai food?"

Vickie and April were compatible; they clicked. They had no trouble sharing their thoughts over dinner. "You're really lucky that you've been happily married to one man," said Vickie.

"Well, we've had our moments, like any other couple; but so far, we've been able to work through all the stages and changes. Now that Karl and I have overcome each of our midlife crises and we're still together, I think we'll be in it for the long haul. Phew. When you marry as young as we did, it's natural that both of us had to make major changes and adjustments."

"Well, I've been married and divorced twice. I *had* a good husband who fathered three wonderful children. He was a great guy, but I was stupid. I fell for a good looker who swept me off my feet. He used me financially, emotionally, and sexually. Let me tell you, it's never worth it for a woman to give up her values and good sense simply by falling for a passionate guy and a lot of sweet talk. You know that old saying: 'If it's too good to be true, it probably is.' Well, it was. I learned my lesson, and it was a hard one. Now I live with my widowed mother in a rented house in Altamonte Springs. I still have a good relationship with my first husband, and he's close to the kids, but now we're just friends. You'll have a chance to meet everyone when you come for the picnic."

CHAPTER 23

"How long do you plan on working tonight? It's after seven," Dr. Peters cautioned.

April looked up to see him leaning against her office doorframe. He shook his finger as if she were a naughty child who needed to be reprimanded. He was one of the gentlest men she had ever met, which was not unusual for physicians who pursued a specialty in pediatrics. A Phi Beta Kappa recipient, he was extremely intelligent, patient, and caring. Tall and slightly built, with thinning gray hair, he was about fifty-five and in a second marriage that didn't seem to be going well—at least, that was the office scuttlebutt.

"Gosh, I had no idea it was so late. I lost all sense of time. I've been working on my goals. Thanks for the interruption. I do have an appointment I need to run to."

"How's everything been going for you? You seem to have hit the ground running since you arrived."

"Extremely well. Everyone's been great. The *esprit de corps* in this office is infectious. I love it here. The leadership has really been successful in developing a cohesive team spirit. This might sound strange to you, but this job has begun healing the wounds I received working at a hospital system, and later, a dysfunctional HMO."

"My informers tell me you've fit in nicely too," he added. "The marketing director said the two of you have begun joint meetings with your staffs. That's a feat in itself, since marketing usually blames medical that they can't sell business because there aren't enough contracted doctors and hospitals in the area. And medical blames marketing for writing bad business that spikes medical costs. I knew you were just what we needed the minute we met. The chemistry has been perfect."

"I do appreciate yours and Mr. Barnett's confidence in me. I'd like to ask you a question. Are you familiar with Rachel Ripley Blackburn?"

Joe dropped down in the chair opposite her desk. "Everybody knows Rachel in this business. Why? How do you know the infamous Ms. Blackburn?"

April explained their meeting and subsequent friendship when she arrived. She gave details about the pressure Rachel had been applying to get a contract with her physician group, describing it as a life-or-death situation to her career. "She's been unreasonable and unrelenting about wanting to contract with us. I told her we have an exclusive contract with another group, and there was no reason to sever our relationship with them."

"That's Rachel. Everything's life-or-death with whatever she wants. She's also got a reputation for using unethical business practices, so be careful. I don't know how she's been able to keep her job. Don't pay her any mind. I wouldn't be surprised if her dramatics were her way of trying to manipulate her friendship with you just to get a contract with us. Now, shut the lights off and call it a day. You're the first to arrive in the morning and the last to leave. Don't burn yourself out. Any good news from your husband about selling the house yet?"

"He says things are beginning to pick up, but nothing firm yet."

"Well, we want you to stick around for a while."

"You don't have to worry about that. I never intend to leave Florida."

"I'll see you in the morning. Now scat!"

She picked up a burger on her way to the furniture store for another spiritual lesson. This time, she had her own notebook. She gladly participated in the hugging and fellowship. It felt good to see faces that had become familiar. The group had begun to feel like home. As she walked out of the kitchen with her coffee, burger, and book in hand, she spotted A. J., Vickie, and Jill.

"Mind if I join you?"

"Not at all. We'd expect it," said Vickie as she handed directions to her house. "Come, sit here in the middle of us." The sectional sofa faced the door and was perpendicular to Breau's chair. "This will give us time to talk about the cookout. I'd like you to be there about two-ish. We'll eat about three."

"Can I bring something?" asked April.

"There'll be about twenty of us. Bring some cookies."

A. J. said he'd bring the beer, and Jill offered things to nibble on. The door closed, and Breau prepared to begin the lesson for the evening. April stared at this captivating man who seemed to be so wise.

"The subject tonight is about love. The Divine is love," said Breau. "The only way we can transition fear to love is by forgiving—forgiving ourselves or forgiving others. When you forgive, you call upon the strength of the Spirit within you and release all your darkness and fear. If forgiveness is the method to transform fear to love, then it must be our key to inner peace. This means that the best way to change the world is by changing our mind about the world and how we see it.

"Whatever we focus on—whether it's wrong or right—will be what we'll receive more of. Did you ever hear the saying, 'whether you think you can or you can't, you're right'? We can't think one way, feel another way, and then be the expression of what we desire. We must put ourselves in a balanced state. Whatever we focus on will be the outcome. If we focus on love, our life will be filled with love. If we focus on abundance, we'll experience abundance. If we focus on scarcity, we'll experience scarcity. We can control our life from within. Remember, Spirit is within each of us."

Next, Breau directed the group. "Close your eyes, and repeat after me. Forgiveness is my function as the light of the world. I will fulfill my function that I may be happy."

"You make it sound so easy," said an elderly man sitting on a padded bench near Breau's chair.

"It is easy," answered Breau. "Go within yourself, and contact God within your heart. All we need to do is ask for anything we wish to do or know. If it's for our own good, we'll sense either a peaceful reaction or a feeling from our intuition, which is nothing more than a small voice from within. How skilled we are at tuning into our voice will determine how loud it is. It could be a gut feeling, a voice, or a thought. If our intuition is on channel five and we're tuned in to channel three, we won't hear the answer. Go within, pay attention, and listen for the answer. Whenever you want to ask for anything, always say, 'I choose this thing,' and listen for the answer. If it's your highest good, you'll never have to worry that you'll bring anything into your life that will make you unhappy."

"Give us some how-tos to help us get started," requested a matronly woman in the back of the room.

"When you need gas, you go to a gas station. When you need food, you go to a grocery store. When you want something from Spirit, you need to go to Spirit, who is you. Go within. You have all the power you need. Tune in to your heart and love. That's the magnet that draws things to you. Love is giving. Love is helping. Love is forgiving. Love is the universal currency for getting what you want.

"Another how-to is found in the use of the word *blessing*. The dictionary gives definitions such as 'approval,' 'permission,' and 'praise.' It can be your key to personal power. When you praise someone, you are recognizing them. How do you feel when someone praises you? Don't you feel good—like a flower ready to bloom? You need to take a few minutes every morning when you're getting ready for the day to attend to your spiritual grooming. Don't you think it would make a difference in your day to unleash your personal power?

"Every morning, before I begin the business of my day, I repeat a few times, 'I praise you, Breau.' And if you try this blessing, then at the end of the day, recall the events and see if there's not a difference."

"Does that mean the way you see the world depends entirely on you, and not what's happening to you?" another voice asked.

"That's exactly right. You cannot change what's happened in your life. All you can change is how you react to what's happened. You don't need to be a victim. It's not an accident—where you are and what's happening to you. Embrace it. Tap the power and strength within you. Love the lessons it's teaching you. Once you've become proficient in blessing yourself, then begin to bless others. If there are enough of us blessing each other and ourselves, eventually, we can produce a collective consciousness that can heal the psychic wounds that divide us, like racial and gender oppression and injustice. Now, that's real power! That's power you can take to the bank—and maybe even solve the social ills of the world."

Jill spoke up. "In my empowerment classes, I give them something they can say to get what they're asking for. For instance, if they need to regain power from pain, they can repeat to themselves over and over until it manifests, 'I take back the power I've given to having pain, and I take it back right now.' If they need to regain power from an illness, like a migraine, they can repeat, 'I take back the power I've given to having a migraine, and I take it back right now.' As you said, it's not the words alone that conjure up the power; it's the feeling along with the words that makes it happen. I don't mean to infer that you wave a magic wand, and *poof*, it disappears. It may not happen the first several times you say it, but repeating this over time can help to regain the power you're praying for. Keep in mind: it is not a quick fix. It will not happen overnight. We all must be willing to speak up for our intentions and be a space for creation."

Jill continued, "I met a woman who thought the only way out of her marriage and her problems was to not be present. Within a short time, her body quickly developed a fatal illness. It was a great way out for her. It was a socially acceptable way out, and she got a lot of sympathy from a lot of people. When she changed her mind and notified her body she wanted to take back her power from death, she was willing now to see what creation really had in store for her. When she undid what she created, the universe supported her in what she now thought should be present. When she was willing to undo that, the illness disappeared. Her body was willing to support her in her speaking. We need to take a stand against negative conversation. Miracles are a shift in perception to the Holy Spirit's way of thinking. Sickness, many times, begins in the mind, not the body."

"It worked for me," a man sitting on a leather wingback chair replied. "I took Jill's empowerment class, and I was able to stop smoking."

Breau continued, "That's exactly what we've been talking about. Ask, and ye shall receive. Your thoughts will always manifest your reality. Just as physical fitness takes time to make the change you want; so too does spiritual fitness. But it's up to you to create that positive change. Thank you, Jill, for offering another how-to."

April closed her eyes and began saying over and over to herself, *I take back the power I've given to having nightmares about my father, and I take it back right now.*

April opened her eyes and began to take small sips of coffee while finishing the last few bites of her burger. She scanned the room and was amazed to see Rachel sitting on a desk chair near the door.

Rachel sat round-shouldered, with her head down, as if all the words being spoken were washing over her without any comprehension of their valuable lessons. She looked like she was in pain and wishing she were someplace else. She had dark circles under her eyes. Her face was flushed, like someone experiencing a hot flash, and her hair was unkempt. The skin around her mouth was drawn tight into a frown. She wore a wrinkled Gap t-shirt with rhinestones sprinkled on the front, which was a pronounced change from the sophisticated, smart dresser April met a while ago on the plane.

Once the readings in the book concluded, Breau began the meditation. April had been practicing meditation every evening at home to get the hang of it. It sounded easy, but it wasn't. It took her forever to learn to sit still and quiet the mind's chatter and nonstop flow of bombarding thoughts. Nightly meditations following tapes by Tony Robbins did the trick, and meditation had become second nature. As soon as April got comfortable, was quiet, and closed her eyes, she was there.

April's body responded to Breau's introduction and settled into a deep relaxation, blocking all thoughts from her conscious mind. She was no longer in contact with outside matters. She stepped out of her skin and began to breathe so deeply she could no longer feel her body, which began to rise above the room.

April entered a beautiful garden sprinkled with multicolored daisies and illuminated with sparkling diamonds. She heard a voice that told her to go to Cassadega, a place she had briefly heard about from Dinah. She walked through a gate, which led into a bright meadow. There was a pine-covered hill overlooking a small lake. An old, rustic, dirty two-story brown house stood in the middle of the field. There was a white sign on the house that read in white letters, *Cassadega.* As April floated through the meadow and opened the door to the house, she saw that A.J., Breau, Dinah, and Isis sat around a table in the middle of the room, inviting her to join them.

The room was filled with gentle music and smells of fruity incense. A soft breeze blew from an open window. Ceremonial items and variegated crystals adorned the walls. A feeling of serenity and perfect bliss enveloped her thoughts. April stood at the table, knowing immediately that the people there were guides who would help unlock the mysteries in her quest for peace. Feeling centered and calm, she resisted leaving the meditation. When Breau began his closing prayers, she thought about how this journey had immersed her into a new world of spirituality that she never knew existed.

Unable to clear her vision and return to conscious thought, April opened her eyes to a glimpse of a woman hurrying out the door. For a fleeting moment, she realized it was Rachel. April began to feel sorry for her and was compelled to go after her, but instead, she remained frozen to her chair. It was half past nine before everyone left the building. April and her friends said their goodbyes, looking forward to the weekend barbecue. On the drive home to her apartment, April wondered who Isis was and why this intruder had appeared in her meditation.

After falling asleep in her double bed, April awakened to the shrill ring of her telephone. Tiredly, she looked at the clock. It was half past midnight. She had been asleep for two hours. Slowly, she lifted the receiver, hoping there wouldn't be bad news on the other end. There was a long, scary silence. "Hello. Who is this?

"A-A-April, it's me."

April gave a bleak sigh. Her heart sunk when she heard the raspy, familiar, cracked voice. By this time, she was wide awake and speechless for a moment. "Rachel, what's wrong?" She cleared her throat. "It's late …"

"I know," Rachel interrupted, "but I need to see you. I need someone to talk to. If I don't talk to somebody soon, I'll go crazy. I don't know what I'll do. Please help me, April. Help me!" She started sobbing hysterically and talking in staccato rhythm again, forcing out words.

"What can I do this hour of the night? What's the matter?"

"I can't tell you over the phone."

"God damn it, Rachel, I can't figure you out. You're making me crazy. I'm not sure I'm the one who can help you." With a death grip on the phone, April slumped down in her bed and felt a chill of anxiety that she hadn't felt for a long time. This call for help brought back a flood of similar feelings from the past, accompanied by a wave of fear and nausea. Her nerves felt frayed. Rachel's penchant for the dramatic made April feel she was riding a roller coaster.

There was another long pause. "Please don't curse at me; I know I've been unreasonable. I have no right to impose on you like this, but I don't know where else to turn. Please, let me come over. I need you," Rachel pleaded, sounding deeply remorseful and penitent. "Help me!"

April turned on the bedside light. She felt trapped. *Shit. Why me? What the hell is going on with this woman? What else can I do? Should I hang up now?* Feeling helpless to a weighty responsibility, it would be impossible to turn Rachel away in such a desperate state. April couldn't see a graceful way out. She relented. "All right, come over. I'll put on some coffee."

April turned on the lights in the living room, made a pot of coffee, and waited anxiously for her midnight visitor.

Two hours later, Rachel was nowhere to be seen. April called her house. There was no answer. *That's it! This woman is crazy, and is slowly driving me crazy. I don't need any more of this in my life.*

April unplugged the coffee machine and the telephone, turned off the lights, and went to bed.

CHAPTER 24

Light was beginning to peek through the shutters. April needed to be on her way out the door early this morning. First on her agenda on this beautiful holiday weekend was an appointment with Dinah at Cassadaga; then on to the Memorial Day picnic at Vickie's.

For the first time since she moved into her apartment, April turned on the oven, then assembled the ingredients. The kitchen was small enough that she could fill the oven with baking sheets of chocolate chip cookies and unload the dishwasher at the same time. There was no worry about too many cooks spoiling the broth in this kitchen. They wouldn't fit.

April called Karl, but hung up, remembering he was golfing this morning. Next, she dialed Michael. "Did I wake you?"

"Nope. I've been up. I'm going mountain biking with a friend this morning. Are you okay?"

"Just wanted to hear your voice. When are we gonna be able to see each other? I miss you and Dad and Joe and Mom. Dad's coming for the holidays. I wish you could come too. I'm gonna move in a couple months. I've begun scouting around to rent a house in this neighborhood. Do you think you can get off for Christmas and New Year's?"

"Funny you should call. You were on my mind. When I mentioned to the CO that you moved to Orlando, he hinted there's a recruiting station there that I might be assigned to for a couple months. Let me see if I can find out more about it and swing something for the holidays. So how's the job coming along? Are you happy you're there?"

"Oh, my God, Michael, am I happy? I've been thrust into an exciting spiritual world that I'll share with you when come here. The job is great. I have two satellite offices, plus the main one in Orlando in an eight-county area. I've been learning my way around the state. I've met some really nice friends that I want to introduce you to. In fact, I'm baking cookies to take to a cookout at one of their houses this afternoon. So, think about coming here for the holidays. I love you."

"Love you too, Mom."

Days grew warmer, and the trees and flowers were in full bloom. Spring winds were beginning to brew, and the harsh, omnipresent Florida sun heralded early approaching summer temperatures and aromas of jasmine.

April left Orlando, driving northeast on Interstate 4 to exit 54 into the town of Cassadaga. She stopped at The Universal Centre on Stevens Street, where she hurried to be on time for her appointment with Dinah. The tiny parking lot surrounding the building was filled with cars. Inside the small, low white house were shelves bordering three walls. They were filled with a vast array of books, greeting cards, and tapes. A woman stood behind a glass display case filled with many of the artifacts and gifts similar to the ones at the Spiral Circle. She welcomed incoming visitors.

April removed her dark sunglasses. "They're pretty, but what's with all the crystals?"

"Crystals amplify consciousness," the saleswoman responded. "Plus, they're beautiful."

April read a pamphlet describing Cassadaga's beginnings. It was founded by a trance medium from New York. A spirit guide urged him to create a community in the South. A spiritualist named Rowley, along with other mediums, established the Spiritualist Center and signed the charter in 1894 in Volusia County because of its unique energy intensity. Its purpose was to promote spiritualist beliefs in the souls' immortality. It spanned fifty-seven acres. Some of its few residents included licensed mediums and spiritual counselors who provided readings along with psychics, mediums, scientific palmists, astrologers, Tarot card readers, and those helping with past life regression. The name Cassadaga came from the Seneca Indians and means "rocks beneath the water." It beckoned visitors to escape from the mainstream to relax and get in touch with their inner spirit.

The little town had a bookstore, gift shop, two lakes, and restaurant in an old-style Mediterranean hotel, which was said to be haunted by a ghost named George, who made his presence known by the smell of his cigar. The energy reverberated like the beat of a tom-tom. Country, one-lane slag and dirt roads lined with pine and live oaks were draped in Spanish moss. Most of the houses—some pink, some blue, all different colors of the rainbow—generally needed refurbishing; many were in dire need of curb appeal, with sagging front porches and peeling paint. History seemed to hang heavy in the spiritualist community.

Approximately 100 psychics and mediums lived in the town. The Center had a list of their names, specialties, and phone numbers hanging on one of the walls. People could be seen without an appointment. April got directions to Dinah's house on Bond Street. It was a mint green, shingle house with an eight-by-five porch and violet shell chimes overhead. A clay pot on the edge of the porch was filled with artificial pink tulips. On the side of the porch hung a wooden plaque entitled *Mother*, which read:

> To one who bears
> The sweetest name
> And adds luster to the same.
> Long life to her
> For there's no other,
> Who takes the place of my dear Mother.

This was a far cry from Dinah's beautiful antebellum house in Orlando. Across the street was a small white house with an attached garage. Two garbage cans and a recycling bin sat under the homemade porch canopy.

Dinah appeared within minutes of April's knock on the door. There was an octagon-shaped table with three old beige chairs and one blue chair in the middle of the room. On the table was reading material: *Reminisce, The magazine that brings back the good times,* issues Sept./Oct., 1988 and Jan./Feb., 1989.

Dinah greeted her. "Let's go into the reading room off to your right."

They walked into a cavernous room. On the wall was an eleven-by-thirteen wooden framed picture of an old English sailing ship. April and Dinah sat on hard wooden folding chairs around a tiny round painted table. There were no windows. A transom over the door bordered with sparkling white Christmas lights was the only opening that provided a hint of daylight. April smiled nervously, finger-combed her shag, and rearranged the front of her jacket. She gripped the sides of the chair with sweaty hands and feelings of heaviness in her chest.

"I want you to relax," said Dinah.

As Dinah spoke, April reached into her purse and pulled out a checkbook and pen.

"Put your money away. There's no charge for you. You're a friend, and I want to help you, because I sensed you had a lot on your mind when we first met. I want you to feel at ease while I tell you what to expect from this reading. No psychic should tell you what to do with your life, whom you should marry, or what job you should take, or leave, or apply for. I hope you came with some questions in mind. People generally seek readings when their lives are in transition—when they're seeking answers and guidance to major turning points in their lives.

"In spiritualist beliefs, the spirit communicates through a medium. I'm the type of psychic who sometimes hears and feels messages from the dead and passes them on. Everyone is psychic to some degree. We all have a natural intuition; however, some are better than others at tuning in to it. Psychics see, hear, and/or feel vibrations from an energy source. My forte is using an inanimate object—like maybe your wristwatch—to feel the vibrations from your energy source. It's called subjective psychometry. Do you mind? Maybe I can give you some valuable insights this morning." Dinah paused. Her chair creaked when she shifted her weight.

April watched her eyes, waiting for her to continue.

"When I hold on to your watch, I'm able to tap into your individual energy, known as your aura. The more relaxed you are, the better I'll be able to access information from your auric field. I focus more on interpreting past events rather than future ones. So, let's see what comes up. I'm going to record this. My phone number is on the tape. Don't be surprised how things will come up later after you've had an opportunity to think about them. When they do, feel free to call me. We could schedule another session or just talk over the phone. When I ask you a question, don't be too quick to answer. Feel free to ask questions at any time. It doesn't help if you lie or try to trick me. Something may not make sense at first, but may change by the end of the reading, when you've had time to think about it. So, let's start off with why you want a reading. What are you hoping to learn today?"

April removed her watch and laid it on the table. "You know my father passed away. He died in an auto accident almost thirty years ago. I'd like to know if you feel any vibrations around him or my son, Michael."

A small candle in a glass jar flickered in the middle of the table. Dinah held out her hands, cleared her throat, and said, "Are you ready to get started?"

April joined hands with her. She stared into the candle flame, imagining a scene from the *Twilight Zone*. Today, the rings on Dinah's fingers were different. Most were silver, except for one. On her thumb was a broad gold band. In the middle of the band was an engraved Egyptian-looking figure with a wide wingspread, a lotus blossom touching each wing, and an Ankh linking to each lotus blossom.

Dinah began with a closed-eye prayer. She asked for a blessing and protection from the dark entities. She picked up the watch and held it tightly in one hand. Next, she asked a variety of questions and took notes as April answered—birthdate, birthplace, hour of birth. With closed eyes and heavy breathing for a couple minutes, she finally began talking.

"I'm sensing vibrations from your past." Dinah looked intently into April's eyes and said, "You're a very strong person, but also very good at hiding your emotions and self-doubts." Once again, she closed her eyes. "I'm going to tell you a simple story about a young woman. She escaped an unhappy childhood by getting married in her teens. An accident occurred that changed her life. She never let go of her dreams and struggled to reach her goals over her husband's objections. She's a hard worker and accomplished a lot in a short time. She excelled in the business world and is an advocate for women. Her family is loyal and loving. Something about this accident in her past continues to trouble her. This accident was your father, wasn't it?" Dinah opened her eyes slowly.

April nodded.

"That happened years ago. Why does it still trouble you?"

"The accident doesn't trouble me. It's the nightmares that I've had for years. They stopped, and now they've mysteriously continued. I don't know why. That's why I'm here."

"What happened before those dreams started again? We need to identify what set this off."

"I don't know. I came to Orlando, met some great friends, joined the group with Rachel. I have a wonderful job. I don't know why the nightmares have recurred. Maybe it's because I miss my husband so much. He can't join me until he sells the house. Do you think he'll be coming soon?"

"I don't see him coming this year. Be patient. There's a reason for you to be alone for a while. There are lessons for you to learn. The recurrence of the dreams has nothing to do with your husband. It's something in your past that hasn't been resolved. It's something about your father's death."

"But he died so long ago, why now? Why again?"

"You need to go deep into your soul to understand what might have triggered this. Maybe that's why you're meant to be alone—to learn what it is you need to resolve. I'm not getting anything more from this. No messages are coming forth from your father. I know he was a troubled soul, but he shouldn't be troubling you this way."

"Did he reincarnate?" April leaned back and waited with baited breath for Dinah's answer. April's body became rigid. It was as if she was looking at Dinah in a fog. The candlelight flickered over Dinah's face, making it almost impossible to focus clearly on her.

"First, it's very unusual that someone can make a quick reentry. If they do, usually they don't reenter into the same family. I'm not sure he reincarnated. Remember when we met, I told you I sensed you were on a spiritual odyssey. Be patient. The answers will come. Maybe if we continue our work another time, we could solve more of your mystery. I'm not getting any more about this now. I can tell you that your husband and child will both be joining you in Florida. You'll be getting a call from your son soon. He'll be coming to stay with you for a while."

"That's funny. We talked this morning before I came here. He might be assigned here temporarily."

"I think it's going to happen. They'll both be with you soon. You'll be very happy."

"Do you see anything about my job?"

"Just that you'll be very successful. It's everything you've always wanted—worked for in the past. You've worked hard for a long time to make it happen. You'll be there until you're ready to retire. I also see Isis."

"That's funny. She appeared in my meditation the other day. I didn't know who she was, but her name popped into my head. Who is she? Why did she show up in my meditation?"

"Isis was an Egyptian goddess who was worshipped as the ideal mother and wife, as well as matron of nature. Obviously Spirit is telling you that you have fulfilled those attributes with your family. Didn't you tell me you were a nurse? Nurses are nurturers, just like Isis. You're to be commended. Do you see this figure on my ring—the one with the wide wingspread? That's Isis. She was a goddess worshipped by the Egyptians for years."

When the session ended, April walked across the street and down a few blocks to a big pond. Her legs were shaky. She sat on a park bench and closed her eyes. She stuffed her cold hands through the sleeves of her sweater to warm them. Lifting her head toward the sun, she needed to reflect for a few minutes on what had just happened and regain her composure. She was left with more questions than before, but she was certain about one thing. Orlando was filled with spiritual energy. Who would've thought that the city had so much more depth than its worldwide symbol of a *mouse?* Dinah didn't provide much information about Josef, nor if he was reincarnated. April wondered if her question would ever be answered.

******

April parked in front of a beige Cape Cod house with black shutters. An American flag hung from the porch railing. Variegated Aztec and pampas grass lined the driveway. Red azalea bushes surrounded a grove of oak and pink crepe myrtle trees. People were moving in and out of the house, setting up tables, chairs, and games in the backyard. April walked up the drive with her cookies packed in an aluminum foil pie plate. She was looking forward to a good old-fashioned family picnic with children, games, and lots of activities.

"Hi. You must be April, the Buckeye who got transplanted to Florida," said a smiling young woman hurrying out the backdoor. "We've all heard a lot about ya. I'm Vickie's older daughter, Iris. Welcome. Join us in the backyard."

"I'm glad to meet you, Iris." As April and Iris walked through the garage, Jill came out of the house carrying a covered pot of baked beans. The smell of beans and bacon reminded April how hungry she was. She spotted Vickie smoothing a red, white, and blue checked plastic tablecloth on the picnic table. In the center was a small pot of yellow and white daisies.

Vickie turned and saw April. She walked over to give her a big hug. "I'm so glad you're in my life, young lady," she whispered in her ear. "Don't you look cool in your Bobbie Brooks yellow gingham summer outfit?" Vickie grabbed the tin of cookies and put them on the table next to the chocolate cake. "Holy cow, did you make these? They smell like they just came out of the oven."

"I did, and they did—early this morning. It's the first time I baked anything in my oven, and it even worked without a hitch."

Vickie intertwined her arm through April's and led her toward the house to introduce her to the rest of the family. April quickened her pace to walk evenly with Vickie and expressed how grateful she was to have new friends in her life. The two women turned the corner into the garage and stepped over the threshold. The smell of corn on the cob drifted through the screen door, and the glare of the sun almost blinded April as she approached the entrance into the house. She and A. J. almost collided as he bounded out the door, carrying a bag of charcoal briquettes.

"The meat will be ready in just a few minutes," he said, returning to the backyard.

As they entered the kitchen, Vickie's son doggedly insisted his two boys take their tug of war outside and leave some peace and quiet to the adults in the house. He was dressed in cutoff shorts, a tie–dyed t-shirt, brown Docksiders, and an FSU baseball cap. He appeared to be in his late twenties.

"Nice to meet you, April. Excuse me while I take these Hardy boys outside before they drive their great-grandmother crazy." He gently grabbed both of them by the scruff of their necks and followed them to the backyard with the plate of burgers and dogs ready for barbecue. "I'm gonna fire up the grill. Everything'll be ready in a jiffy."

Vickie's mother sprinkled paprika on the deviled eggs and then arranged them in a divided dish next to the kosher pickles.

"Mom, this is April."

Vickie's mother quickly wiped her hands on the front of her apron and extended them for a greeting. She said she was glad to have April join them. She introduced April to Vickie's younger daughter and grandchildren. She handed April the bowl of potato salad and condiments to carry outside. April's stomach was growling in anticipation of the holiday picnic.

April sat next to Vickie and across the table from A. J. and Jill. The children sat at the other end with their parents. The barbecue was full of laughter and talk. April was lost in thought, gazing at her new friends during brief periods. *Life is always brimming with surprises—what an example of Breau's synchronicity this is—my new friends. I need to seek their advice about Rachel before I leave today.*

197

"Where are you, April?" asked A. J.

A wisp of wind touched April's face as she stared long and hard, studying the outlines of his well-chiseled chin and clean-shaven face. She simply replied with a nod and a smile. "I have some things on my mind that I need to talk over with you all later."

Jill looked serious. "I'll bet it has something to do with Rachel."

"My God, Jill, do you also read minds too? There are no accidents. Spirit knew I needed all of you as my friends. I feel blessed having been dropped in your midst. You're all so full of love and acceptance."

The friends retired to the living room after the cleanup was finished.

"Let's hear what's on your mind. Enlighten us," said A. J.

"Rachel's a puzzle. She keeps me off balance with her bizarre behavior. In the short time I've known her, either she's overly obliging and doing everything she can to befriend me, or she's abrasive— promising to do something, yet never following through. She promised to pick me up for the Regression Workshop, then never showed up or even called. I feel like she's controlling me. It's like she has me dancing on the head of a pin. I'm on a wild ride and can't get off."

"Remember Breau's discussion on empowerment?" added Jill. "You're relinquishing your power to her. You need to take it back right now. It's a perfect example of how insidious giving power to someone can be. It can devastate your life."

"That's easier said than done. I've attempted to break away. And just when I think it's over between us, I get a life-or-death call that she needs me."

"It's time to sever the relationship for good," said A. J.

"I feel obligated to respond. She's like a manic-depressive, and I sure don't want to be responsible for something that might happen to her."

"You're a smart cookie," said Vickie. "You'll figure it out. You know we're here to help you any way we can. Maybe a session with A.J. would help."

April lifted a curious brow. "You too? A dentist by day. A therapist by night?"

"No, a therapist on the weekends," he laughed. "What do you mean, you too?"

"I just had a session with Rachel's mother in Cassadega this morning. She's a psychic. I was dying to ask her about her daughter, but felt it inappropriate. So what kind of sessions do you conduct, A. J.?"

"Nothing like what you experienced with Dinah. Mine is different. Maybe we could meet for lunch and talk in more depth."

"Thank you all for listening."

A. J. walked April to her car. "Did you know Rachel's a recovering alcoholic? There's a pretty tragic story about her and her father when she was little. I was told she shot and injured him years ago."

"No. I had no idea, but it makes sense. There had to be an explanation for her bizarre behavior. Even the necklace she wears. You can't help but notice it. It's so garish."

"That necklace is a symbol of death. She's bent on punishing herself for what she's done."

"That explains a lot." April watched him in silence for a moment while she thought about the new information. She started to say something, then stopped and stared at the ground.

"April, the key to acknowledging emotions is to become fully conscious of your feelings. Like Jill said, don't give your power to Rachel. You're certainly externally comfortable, but not yet internally comfortable in your own skin. Rachel might be bringing up something in your past. Only when you begin to understand what it is that's causing those feelings will you be able to put them away forever. I might be able to help you confront them, resolve your anguish, and return you to a state of love and peace. Think about it. Give me a call to schedule an appointment when you're ready."

CHAPTER 25

April was gripped with anxiety as she drove to A. J.'s on a sunny Saturday morning. She had no inkling of what to expect, and maybe that was best. She trusted him. His grand Victorian home was surrounded with thick green hedges and tucked far from the street among gardens of wild flowers, rhododendrons, magnolia trees dripping with Spanish moss, and huge fir and oak trees. It almost looked like an historic scene from a Hollywood movie.

When A. J. answered the door, he immediately withdrew his hands from his pockets, hugged April, and gently kissed her cheek. He looked like a middle-age Michael J. Fox—a small-built man with narrow shoulders and small neck with prominent veins. He was dressed in denim frayed shorts, black flip-flops, a white t-shirt with a peace sign emblazoned in red, and a small gold hoop earring.

April and A. J. walked through a foyer entry. A rose-colored Tiffany chandelier hung from a twelve-foot ceiling. The foyer doors with transoms, front staircase, and mantel all matched the butternut woodwork. A guestbook lay face-down on a half-moon-shaped wooden table. A. J. led April through a living room, across a hallway, and into a gathering room that was lined with small-paned windows from one end of the room to the other, overlooking a marsh. Candles and jasmine incense were burning in wooden holders.

April settled herself comfortably on a maroon leather sectional sofa. New Age woodwind music played in the background. An anxious silence filled the air. A. J. began to guide April through a closed-eye meditation.

"April, I want you to visualize yourself walking along a garden path of variegated flowers—the colors of the rainbow—red, orange, yellow, green, blue, indigo, violet, and white. Right now, you're walking among the red flowers—beautiful, pure red. I want you to tell me how that color feels to you. What does that color bring up to you?"

Having left the office after working most of the morning, it took April an hour to complete the descriptions that each of the seven colors symbolized for her. When she got to describing her impressions of white, her eyes began to moisten, and sadness poured over her. She began sobbing uncontrollably until she was finished with her description.

"Next, I want you to find yourself face-to-face with a lion. Tell me what happens."

"We kind of stare each other down." April paused for a long time before continuing. "And then we kind of become friends. She realizes I'm not afraid. Isn't that symbolic?"

"I think that you refer to the lion as *she* is very symbolic, but we can discuss that later. Walk with this lion, now, down the garden path. Know that the strength of the lion is your strength. Find yourself walking through snow. Tell me how it feels."

"This is strange, but it feels pretty regal—pretty inflating."

"Give the lion a hug. How does it feel?"

"Powerful—pretty powerful that I could hug a lion."

"Find yourself by the lion in school. How does that feel?"

"Pretty all-knowing, like I'm on the highest plane of knowing." April sighed and paused again for a long time.

"Now, I want you to find yourself lying down and going to sleep next to the lion. Just rest. Just rest. I'd like you to take some very deep breaths—slowly. If you're clear and comfortable, I want you to find yourself back here on the couch. When you're ready, open your eyes." A. J. leaned toward her and handed April a mirror so she could look at herself. "You look good."

April opened her eyes and looked into the mirror. Everything looked hazy—like she was looking through an unfocused set of binoculars. Then she looked around the room as if it was the first time she had seen it. "You certainly do have a lot of mirrors in this room, don't you?" Her voice faded off as she glanced around the room, where several mirrors were hanging.

"One must look at oneself," A. J. said.

"I guess so. Well, do you think we got to the bottom of anything?"

"I'm going to go over it—what we did here for you—to review some of your insights. We started with the color red, which is your connection to the earth—your grounding. It's your base chakra.

"Chakras are the basic energy centers in the body that correlate to levels of consciousness, colors, sounds, body functions, developmental stages of life, and much, much more. Your response to your feelings about red were warmth, love, beauty, and a bullfighter's cape. Red is the color associated with passion, energy, health, and general well-being. Do you have many red clothes? I notice you're wearing black and white today. Why?"

"Yes, I do, but I probably wore black because today represents the death of the old me that I'm trying to leave behind. I didn't feel like wearing color this morning."

A. J. smiled and continued, "Orange is the chakra that represents your sexuality. You said it's your favorite color; you feel pretty in it. You feel you're pretty comfortable with your sexuality."

"I guess I do."

"Yellow. Your response to that color was buttercups and sunflowers. Yellow is your gut feeling and knowledge being more rooted in the earth and comes from a higher connection with Spirit. You said warm and fresh.

"Green is the heart chakra. You said neutral—it doesn't affect you one way or another."

"I guess that means I'm not letting my emotions out," stated April.

"You're very bright. You've let your head rule your life for a long time. You're good at compartmentalizing and hiding what you really think. That's helped you to be successful in business. But now you're getting a connection with your gut, and your heart is getting in the way. Your heart wants to be heard. That's what your tears were showing when you began to cry. Pay attention to it. You're thinking an awful lot when you should be feeling. You've always let your brain tell your heart what to feel. Help me understand why."

"Probably because I was a child of an alcoholic and always tried to protect myself from my father's irrational outbursts." April felt tightness in her chest.

"Then, as a child, that's what happened when your father was in one of his rages. Your brain took over and told your heart what to feel, because it was easier for you. It buried the hurt. You don't have to do that anymore. You can change that pattern now."

"I know, because I'm surrounded by love now—except for Rachel."

"We can discuss that later. Now you can be vulnerable, because there's no need not to be. Blue is communication and is located in the throat area. All you said was cool. You don't let a lot of emotion show, and what you're really feeling is making you more vulnerable rather than less. Cool works for you in your corporate world, doesn't it?"

April nodded affirmatively.

"Violet is the third eye—your intuition. You had a hard time visualizing it. You were resisting it. Indigo is the top of the head chakra; it's your connection with Spirit. It's the highest frequency in the visual spectrum. You said that's where you want to be. You are attempting to connect with your higher power.

And white—that's the soul, your core. They are inseparable from each other. It is the essence of our being. You can't hide from it. You said people can see the inner part of me, transparent, faith.

And that was your goal today—to open the door just a little bit to your soul. You were very confused talking about faith. Part of you delighted in hiding faith, and part of you is very sad in it being hidden."

"I never had any faith. God was never around when I needed him. I guess I've just been keeping myself from myself. There's nobody to be afraid of anymore—least of all me."

"You don't need this protection anymore. And the lion—that felt pretty darn good to you, didn't it? You referred to the lion as *she*. You have lots of male qualities, April. You're strong, cool, a successful businesswoman. You've done well in a man's world. You learned how to compartmentalize—how to hide what you're thinking. You've got that down. It's the woman now that you want to develop. The lioness is your strength, symbolically."

"Because I was my father's favorite—he was a very strong person," April said. "He delighted that I was strong and outgoing like him. I got positive reinforcement from him. It also helped me to be a survivor, but I don't need that protection anymore. My father praised me for my strength, and my mother criticized me for it."

"So you developed the one you were praised for, and suppressed the one attached to criticism," A. J. responded. "Usually what upsets people in others is something they're dealing with themselves. May I suggest you begin to wear the colors you had problems with—green, blue, and anything white—and meditate on this session? Green will help open your heart, so it won't be overcome by your brain, and the color blue will give a voice to your heart. And white is the most important, because it will help open your soul. Remember what Michelangelo once said: 'I saw the angel in the marble, and I just chiseled till I set him free.' Chisel yourself free, April. Go deeper to mend the hole in your soul.

You must go through the grieving process to feel your child's pain that you've repressed all these years. Mourning is the only way to heal your soul. You must forgive yourself and your parents. Your guilt is a symptom of the family dysfunction that was present when you were a child.

You wonder what purpose Spirit had with the entrance of Rachel into your life. Think about it. Her characteristics are similar to your father's—controlling, an alcoholic, volatile mood swings—all the things you thought you left behind with his death. That's why you regress into feeling like a child when you're with her. She becomes the parent, and you, the child again."

"My nightmares have returned since I came to Florida. I've tried all my life to understand those dreams. I keep thinking, if only I could find the thread … it would all fall into place, but it never did."

"Dreams help us deal with realities in an unconscious state when it may be so hurtful that our conscious mind is too fragile to handle and help heal it. Your dreams helped you realize that you had not reconciled the death of your father. Spirit put Rachel in your life to show you that your pain from the past had not been resolved. Once it is, you'll be able to stay in the present and enjoy the life you were meant to live. Being in the present is one of the most powerful spiritual places to be. Remember, she was the one to introduce you to the beginning of your spiritual journey. When she entered your life, you were forced to directly confront your trauma.

We can do another session when you're ready. Now you need to be gentle with yourself. When you feel you're ready, listen to this tape; then call me, and we'll see about another meeting."

A. J. and April walked into the backyard in silent friendship, where they sat on a swing in silence, sipping iced tea and listening to the chirping birds. Some osprey and blue herons were walking along the edge of the marsh. A woodpecker busily burrowed a hole into a tall, thin raintree. A large bald eagle flew overhead. April got up slowly and embraced A. J. "What do I owe you for this?"

"My only price is that you finally heal with my help. You're my friend, April. That's all I want from and for you."

As she drove home with the sunroof open, April admired the beautiful blue sky that was a pallet for billowy marshmallow clouds. She thought that A. J. could help her sculpt a new beginning. She basked in the warm air. The weather was different from the gray, clouded, Rust Belt, pocked with deserted furnaces, spewing bitter mill smoke. She felt deeply grateful to A. J. for putting her on the right path to self-discovery. She was convinced he could help her seek out aspects and awaken to a clearer sense of herself.

April realized she could never change her history—but in time, and with A. J.'s help, she might change her understanding of it. She sat on a bench at her apartment complex and closed her eyes. There was a faint trickling movement from the fountain. The air was cool and sweet. There was a scent of wet grass. A looming hot coral sunset was descending. She was spellbound, thinking she had finally found someone who understood her and might be able help unlock whatever she had repressed all these years. The annoying mosquitoes and no-see-ums were out in full force in the early evenings. She quickly returned inside for relief.

CHAPTER 26

The shrieking sound of a car alarm interrupted April's nightmare. Maybe if she kept her eyes closed long enough, the haunting images would disappear. She hated the aftermath of the nightmares, which loomed like a dark cloud, shrouding her thoughts for the entire day. *This keeps happening over and over. Something's got to give before I go crazy. A. J.'s my only answer. I have nowhere else to turn. Breau said with enough energy and intention, there's nothing that can't be healed—even war and world hunger. I'm more than ready to get this monkey off my back.*

April felt her metamorphosis was imminent. Leaving Ohio was the initial crack in her cocoon. Now the time had come to emerge into the new and break it completely open. Her intention and energy reached a new level. She was ready to jump and take flight to total freedom. Whatever that may be, it would have to be better than this.

Fatigue overwhelmed her. She put on her horn-rimmed glasses and opened one eye to look at the clock. It was 8:00. Familiar noises had already begun around the complex—lawnmowers, leaf blowers, hedge trimmers, running water from the adjoining apartments, and sirens wailing down Kirkman Road on their way to Florida Hospital.

Sunlight streamed into the front windows as April adjusted the plantation shutters, which faced east. The sky was bright, with dark clouds evident from the north—not a good sign. Hurricane season was in full force, but there had been no warnings to date. It must've rained during the night. The roof and surrounding trees were dripping water. There were puddles along the walkways. Humidity hung in the air like a smothering blanket. The annoying, harmless black love bugs mating while airborne swarmed everywhere. Slowly, April was adjusting to the southern climate.

She made her way conscientiously into the kitchen to brew some coffee. A fresh cup was always the best way to start a Sunday morning. The theater section of the *Orlando Sentinel* had an article about the successful long run of the movie *Dead Poets Society.* It was a reminder she needed to spend part of her day at the movies if she was ever to extract important personal messages. April wanted to make the best of this synchronicity. If she was ever going to begin sculpting a new beginning, this might be the place to begin enlisting Spirit as her co-creator. But first, she needed to get ready for the morning group meeting. Sundays were the most crowded, but she knew her friends would save her a place. As she scrubbed her skin with perfumed body wash, she mused how her spiritual journey fit with her non-religious convictions.

Thinking back to a book by Sue Monk Kidd, *When The Heart Waits,* April remembered the author's description of a spiritual journey, which said it's "a lot like a poem … it falls on you like a teardrop or wraps around you like a smile." All of a sudden, April experienced an epiphany. *Moving to Orlando was my journey. It gave me the opportunity to wait and be still. Spirit literally dropped me into a circle of new friends—my spiritual teachers. They wrapped around me like a smile. Even my dreams drew me to find A. J. Wow. There's so much more to learn. Amazing how things are beginning to connect and fall into place. The last piece of the puzzle is to find the answers to Daddy's accident. Forget looking into NOW meetings for new friends. That's the past.*

April barely heard the phone ringing while she dried her hair. "Hello." There was no answer. "Hello." Still, there was no answer. "Who is this?" *Click.*

That shook April out of her deep reverie. A few minutes later, the phone rang again. "Who is this?" she yelled abruptly into the phone.

"Good morning to you too! Got up on the wrong side of the bed, did we?"

A cramping pain seized April when she heard Rachel's voice. April wanted to close her eyes and hang up. She paused instead. "Did you just call me a few minutes ago and hang up?"

207

"Now, why would I do that, sweetie?"

As Rachel spoke, April could clearly see that plastic smile in the back of her mind. *Here we go again with that syrupy façade.* "I don't know, but there's a lot of things you do that I can't explain. Someone called and hung up after I said hello a couple times. That's why I answered so hastily. So, what's up with you this morning?"

"I wanted to invite you to go with me to the group meeting today. I'd love to pick you up. Maybe we can do some fun things after the group session."

"I'm sorry, Rachel. I've already made other plans, but I will be there this morning."

"So I'll see you there. Do you want me to save you a seat?"

"No, thanks. I'll be sitting with some friends. Why don't you join us? You know A. J., Jill, and Vickie. Why don't you sit with us?"

Rachel's voice became sharp. "Never mind!"

"You know, Rachel, I don't appreciate your sarcasm and mood changes. They don't become you ..."

The phone went dead.

Fine, go ahead and hang up on me again, but I'm not gonna be bullied by you anymore. But as much as April told herself that she was in control, her body's visceral responses told her otherwise.

April needed to brace herself for the long, humid summers that were in full swing. She debated what to wear as she scanned the clothes in her closet—dress warm for the air conditioning and cool for the humidity. Temperatures had been climbing into the mid-nineties. Maybe her new green cotton sweater set would work. She toasted a pumpernickel bagel and filled a Styrofoam cup with coffee. Just as she was about to bolt out the front door, the phone rang again.

"Hello," April barked.

"Hi, Mom, it's me."

"Michael! It's great to hear your voice. I was just on my way out."

"I won't keep you. I have some great news. I've been given a three-month temporary recruiting assignment at the naval base in Orlando. Would you like to have some company?"

"Would I? I'd love it! The base is around the corner from my office.

They're moving the furniture from Ohio next week. I rented a new house with three bedrooms, two baths, kitchen, living, and family room. I've been lonely, and you're just what the doctor ordered. How soon can you be here?"

"In two weeks, if that's okay."

"Okay? The sooner, the better, honey. Wait till Dad hears. He'll be jealous. I'll even let you hook up all the electronic equipment and hang my pictures. Let me know when you're leaving so I can make sure you get the directions in time. I need to run now, but let's keep in touch."

April hurried out the door, thinking about Dinah's prediction. She had been right about Michael joining April soon. The heavy, hot air smelled stale. April wondered how anyone ever lived in the South before air conditioning.

******

Dozens of people filtered into the furniture store. It was heartening as more and more of the faces had become familiar to April. She loved hugging each person and basking in the loving energy. As far as she was concerned, Orlando was a Mecca for spiritual growth. She spotted A.J. from the corner of her eye. He glowed like a yellow sun. He put his arms around her shoulders, nodded, and squared up to face her directly. He pointed to where Jill and Vickie were sitting.

"The ladies have saved a seat for us over there on the sofa. Come walk with me to the kitchen."

"A. J., you'll never guess who called me this morning out of the blue. Three guesses, and the first two don't count."

"It had to be Rachel."

"Yup."

"And how did you handle it?"

"I guess I handled everything okay, but the sick and nervous feeling flattened me like a bulldozer when I first heard her voice. She invited me to come with her this morning, but I told her my plans were already made."

"Just be patient with yourself. It'll take time to completely overcome your feelings from the past."

As April and A. J. headed back into the main part of the store, people were seated and waiting for Breau to begin. The smell of fresh coffee filled the air. A. J. stretched his small frame at one end of the sofa, removed his cap, and laced his fingers over his chest. Jill sat on the other end, with Vickie and April in the middle. Vickie nudged April with her elbow and nodded in the direction of a stately woman who had just entered the room. Rachel looked out of place dressed in a tailored black St. John suit with that gold medallion hanging low around her neck in all its glory. A few stragglers filed in behind her and looked for empty seats, while she just stood there, panning the room.

"Come in and shut the door, Rachel," said Breau. "Don't be shy." He looked surprised as she stood in the doorway with her hands on her hips in an obstinate posture. She didn't move. Two sailors walked in behind her and finally closed the door.

Although April was surrounded by her new friends, she felt her muscles tighten while memories of dread and fear surfaced. It was as if she was that little girl again, waiting for her abusive father's next move. Her body stiffened. She gripped the edge of her notebook. A. J. carefully encased her hand in his warm one. A wave of anger crossed Rachel's face when she noticed A. J.'s gesture.

April made a purposeful turn to face Rachel's steely stare head-on. Rachel's face looked gaunt. She had dark circles under her eyes and a sallow complexion, almost appearing as if she was at the end of her tether.

April smiled at her for an instant before looking away. *There, that didn't hurt.* She even sat straighter in her chair. Her power was intact. A.J. squeezed her hand to acknowledge her newfound confidence.

About fifteen minutes into Breau's presentation, Rachel retreated. She inched out slowly, shriveling away like a wilted daisy, quietly closing the door behind her. April held her breath until she saw she was gone. She gave a sigh of relief. A. J. patted her hand before returning his hand to his lap.

Breau ended the meditation with a prayer. "We ask Spirit—who is perfect, good, loving, and resides in each of us—to help us forgive others and ourselves. Only then will we be overwhelmed with joy at the results. Amen."

April put her sunglasses on as soon as she opened her eyes at the conclusion of the meditation to adjust to the sunlight that poured into the room once the front double doors were opened. She embraced her friends and told them they would be meeting her son in a couple weeks. She asked to schedule another session with A. J. as soon as possible.

His expression warmed. "Give yourself more time to heal from our session. Meditate on it a few times; then call me. I think you've reached a new milestone this morning. You showed great strength in your reaction to seeing Rachel. I'm glad you took my advice about wearing green. You look pretty today."

April peeled off her cardigan and tied it around her waist.

A. J. walked April to her car. They embraced before she left. She hurried to make the movie matinee.

******

A gray twilight had descended across the horizon simultaneously to a burnt, golden sunset. On April's drive home from the theater after seeing the movie for the second time, she recalled the most poignant and personal messages elicited. *Carpe diem* was the film's theme. *Seize the day.* April was living *carpe diem*—migrating alone to a different geography, culture, and life. If that wasn't seizing the day and non-conformity, what was?

The antagonist of the movie was a controlling father not unlike April's own father. It had taken her years of striving to find her voice, discover new ground, and shed a life of quiet desperation. Now she realized that her uncontrollable sadness from the movie was not only caused by the recent news of her friend's suicide. Rather, she identified with the young man in the movie who took his life. Like April, he had no freedom, was controlled by his father, and had a mother who was not always present as his advocate.

The most profound epiphany was the professor's metaphor for changing the way one sees the world. He forced his students to challenge their ideas about the world and their place in it—in this case, he had them climb onto their desks to see things from another angle. The important inspirational lesson was crucial for them to find their own ways to approach the world as they struck out on their own. What they saw would be the same, but how they saw it would be different. What intrigued April most was the movie's subtext—viewing the world from a different perspective was a way the professor also demonstrated non-conformity and freedom. A poem the professor recited kept whirling around in April's brain like an earworm: "Only in dreams can men be truly free. Was always thus, and always thus will be."

On the car radio, Stevie Wonder was singing April's favorite song, "I Just Called to Say I Love You." She pictured Karl singing to her on bended knees. She smiled. *Synchronicity—there are no accidents*. At that very moment, Stevie Wonder was singing the song on the radio especially for her. Spirit had reminded her how much she missed Karl and wished he could be joining her soon in this enchanting city.

CHAPTER 27

During the next two weeks, April followed A. J.'s instructions. During each meditation, she played her favorite tape, *Miracles*, as background music. It was an instrumental tape, with harps, strings, and woodwinds. Within minutes, she'd begin floating into a relaxed meditation.

When Joe came into town on business, he stayed with her for a couple nights. Together, they enjoyed a deep meditation, which was an exercise he religiously practiced to maintain his balance and stress level.

******

It had been three long weeks since the session with A. J. April remembered to wear the colors he suggested and listened to the tape multiple times, but the nightmares continued. She'd wake up with tightness in her chest. The nightmares were beginning to interfere with her concentration at work. Her mind would wander at the least opportune moments during important meetings. *That's it. I can't go on like this. I need to get to the root cause of these nightmares once and for all.* She contacted A. J. and scheduled another session.

On April's ride to A. J.'s house, she had an intuition that the day might finally reveal important answers. April was lost in thought while she listened to the birds through her open sunroof when a bolt of lightning shot through the sky. It roused her out of a trancelike state. She quickly closed the sunroof. A small rain cloud pushed her way for three miles with a downpour, which lasted about fifteen minutes.

April drove onto the East-West Expressway that was lined with freshly planted groves of small fir and palm saplings and white oleanders. Just as she turned onto the exit which led to A.J.'s house, she witnessed one of the most beautiful rainbows she had ever seen. It stretched for miles. The colors were brilliant. She thought it was an omen to validate that the day would finally reveal the answers and basis of her nightmares.

A. J. was in the yard, trimming two ten-foot holly bushes at either end of his front door as April parked in front of his house. He put down his pruning shears and gave her a warm hug.

"I just saw the most dazzling rainbow on my drive here this morning."

"Perhaps it's a sign that Spirit's ready to guide you through your storm. Maybe you'll even find a pot of gold at the end. Do you feel how purposeful it is that we're doing this today?"

"Yes, I do. I knew the rainbow was my good luck sign."

April heard music as she entered the house. It was *Miracles*. The energy in the room was very calming. Once again, she sat on the sofa across from the massive window which overlooked the garden of magnolia trees and coleus bushes along the edge of the marsh that had become familiar. She took several deep breaths to absorb the strains of the music in all parts of her tissues and cells. She and A. J. sat in silence for a few minutes, admired the view, and enjoyed the music.

"If you're ready to begin, I want you to close your eyes. Get comfortable, and tell me when you're ready."

"I'm ready. I feel very dreamy and calm. You won't believe it, but you're playing my favorite tape. I listen to it as background music during my evening meditations."

"Good. April, I'm going to take you through the colors again, but in a different way. So, I'd like you to use a bit of your imagination and find yourself in a place that brings you peace. Where would that be?"

"In Treasure Cay, Bahamas."

"Tell me what you're doing when you're able to find yourself in Treasure Cay."

"I'm in the water."

"What color is the water?

"A beautiful, sparkling aqua."

"How does it feel?"

Without hesitation, April answered, "Great! I was there several months ago with my husband."

"What I'd like you to do is use your imagination now to change the color of the water and yourself as you float to a beautiful, bright red. Let me know when you've done that."

"I don't want it to be red. You want me to go with what I feel, right?"

April's imagination struggled but was eventually successful as A. J. once again led her through each of the colors of the chakras until they reached blue.

"Make the water blue, and let me know when you've done that. Let me know when you're also that color."

"I'm working on it. Okay, I think I've got it."

"How do you feel being blue?" A. J. asked.

"Cool. Not me." As soon as April said those words, memories came rushing back. They were deep into the session. There was no turning back. Her heart pounded like a piston. The world had begun to spin on a different axis when she realized who it was.

"Who, then?"

"Somebody else." She suddenly sensed a gnawing nervousness and anxiety. She listened to the music to help calm herself.

"If that person had a name, what would that person be called? April, I want you to allow your conscious mind to step aside. Let your subconscious step forward."

Seconds passed before April finally answered, "Probably Josef." As she said this, it was as if she was ten years old, and the power of the auditorium curtain was lifting. But now the curtain was lifting to expose much more than just her father in the audience to show his love for her. She couldn't quite put her finger on it just yet, but she knew something was coming that made her very nervous.

"Is this someone you know?"

She jerked out of her reverie and finally made an attempt to answer. "Um-hmm."

"Who's Josef?"

"He was my father."

"Why is he here?"

"I don't know. He always ends up coming back to me in nightmares." April's mouth became very dry. A sick sensation came over her. Her eyes filled with tears.

"Is he coming back?"

"He died over twenty-nine years ago. What a long time ago that was."

"How old were you when he died?"

"Twenty."

"Were you close?"

"Yes."

"What were the circumstances?"

"I was his favorite. I was the most like him, and when I was little, I wanted to be like him—but that changed."

"That changed?"

"Um-hmm."

"I spent my early childhood worshiping him, but he became a real disappointment. My feelings changed. The person I loved began to disappear, and a gray shell of who was left was no longer the father I loved. For all his miserable failures, I owed him a good deal of my achievements in life."

"He disappointed you?"

"Um-hmm."

"In what way?"

"He was an alcoholic. There were a lot of things I admired about him, but when I got older, I realized I didn't want to be like him. He let me down. I couldn't depend on him. But he was the greatest influence in my life."

"Do you realize that Josef helps you sometimes?"

"Um-hmm. I wouldn't be where I am today without him. He gave me all the drive—the ambition necessary in the business world. So, I know he's helped me."

"Can we go back to the time when your father was still alive—near the end of his life? Where are you?"

"In the kitchen at his house."

"What's happening?"

"It was really sad before he died. He and my mother weren't getting along, and she was close to a nervous breakdown. I was the only one who could talk and reason with him, so I asked him to leave my mother and not come back until he straightened himself out," she concluded miserably.

"How did that feel?"

"Scary and sad—like, when was this ever gonna end?"

"How did he take it?"

"As usual, he thought nobody understood him—but he listened, he left, and he died one week later."

"Were you with him when he died?"

"No. He died in an auto accident."

"When was the last time you saw him alive?"

"The night I asked him to leave his house."

"April, there's great learning to be had right now, and I want you to allow it to happen. Tell me what comes to mind as you put yourself back in time."

"After he died, I used to have a lot of dreams that he was alive, and I wanted him dead. They were always bad dreams. They stopped years ago and came back once I moved here."

"Guilty, huh? You felt guilty, didn't you?"

As A. J. began digging further getting deeper into the session, a groundswell of awareness surfaced. April began sobbing, and she was unable to speak. She felt a strange sensation—like the past was coming to life. She couldn't hear or see. She was in another time and place. She didn't want it to come to life, but a curtain lifted and began to expose the truth—something she never realized. It struck her at this moment—at this culmination. *Guilt, oh my God, guilt—I have repressed guilt. It's high time to forgive myself.* Her mind raced. Soon, she was flooded with thoughts. *If I just hang in there, I might finally be at peace. It's as if all of Breau's forgiveness lessons have been especially for me. These nightmares are driving me crazy. I want to get up and leave. I want to go home. If I do, I can't go home. I have to find out. I have to stay. How am I ever gonna find my way*

*back to peace? Trust your gut, for God's sakes. There's no turning back. Go
with it. End it.*

"April, come back. April, can you hear me?

"Um-hmm. I hear you."

"April, I want you to get in touch with your feelings and your
emotions, no matter how painful they might seem. Only if you face
these feelings and confront them head-on can we unlock their mystery
and begin to understand why you have these dreams. Stay with me.
Dreams can be an outlet—an escape valve for all the negativity you're
holding in your conscious mind. Tell me what's happening. Why are
you having trouble speaking right now?"

Somewhere deep in the pit of her stomach, she knew it couldn't
be true. *How could I have been so blind?* Suddenly, she was twenty and
pregnant, sitting in the funeral home. The sudden memory of her father
lying in the coffin, his face almost unrecognizable, the smothering smell
of flowers and candles filling the room—it all came rushing back. All
her unsaid words went back to where they had been all these years. *How
could I have been so blind?*

"April, come back. What's happening?"

April opened her eyes and stared into space. Her face was
expressionless. She listened to the woodwinds in the background. Her
heart was so heavy with regret, she couldn't speak. Sunlight slanted
through the picture window. She watched the egrets carefully step
around the marsh. In the background, the sound of the air conditioner
kicked on to relieve the stuffiness in the air.

"April. Talk to me," pleaded A. J. "Why are you having trouble
speaking right now?"

"Because I never thought about guilt—I failed to see it, but I guess
that's what it was, and it won't let me go, huh?" It was too painful to
keep her eyes open. April closed them again. "People blamed me. Even
my uncle said my dad committed suicide because I turned him out of
his own house, and I was so adamant that it wasn't true—that it was an
accident. But it had to be. He had to leave. I was haunted with these
nightmares for a long time," she rambled on with unsteady breathing.
"They stopped, and now they've come back since I moved here. I don't
want to sob, but I can't help it."

"Yes, you do. You've been holding it in for a long time. It's cleansing, and it's needed. Allow it. Remember that many of our memories are held in our subconscious, and the key to unlock those memories is released in our dreams, like ticking time bombs. Your nightmares are a release of harboring negative thoughts so painful that you've locked them away in your subconscious."

April's head was spinning, and her body shivered with spasms of sadness. "I just wanted things to be different, but they couldn't be. I wanted his whole life to be different," she said, sobbing.

"April, I want you to go into the center of that feeling. You're headed there. Let that come out. You need to express that. It's crying, and it wants to come out. Talk about it. What're you feeling right now?"

April's sobbing stopped. With tightened eyes, she searched for answers. "Oh, gosh, there's too many. I don't know—shame, sorrow, anguish, frustration. I don't think I feel guilt. It had to happen."

"You don't feel guilty about telling him he had to go?"

"I didn't think I did. It was a choice between my mother and my father."

"Did you feel guilty about the dreams after he died—about him being alive and you wanting him dead?"

"Well, it wasn't only in dreams. When I'd visit my mother, I'd expect to see him walk through the door, and I'd feel—wow, what a relief that he wasn't going to. It was over, but I didn't want it to be that way. That was his choice, and nobody could change it. I couldn't. I tried."

"What was Josef like?"

"Josef did everything with a passion. He was a man of extremes and had a voracious appetite for food, drink, love, business, money. But for all his shortcomings, he was the biggest influence in my life. He was my role model. But he lost his way. He was tired and at the end of his rope. He was riding high—but like Willy Loman, those days were gone, and he was sinking quickly. The days of King Midas were over. It was just a very sad story. He had a terrible childhood and was obsessed that if he was smart enough and made enough money, maybe he would be worthy enough to win his mother's love and approval."

"April, I want you to imagine yourself becoming Josef. It's gonna be very valuable for you. I want to talk directly to Josef, and I want you to feel and hear his feelings about life. I want you to go to the time when you're talking to him in the kitchen and you see his eyes. Do you see them?"

"No, because he's always looking down while he talks."

"Will you imagine yourself as Josef?"

"It's really painful, because he feels no one understands him."

A. J. continued. "Josef, how do you feel that April's asking you to leave?"

"A. J., you're almost making me feel like it's my fault that he chose to die. I've been blamed by others. I could never accept that. I only want to think and believe he's happy now." April was having difficulty assuming her father's persona.

"April, just go with it. Have the courage to do this in spite of your fear. That's what real courage is. Risk it. You know it's not your fault; he *chose* to die. You've learned that people make their own decisions, even selecting when it's their time to go to the other side."

"But it's like I gave him his final failure, and there was nothing else for him to hold on to." April became aware of her heartbeat pulsating behind her eyes.

"There's a beautiful lesson here for you. This is the door we need to open to understand what's happening to you now and why you're having these nightmares. It's a beautiful opportunity. If you choose to take it, it's there for you. No judgments. Just experience. A lesson will be clear. Don't judge yourself."

"I'm not, but it's the awareness when he decided that—that it had to be. There was nothing left, and he couldn't change, and there was nothing left to hang on to. And that was the only way to redeem himself. I didn't want him to do that. I just wanted him to change."

"He knows that. You can let go of that. Remember, there is no time and space in Spirit. I want to talk to Josef."

"Josef would never talk about it. That's why he drank." April continued to resist.

"He's in Spirit now. Josef, I want to talk to you now. It's safe, and it's with love. Don't be so frightened. There is only love here. Josef, this is your opportunity. You're a beam of light. What happened that day when you decided to have that car accident? Tell me what happened. What were you feeling?"

April felt her father trying to scream something at her from across the distance between his death and her nightmares, but she couldn't make out the words. April surrendered. Her father finally emerged. "I was feeling love for my family, and I wanted to give them peace. That was the only way I knew how. It was a decision I made."

"Through love?"

"Through love and through exhaustion from the struggle of hurting others and hurting myself. I had to leave. I knew my family would be better off with me gone. That was the only way I could finally bring peace to them and peace to myself. I couldn't bear not being in their life anymore."

"Josef, I want you to go back—just moments before the car accident. Tell me what's going through your mind. What do you feel? Right now, Josef, what do you feel just before your passing?"

"Scared. I guess of not knowing if it will hurt—but when I got in the car, I finally felt at peace. I knew what I had to do. I had to give my family a gift and not do any more damage to them. I had to leave. That was the only way to finally bring peace to their lives."

"What happens at the accident—at the moment of the accident? What's happening?"

"I'm leaving the physical."

"April, your father is about to go into the light. Tell him everything you're feeling. Everything you wish to tell him, tell him now."

"I'm sorry, Daddy," said April. "I'm sorry for the way it ended. I love you very much."

"Josef, do you have anything to say to April?" A. J. asked.

"It's okay, baby. I'll be okay. I'll still be with you. I won't be far. Someday, you'll join me, and we'll be together again. I'll miss you."

"There's no time and space in Spirit," said A. J. "Josef, you're always here, and you'll always be with her. That's the joy of Spirit. There is no distance. The light exists everywhere. Give her that gift of love. Are you going to the light, Josef?" A. J. asked.

"It feels so much better now."

"Josef, now that you're in the light, I ask that you help heal April's deep-seated guilt, which you've created in her. You will help with love, because that's what Spirit is. This is your greatest gift to April." A. J. addressed April again. "April, how does it feel to let your father go into the light?"

"At peace," April answered. "Almost a spiritual sense of peace and possibility." For the first time, she spoke calmly and without tears. "I can't believe I've suffered with nightmares when the truth should've been so obvious."

"Fill your body with warm, crystalline, pure white light. Feel the intelligence that exists in every cell of your body. Feel the beauty that is yours. See yourself now without guilt and remorse, but only with love. How does it feel?"

"It feels great. I feel whole again. I feel peace, contentment, and love."

"If you could describe yourself as a color right now, what color would that be?"

"I am that aqua water. I feel complete."

"It's a new morning for you. It's a brand new day, and now you have full control of your physicality. Glow in it. Bask in the warmth of it. Feel the excitement of it too. There are no words for it. Allow the full expression of yourself to blossom. You have great love for yourself, which others can share. It is now yours to use in every part of your life. In the next several weeks, each day will bring something new. The greater understanding of yourself will continue."

"This whole transplant to Florida has been enlightening." A realization washed over April that she knew in due time would change her life forever.

"The Sunshine State," laughed A. J. "You can open your eyes now. April, do you remember the story of Sisyphus rolling the huge stone up the hill? You were Sisyphus, and that huge stone was your guilt. Until you learned to forgive yourself, you never would have been able to reach the top of the hill and live an authentic life. Then—and only then—would your nightmares be gone forever."

"No wonder I had all these dreams for years after he died. I buried my guilt in my subconscious. Could his influence on me have also been transferred to my son, Michael? I was three months pregnant with Michael when my father died."

"Sometimes spirits are confused about going to the light when their physical bodies die, so they stay in the earth plane. Some aren't even aware of their passing. They can even attach to their loved ones. Josef's attachment to you certainly affected Michael in utero."

"But why did those nightmares return once I moved to Florida?"

"Synchronicity—there are no accidents. Rachel reminded your subconscious that you hadn't resolved your guilt. She brought that all back so you could face it. One relates to the other. You turned your guilt inward. The basis of your dreams was guilt. You were looking in all the wrong places to eradicate your nightmares. The only way to undo your unconscious projection of guilt was through forgiving yourself and releasing it to the Holy Spirit.

"Until you could resolve the blame you had harbored with the death of your father, you would never have been able to deal with Rachel. Until you learned how to forgive yourself, your dreams would have continued and hindered your spiritual growth. It's not important to know whether your father's accident was intentional. While we fear death consciously, we are attracted to it unconsciously. Your last meeting with your father helped release him from his inner turmoil— from his pain, guilt, and suffering. That was your gift to him, and his accident was his gift to the family—a supreme sacrifice. You gave each other blessed gifts."

"How amazing and reassuring that in the span of such a short time I've lived here, your guidance has helped cure my troubled heart," responded April. "It's been cathartic to tell you my story, only to have you interpret what I've repressed for too long, never knowing the guilt I harbored because of my father's death."

"Fear binds the world. Forgiveness sets it free. You know, we spend our lives trying to prevent death, when death just might be a gift."

"I'm awestruck. The past was a place to visit, but I don't want to live there anymore. My metamorphosis began when I moved here, but it took time for my cocoon to completely break open. You helped give me the courage I needed. How can I ever thank you?"

"When the student is ready, the teacher will appear. I'm sure you've heard that before. James Van Praagh once said, 'Each soul comes to his own truth in a personal, unique way and at the proper time.' April, it was your time. Your soul was ready."

******

April drove home humming softly to herself. She felt free for the first time. The anvil that weighed heavily on her shoulders had been lifted. She drove back to the apartment and called Karl. She couldn't wait to hear his voice.

"Are you listening to me?" April asked. It was as if the kitchen clock ticked like a time bomb until she got everything out that she wanted to—everything about A. J. and her sessions. She was excited.

"Yes, I'm listening. I wish I could be there to hold you, like old times."

"I do too. When is it gonna finally happen for us? When will that condo sell? We've been apart much too long."

"Be patient, honey. It'll happen."

CHAPTER 28

Four men from the Florida Moving Company backed into the driveway of the new rental home. It was a challenge for April to singlehandedly manage *and* direct all the moving activities simultaneously. April checked the invoices against the boxes as the men unloaded them from the truck. She directed the movers to where she wanted the boxes unpacked and the furniture arranged in the house. Unloading and arranging furniture and goods from an Ohio twelve-room condo to a seven-room Florida house was a masterful feat. Overflow ended up in the garage.

Eight hours later, April collapsed at the kitchen table with a sigh of relief that this mission was accomplished. She spent the next two days putting everything in order and stocking the pantry with groceries in anticipation of Michael's arrival.

For months, April's new life in Orlando had remained completely separate and estranged from life at home in Milltown, but now it was starting to come together. She hurried to get out of her nightgown. It was an unusually foggy, misty morning. No sooner had she changed into her jeans and sweatshirt than she heard a car pull into the driveway. She hurried outside and ran into Michael's arms. She breathed in his smell and kissed his neck and cheeks. His arms tightened around her— the arms that were longingly familiar. "I've missed you so much. You have no idea what having you here means to me," April said, her face shining with tears.

Michael held onto her shoulders while stretching to look her over.

"It's been almost a year since I last saw you, Mom. You look wonderful. Your face has even changed. Is this what the South does to people?"

"Only when they're finally in the arms of their loving son," April cried. "I just don't want to stop hugging you."

"Well, I'm gonna be here for a while, so you'll have plenty of opportunity." Michael and April walked inside.

April took him on a tour of the house. He dropped his luggage in one of the guest rooms. "You mean, you just moved in two days ago? Looks like you've been here two months. Everything looks so organized and complete."

"I wanted to get it all ready before you got here so there wouldn't be any time wasted. All you need to do is hook up the TV/VCR and hang pictures."

Later, April and her son grilled salmon steaks, tossed a salad, made a pitcher of iced tea, and spent the rest of the evening catching up on their lives from the last time they were together. April told Michael about her spiritual friends and the newfound peace in her life that she was able to discover through meditation and self-study. They talked into the wee hours of the night. She was so thrilled her son would be all hers for at least three months that she had difficulty falling asleep that night.

Eager to greet the morning when the first hint of sunlight peeked through the blinds, April looked at her clock. It was only 6:15. The neighborhood was still asleep. Everything was quiet. There was no hint of trickling fountains, blaring cars or sirens, running water, or neighbors bustling about. The only thing she heard in the background were birds chirping in the distance.

April pulled on a pair of comfortable shorts and matching golf shirt and walked outside to examine her new environs. There was a hint of jasmine in the cool morning air. The sun threw a gleaming brightness across a grove of blossoming magnolia saplings planted along the house. A young boy was delivering the Sunday papers on his bike with the nose of a Schnauzer peeking over his basket. He waved to her as he rounded the cul-de-sac.

One contractor built all the houses in the subdivision. The neighborhood featured a combination of one- and two-story stucco homes, which all looked the same—three bedrooms and baths, a family room, and a kitchen overlooking a small backyard. The neighborhood was about two years old—a fine place for young couples to begin their lives. April's landlord lived around the corner and was managing the rental for the owner, who was living in Hawaii. He was an accountant for the TV weekly detective series, *Jake and the Fat Man.*

April could smell the coffee brewing as she approached the front door. Michael was awake and sipping his espresso on the patio. She tapped the newspapers against his chair and kissed his forehead. "Did you sleep okay?"

"Like a dead man," he said, and he laughed.

When they finished their coffee, April offered to help him unpack. Frozen in her tracks, she screamed, "Michael!" as she lifted the missing statue out of a box of civilian clothes. She wanted to cry from happiness.

Michael came running from the bathroom, out of breath. "What's wrong?"

"My statue! Where did you find it? How long have you had it?"

"My God, I thought you had a heart attack. Don't scare me like that." Michael looked as if he was caught with his hand in the cookie jar. "I took it when I left you last Christmas. I was drawn to it when you shared the story about your father. I guess I forgot to tell you."

"I looked all over for it when I was packing to move here. I couldn't imagine what happened to it. Thank God you had it. You know, your grandfather had that statue for years. It was clutched tightly in his hands when they found him dead in his car. You were named after that statue.

"Remember our conversation about the misgivings you had about being my father in another life? There may be a kernel of truth to that." April related the sessions she had with A. J.

"Michael, you are not my father reincarnated. I was so deeply affected by his accident that some of those feelings could've been inadvertently transmitted to you before you were born."

Michael and April dropped down on the side of the bed together. He sighed and rubbed his eyes. "You must miss your father very much."

They sat there for a while, silently holding each other.

******

Weeks flew by. Life in the rental house was delightful. April and Michael became better acquainted than ever. Together, they laughed, cooked, meditated, prayed, rode bikes in the rain, and most of all, shared many special moments in their new hometown. Whenever friends and relatives came as house guests and stayed for any length of time, when they left, April and Michael would stand in the middle of the family room and hug each other, happy that once again, they were alone to bond and discover more new adventures together. Michael even set up one of the bedrooms, which he called the nerve center. He used it to begin his research for possible graduate business schools. While living with April, he applied to the Rollins College business school, was accepted, and planned to attend following his discharge from the Navy.

Michael accompanied April to the Sunday self-study group sessions. Regardless of the age difference, he fit right in with her friends. It wasn't long before he internalized the spiritual teachings.

Following one of his meditations, Michael announced, "I'm not gonna be able to stay for the holidays. I heard a voice. It said I should go back to my roots. I'm going to Ohio to spend the holidays with Gram. I need to be with her."

"We've never been apart for the holidays. You know Dad will be here. We'll miss you, but I understand."

The phone rang late one night after Michael returned from his bike ride. He had his walkman on, and the Eagles were blaring so loudly, April could hear strains of *Hotel California*. He was oblivious to the ringing phone. April doggedly debated whether she should answer it. With lingering abandon, she finally answered after the fifth ring. Before she could get the receiver to her ear, Rachel's voice sent those familiar visceral connections throughout her body.

Michael became alarmed when he noticed April's terrified look, and he saw a transformation he had never seen before. He approached her, immediately removed his Walkman, and laid a consoling hand on her shoulder.

April made a sweeping motion with her arm, as if to say, *It's okay.* She knocked over her glass of wine, spilling it on the beige carpet. She waited and was frozen for minutes. Her chest heaved deep breaths. *Why me?* she thought as stillness slowed her breathing. She could almost feel the negative energy begin to shift away once she remembered Jill's admonishments. *Reclaim your power, and don't relinquish it to anyone.* She held tightly to the receiver, straightened up, and took a few deep breaths. Soon color began to return to her face. She focused warily and listened to the ranting on the other end. Rachel's words were slurred.

"I'm in so much pain, I can hardy bear it anymore," Rachel cried. "N-n-nobody unnerstans me. Somebody gotta help me. I need to you. You're the ony one I can talk."

"Rachel, I ..."

Rachel interrupted in a cracked voice, sounding as if she were on the far side of the world. "I know I-I-I kept thins from you. I know it c-cost me your fr-fr-friendship, but it was your own good. Now I wanna tell you the tr-tr-truth. Please, I g-g-gotta tell you the tr-truth about me! Pul-eeeze!"

April's mouth dried. She paused in thought and then suggested they do this another time. It was late. She admonished Rachel, saying that she shouldn't be driving in her condition—and besides, they hadn't even spoken for weeks. April said she didn't think she was the one who could help her, but Rachel moaned on and seemed to grow more desperate, crying that she needed someone to talk to immediately. It was impossible to refuse her call for help. Breau said every phone call was either a call for help or a call for love. This call was for both.

April reached for the tissues on the coffee table. She wiped her eyes, took a deep breath, and relented. She suggested they meet at April's office, where they could be alone. She hung up the phone and told Michael not to worry. "This is something I must do."

Michael begged her not to leave, but he was unable to dissuade her. April reassured him that she was fine. She grabbed her sweat suit from her dresser drawer and proceeded to the bathroom to throw some water on her face. Looking at herself in the mirror sans makeup, she wondered what it must be like to be addicted to alcohol.

There were no sounds in the neighborhood. The suffocating humidity and heat of the landlocked city overwhelmed April. It steamed up her glasses as soon as she opened the garage door. The only sign of anyone awake in the cul-de-sac was a ghostly, flickering blue light from the neighbor's television. As she started up the car, the radio blared some New Age music. She hit the tape eject button for fear of waking the neighbors.

Even for a city that flourished with travelers from all over the world, there were few cars on the road at this late hour. The expressway was ominously deserted. April watched the rushing white lines of the highway masked by a slowly rising fog from cool air connecting with the warm pavement. She rolled down the window to let in some night air. She put on the defroster to clean off the windshield's condensation. Smells of freshly baked bread permeated from the Merita Bakery downtown. During the eight blackened miles along the expressway, she only passed three cars. She fumbled in her wallet for change at the exit and waited behind an *Orlando Sentinel* news truck that lingered to pay the toll. She looked at the full moon that rose above the trees as she exited the expressway.

When she turned onto Colonial Drive to her office, she heard loud music from a passing car filled with teenagers—three boys in front, and two girls in back. As she approached the Fashion Square Mall, which was across the street from her office, her car radar detector went crazy. She heard the wail of police sirens. There was a choking smell of rubber and metal burning. All at once, yellow and orange flames shot ten feet into the sky, with clouds of billowing gray smoke floating, over and around a tree.

Lights were flashing. A barricade with fire rescue, ambulances, and police cars blocked westbound traffic. A car had flipped over, causing a municipal bus to lose control on the service road. April felt her muscles tighten. By the time she slowly turned into the office parking lot and opened the car window, she was overcome by the humidity while waiting for Rachel's Buick. She sat in the car, dazed, and watched the professionals do battle with the flames, while across the street, the EMTs, with smoke-blackened faces, carried a gray, wool-blanket-covered gurney into the ambulance. And then it struck her, the obvious thought. *What if that's Rachel?*

For an instant, April was back in Milltown. Once again, she felt the dreadful sensation and dark feeling open up inside her the night she walked into the hospital grieving room. Her head pounded, and the air suddenly felt suffocatingly damp. Her past had met her present. She looked up at the sky and thanked God she was alive.

Rachel never showed. April drove home. *That's it. I'm going to expunge this woman from my life.*

CHAPTER 29

After parking the car in the circular driveway at the entrance of Dinah's beautiful house, April hesitated. Heavy breaths along with a sigh of finality and peace ensued as she awaited the meeting with apprehension. She shifted her weight from one foot to another, the heat creeping through the soles of her sandals, before finally ringing the doorbell. When April was about to ring it for the second time, Dinah appeared in the doorway and apologized for keeping her waiting.

Her face lit up with a welcoming smile when she opened the door. They walked through the house to the patio, which was shaded by an old magnolia tree. A staghorn hung from one of its massive branches. Green spindle leaves had sprouted from all sides of its brown-covered cocoon.

The two women sat facing each other in the morning sun, shaded by a green-and-white-striped awning. Dinah nervously busied herself, straightening each fold in her pleated dress around her diminished frame, as if it was the most important thing to do at the moment. She looked dignified as usual, yet vulnerable and so fragile that a gust of wind might surely blow her away. April was silent momentarily while she gazed around at the surroundings and waited patiently for Dinah to contain her composure.

"Thank you for seeing me so quickly after the funeral," said April, breaking the silence. "I am so sorry for your loss."

"Well, you sounded pretty troubled. I didn't want to keep you waiting."

"I didn't know what had happened until one of my friends called and told me. You don't know this, but I was there when the ambulance was leaving. Rachel had called me at home and asked me to meet her near my office. I could tell she had been drinking, and I begged her not to drive, but she insisted. When I arrived, the ambulance was leaving, and the car had already been towed. I had no idea it was her. I waited in the car for almost an hour and eventually drove home. It must've happened shortly after she called me.

Our relationship was volatile almost from the very beginning. You know, I wanted to say something to you when we met at Cassadega, but realized it wasn't the proper time or place. Some of our problems originally stemmed from business, given that she wanted me to pull strings at my company, but it went much deeper than that." April continued to detail the on-and-off episodes with Rachel's erratic behavior.

"Honey, I'm not surprised." Dinah paused in thought while she continued to straighten her dress. Her eyes darted from April to her dress, then back to April, as if she was unable to focus. Her voice trembled, and her lips began to quiver as she tried to garner the strength to begin talking again while scratching nervously at her palm.

April touched Dinah's hand in a gesture of support. "I had been told about the incident with her father. Dinah, I never considered judging her. I even beat myself up trying to understand her. One time, when I asked her about the medallion, she got so angry with me, but never did answer my question. I had intended to end our relationship the night the accident happened. Given the background with my father and his alcoholism, I should've been smart enough to figure what was going on with her, but I wasn't."

"Then you know the basis of her problems," Dinah said. "My husband was an alcoholic and abused me. That's when Rachel grabbed the gun to protect me and almost killed him. She was just a teenager when it happened. She bought the medallion, knowing it was a symbol of death. I think she wore it to punish and remind herself what she had done. She and her father were so much alike. It's sad how she followed in his footsteps. He left us after that incident with the gun. It even

233

affected her marriage. Her husband left her because of her drinking and erratic behavior. She was sole support of the twins. Believe me—I tried to reach her, but it was impossible. She buried so many mysteries deeply inside that no one could reach her. She had been sober for two years. I don't know why she began drinking again. I guess her pain was intractable." Dinah lowered her head and stared at the patio floor, slowly shaking her head back and forth. "Sometimes I think it's all my fault—"

"You, of all people, know that's not true. It took me years to forgive myself and realize my father's accident was not my fault. You know you'll never have peace as long as you continue to blame yourself. Don't make the same mistake I did. I'll be forever grateful to Rachel. She befriended me when I arrived and introduced me to the spiritual study group."

As April walked to her car, she realized Rachel had been caught in her own personal Milltown.

On her way home, cars had begun to slow down and pull over along the shoulder on I-4. She drove onto the median, stopped the car, left the radio on to listen to the announcements coming from Cape Canaveral, and stepped outside onto the berm. The countdown was in process—"ten, nine, eight, seven … three, two, one." There was no sound when the announcer said, "engine ignition and lift off." All of a sudden, April heard a thunderous rumble of roaring booster rockets. A stream of fire and light emblazoned the sky throughout the bone-jawing thrust and liftoff. Within seconds, there was a stream of fire. Light emblazoned the sky.

She was overcome by an exhilarating adrenaline rush. Tears flowed down her cheeks as the fireball shot higher and higher toward the heavens throughout the liftoff. In a split second, she felt Josef's presence. In that moment, she was one with Spirit. It was a true miracle—synchronicity. Spirit had presented her with a beautiful metaphor—a virtual symbol of inspiration—her new beginning. The pressing weight of her past guilt and dark cornerstone of daunting unforgiveness lifted into the heavens with the Atlantis space shuttle.

EPILOGUE

Karl spent the Christmas holidays with April in Orlando. 1989 would go down in the history books as the coldest winter yet. The temperatures in Orlando were so cold, electricity was turned off by the utility company every two hours to relieve the drain on residential usage. The cold spell brought a dusting of snow to parts of central Florida. Temperatures in the area dipped to the low forties, with wind chills into the twenties in parts of north Florida. The Jacksonville airport and bridges were closed because of ice.

While Karl and April sat on the sofa with a heating blanket over their legs on Christmas morning, he complained, "So much for coming South to keep warm for the holidays. These heat pumps don't do a very good job."

"No, they don't warm the house like a furnace. My friends at work said that it's not unusual to get freezing temperatures from time to time—but never lasting this long, and with snow. This is a real fluke. It just never happens down here. Maybe you brought it with you. But what's worse—cold, cloudy, and whiteout snow storms most of the winter, or a couple cold days with a sprinkling of snow? I can get used to it."

"Well, I guess I better too, now that we sold the condo."

"That's the best gift you've ever given me. I can't believe you'll finally be joining me."

"But remember, I said I'll need to finish up a major project at work before I leave. I probably won't be able to join you until sometime in the spring—maybe when you come up for your mother's party."

Michael's Christmas with his gram was extra-special too. He called later that evening to wish his parents a Merry Christmas. "I've been having a wonderful time here with Gram. I probably gained ten pounds already with all the good food she's been feeding me. I have some news. I think I met my future wife. Hold on now, Mom; I know you've heard this before, but this time, I'm really serious. I met her while I was out with friends, dancing at one of the clubs in town. I spotted this good-looking woman across the dance floor, and the rest is history. She has stolen my heart. You want to hear the best one yet? Her birthday is the same as Gram's, she lives around the corner from Gram, and her name—hold on to your hat—is April. Do you believe this? No one would ever believe these coincidences. Boy, am I glad I listened to the voice that beckoned me back to Milltown for the holidays. I just know she's the one, Mom."

"Then what? Now that you're being discharged from the Navy, and soon going to grad school, it'll be difficult with you in Orlando and your sweetheart in Milltown."

"I know, Mom, but we decided we'll just carry on a long-distance relationship until I'm through and see what happens. If it's meant to be—and I'm confident it is—everything will work out. You'll get a chance to meet her at Gram's birthday party. I know you'll like her. With a name like April, how could I go wrong?" Michael said, laughing into the phone.

******

Joe had planned a surprise birthday celebration for Julianna. It was held in a beautiful park pavilion in Milltown that could accommodate 100 people. There were lush rolling hills for the young ones to run and play games. About sixty friends and relatives attended. The family met the young April, and was delighted with Michael's selection.

Julianna was elated to see how many had traveled to join in celebrating her seventy-five years. Joe requested that some of her loved ones write treasured memories to be read following the cookout and cutting of the cake.

As April watched her mother, she was struck by a familiar feeling.

It was almost as if she could hear her humming in the kitchen again. Although left with thin hair and weathered skin, Julianna's good looks remained. The apples of her cheeks were pink and plump with pleasure. She looked surprisingly young and lovely with her silver hair done in soft curls. She was smiling from ear to ear.

April and Joe cuddled up on either side of the family matriarch at the picnic table. There was a sea of happy faces. All eyes were on the guest of honor. The voices of the onlookers were dampened like distant music as the partygoers waited for Julianna to begin speaking. Karl was ready with the movie camera. Julianna began reading each card and letter. At times, someone had to take over when she was too choked up to continue. Tears flowed from many of the well-wishers as they listened. Everyone laughed when she opened Michael's heavy birthday card. He had taped seventy-five dimes to it. Julianna's trademark with the children when they were growing up was to tape one dime in the card for every year of age. It was something they always looked forward to whenever they received her birthday cards.

Julianna grinned and gave Michael a victory sign.

"Touche, Gram," Michael said with wet eyes. He winked and gave her a thumbs-up and one of his bear hugs.

Wild applause and laughter followed.

******

April awakened the morning after the party to an ecstatic feeling of relief. This was an extra-special celebration for the Dunlaps. Karl was packed and ready for the drive to Orlando to finally rejoin April at the conclusion of the weekend celebration.

The Dunlaps spent the last day driving past old haunts, which included schools and neighborhoods. A new house had been built next to Julianna's. At the back of the house was a large new addition that completely blocked the view of the Croquet Court from April's bedroom window. The two buckeye trees in front were massive, with pendulous branches that ballooned over the driveway.

The last haunt on the trip down memory lane was the cottage on Lake Erie. It brought smiles and thoughts of all the happy family summers that always began with breakfast at the Pancake House across the street from the only general store in town, called The Big Wheel, which the family jokingly referred to as Big Willy's.

The final excursion ended at the cemetery. The sky was a brilliant blue, and the air fresh-smelling and clear. April felt at peace approaching the gravesite. High grass had grown over the name, and only the words *Josef* and *1913* were visible on the headstone. April and Karl kneeled at the apron of the stone. They cleaned out the onion grass until all the letters were revealed. April paused to watch one of the biggest daddy longlegs that lived at the bottom corner of the grave crawl slowly up her arm and rest on her shoulder. A realization and full awareness washed over her for a second as she observed the insect leisurely inch safely back down. She thought of herself as the hopeful young girl she had once been and the woman she had become.

Not much had changed in Milltown, but despite the sameness, everything looked different somehow—perhaps because the town was no longer the epicenter of April's universe. It was just a small Midwestern town where she happened to have grown up. There were no seeds of guilt wedged in her chest. The city would never bring thoughts of dread or despair again. There was no misery to push into the back of her mind—all that was gone forever. Her universe was elsewhere, but at least it seemed now that all her memories had a purpose—every heartache, every happiness, and the lessons learned from being born into the Stratka family. Each had a purpose leading to the woman she had become.

A reflection of her childhood and the unforgiving judgments she had harbored brought

T. S. Eliot's words to mind: "And the end of all our exploring will be to arrive where we started and know the place for the first time."

April Dunlap, a middle-aged woman with never-look-back determination, was living the life her father had dreamed for her. Happy memories would return at odd moments: Josef sitting in the audience at her President's Day play, the smell of his Brilliantine on her fingers, the mansions in the park, gardenias on Easter Sunday, and her daddy saying, "You're my baby, April; you'll always be my baby." Now April was taking her family to her place in the sun.

RITA MALIE is the award-winning author of Goodbye America, a memoir of her mother's childhood. The legacy of growing up in an alcoholic home inspired her to write Supreme Sacrifice to help others overcome and prevent ghosts of the past to influence the present and future. She lives in Florida with her husband and children.